THE CALLING

DREAM OR REALITY SERIES NOVEL ONE

BETH M JAMES

The Calling

Dream or Reality Series Novel One

Beth M James

Written by Beth M James

ISBN 978-0-9889428-8-2 (eBook)
ISBN 979-8-9893449-3-2 (Paperback D2D)
ISBN 978-0-988-9428-2-0 (Paperback)
Cover Photography: Maryia Bahutskaya at Dreamstime.com and Canva

This book is dedicated to:
My dad and brother Mike (in memory)
My brother Danny

Acknowledgments:
Thank you Ellis, Mike, and Sheryl for your hardcore review and edits.

Prologue

Chicago, IL
Present Day

Walt pressed his forehead against the window as he watched the Chicago sky fade to darkness. The sun disappeared behind the buildings, and the temperature dropped into the teens. He could be anywhere in the world—Belize, St. Thomas, Mexico, or even San Diego would do. Anywhere would be better than stuck inside the Billingham Hospital on the loneliest night in the world.

Three months and seventeen days had passed since the fire, and his fiancée was still unresponsive. The rhythmic flow of oxygen pumped through the respirator to remind him of life and death.

"Walt." Helen Arbol's voice brought him back to the present. He lifted his head off the glass but still couldn't look at his mother. He stared at the floor.

She sounded tired and impatient as she shifted in her chair. Her powdery perfume clouded the room, and he wished she'd wear something else. Jessie wouldn't wake knowing Helen was in the room.

The chair squeaked when she stood and moved toward him. The click of her heels seemed heavier than usual before she stopped behind him. "You've waited long enough. You can't ignore the facts. Make a decision. You have responsibilities."

His head down, Walt caught the puckered skin coming out of her pale blue pumps as he turned to face her. He loved his mother. Truly, he did. But the last few weeks she had started to pressure him. And now it continued. Family duties called. He had to get back to work.

"You sit. You wait. This isn't good for you or her. You stay with her, day and night, hoping she'll wake. What if she does? Have you considered the consequences?"

"I get it, Mother," he said and crossed his arms.

She had her arms wrapped around her purse. The wrinkles on her usually smooth face showed signs of weariness. At fifty-eight, she tried masking her age by wearing a little too much makeup and dying her hair jet black.

To avoid his mother's closeness, Walt moved away and went to stand by Jessie, whose face was hidden behind tape and tubes. A strand of her blonde hair fell across her cheek. He lifted the curl with his finger and brushed it aside.

His mother sighed heavily as she walked to the end of the bed. She smoothed out the red prayer blanket a lady from her church had made for Walt and his fiancée. "You heard the specialists. They can't predict what will happen when Jessica wakes. There's no guarantee. Her memory may be gone. She may not be able to talk. You'll have to put her through months of therapy to get her back to normal, if at all. Keeping her on support isn't helping—you're only prolonging the unknown."

A new beep, loud and intrusive, came from one of the machines near the bed. Jesse's heart rate went up and became a jagged line on the monitor. This had happened numerous times. No one understood why, but he believed it was her way to protest.

"Stop it, Mother," Walt said, as if his fiancée could hear them talking about her.

Carol, the head nurse, rushed into the room and checked the monitor.

Walt reached underneath the blanket for Jessie's lifeless hand and squeezed, hoping for a response. They watched the machine until her heart rate went down again and the beeping stopped. Her hand felt cold as he stroked it.

"Only another hiccup," Carol said as she pressed some buttons. She surveyed the room and frowned, as if aware of the tension in the air between Walt and Mrs. Arbol. The nurse smoothed her hair while she excused herself and left the room.

Helen Arbol moved toward the vinyl green chair and collected her fur coat. "The two of you have been through enough."

Walt cleared his throat, irritated that she had to get her last words in before leaving.

"I can't stand seeing you this way. You practically live here and it's not good for you." She looked around with pursed lips. The bounty of flowers—roses, carnations, and orchids—colored the room but couldn't mask the starkness of their present situation. "Even your father agrees with me on this one."

Walt rolled his head to stretch the muscles in his neck. He wished he could reverse the last few months and start over. If only he had convinced Jessie to stay in bed the morning after their engagement party. He should have gotten out of bed and gone jogging with her. Instead, he went back to sleep to coddle his hangover. He should be the one in a coma.

Walt tightened his jaw to keep his emotions intact. His head pounded.

"Your father returns from Paris tomorrow," his mother said. "He will be home for lunch. Please, join us. He'd like to see you."

"I will," he told her without thinking. He'd do as his father wished.

Helen's heels clicked against the floor. She gave him a kiss goodbye, patted his shoulder, then left him alone in the room. Her steps echoed down the hall until she reached the elevator.

Walt tucked Jessie's hand underneath the blanket. He paced the room, twisting his back while waving his arms to relieve his stress. He stopped at the window and looked down at the street. The wind picked up and swirled the snow across the road. The weatherman predicted more snow for tomorrow.

His mother was right. He couldn't go on like this. Each day he waited for a twitch, a moan, a gasp, but nothing came from her. This wasn't Jessie. It killed him to see her so lifeless. But how could he give her up? Why did so many people expect him to pull the plug?

A tear rolled down his cheek, and Walt wiped it away. Jessie always put others before herself. She always reached out to him for a decision. Was he being a coward by not making a decision now?

Footsteps shuffled into the room. "Hey, how's it going, Walt?"

Hearing his best friend, Walt straightened. "Hello, Sam."

His friend worked two miles from the hospital and came to visit every other day, either during lunch hour or after work. He sympathized with Walt, but he wasn't one to dwell on it. He kept Walt sane throughout the weeks by keeping their conversations real.

Sam glanced at Jessie, motionless and mummified within the blankets. "Any change?"

"No. No change." Walt hated repeating the same words each day.

Sam went straight to Jessie and found her hand. He leaned forward. "Hey, Jessie. It's Sam. Yes, again. Wake up." He waited. "The ocean's calling."

At twenty-eight years old and slightly overweight, Sam was single for the third time. He worked too many hours at his law firm. Both wives found other interests less than two years after they walked down the aisle.

Sam greeted him with a fist to the shoulder. He stepped back and frowned. "You catch a remote glimpse of yourself lately?"

"No," Walt grunted. "I avoid looking into anything that resembles a mirror."

"Good thing. When was the last time you slept?"

Walt shrugged. "A few hours ago?"

"No, no, no. When was the last time you slept at home and had a good night's sleep?"

Walt pressed his fingers against his forehead to think. The days blended together. His daily routine consisted of answering e-mails and messages before breakfast, staying with Jessie until lunch, heading into Arbol Publishing, and then spending the evening with Jessie again. Overnight was at the hospital or a few hours at his parents' estate.

"You need to get out of here. You want me to stay tonight?" Sam checked his watch. He set his overstuffed briefcase on the floor. "I can if you want."

"My duty. My shift."

Sam sat on the couch and stretched his legs out. "Have you made any decisions?"

Walt's head shot up. "Have you been talking to my mother?"

"She cares about you." He yawned as if ready to take a nap. "But no, I didn't. I talked to Senior. He called me from Paris to find out my take on how you're doing."

Walt nodded and rubbed his forehead. He knew his father too well. He was preparing to give Walt the same lecture his mother gave but more detailed. "What'd you tell him?"

"You're great under the circumstances."

Walt snickered. "I'm not so sure. I snapped at my mother before you got here."

"That's understandable."

"Everyone wants to know when I'm going to get on with my life."

"And what do you tell them?"

Walt mumbled how it wasn't his choice.

The doctors had placed Jessie in the coma to allow her head and internal organs to heal. Twice they tried to wake her out of it, but she refused. They had seen nothing like her case. Specialists came in to study her chart. No one offered him hope. She was merely a curiosity to them.

"You can make the choice," Sam said. "We gave you the authority. In court. Remember?"

Walt snapped, "What would you do? Let her go?"

"I can't make that decision for you." He raised his hands in defense.

"Why not?"

Sam gave him a nervous laugh as if knowing the dangerous territory he was about to enter. "I can handle criminal actions, not emotional decisions. Remember, I'm the one with two failed marriages."

Walt rubbed his chin, annoyed at his friend's safe response. "If it were Sarah or Kelly, would you have pulled the plug?"

"Before or after the divorces?"

Unlike his friend, Walt wasn't in the mood for humor. He joined him on the couch. "I don't think she was happy, Sam."

The night of the engagement party was a telltale sign. He saw the expression on her face when they toasted, and his mother didn't raise her glass. Jessie had needed some kind of acceptance from Helen, but none was offered.

"Why do you say that?"

Walt shrugged and rubbed his eyes. They hurt from lack of sleep. "I don't know. Me, having money. My family. The business. I know she loves me, but I think the wedding was getting to her."

"Isn't your mother involved?"

Walt snorted. "Yes. She's taken over the wedding." His mother was a bit controlling. "Jessie wanted me to elope. If we had, she wouldn't be in this coma."

"Don't beat yourself up, man," Sam said. He rose from the couch and groaned at the effort, then shuffled over to Jessie's bedside. "You can elope once she's awake. If, of course, she's still intact."

Walt shook his head, angry at his friend for thinking like his mother. He kept his temper in check while Sam leaned over to play with Jessie's nose. He gave it a wiggle—his goodbye to her.

"See you again, Jessie. Walt, here, doesn't need a break, so I'm heading home to White Castles and paperwork. Hopefully next time you'll be up and about." Then he straightened and held out his hand to Walt. "You got some thinking to do. I'll catch you later."

Walt stood and shook his hand.

Once his friend was gone, he listened to the swish and click of machines near his fiancée's bed. He pushed his shirt sleeve up. Eight-fifteen. The nurse would be in to check on her soon.

Throughout his career, Walt made decisions. His instincts for keeping Arbol Publishing thriving hit the mark. He worked his way up in the family business, starting in the mailroom and gaining the respect of the other employees. He learned the ins and outs of publishing, every aspect of their five magazines and what it took to keep them successful. After moving around to different divisions until he learned them all, he was appointed president of sales and marketing. Walt proved his worth like his father, Walt Senior, had when he started the business forty years ago.

So why couldn't he make this one decision? Why did he let the world go on while his life was on hold, stuck to this one little room? As long as he let the machines click, Jessie stayed alive. The decision that tortured his heart also prevented him from saying it aloud.

Walt went over to his sport coat, folded across the chair, and dug into the inner pocket. He found her engagement ring, ready for her to wear when she woke. He held it up to the light and then twirled the band around to admire the rare diamond. The minute he saw the brilliant hues of blues and reds, the jeweler had his money. Six months ago, Walt had placed the ring on her finger as they walked the beach in Carmel. They played in the waves and kicked up the sand after she said yes a dozen times. They'd been like little kids.

Walt slipped the ring on her finger where it belonged. The diamond came off sometime during her courageous effort to get the children out of the burning house. His father found the diamond on the ground near where she fell off the roof. One earring went missing. The other was still in place on her right ear, safely locked in place. Why the hell hadn't the other one stayed locked? The jeweler guaranteed she would never lose them. So much for the man's word. Walt snickered in contempt.

He bent down to kiss Jessie's forehead. Kissing her lips was one of the things he missed most.

"Come on, Jessie. Open your eyes for me." He caressed the top of her head. "I will always be here for you. No matter what." He hooked his fingers around the black band holding her hair in place and pulled it away. Her blonde hair, dull from lack of care, fanned out across the pillow. The nurse had wanted to cut her hair short, easier to maintain, but Walt refused. Jessie would've been livid.

Standing up straight, Walt's six-foot-four frame towered over the bed. He checked one more time to make sure the ring was centered, the right earring was locked, and her hands were comfortable at her side. He smoothed out the sheet and blanket covering her.

Walt stepped away from Jessie and headed toward the nurse's station outside the door of her room. Disinfectant hit his nose as the night crew started their cleaning.

Carol, the head nurse, smiled at him when he placed his hands flat on the countertop. Her expression changed to concern the instant she saw his face.

"I'm ready," he said. The words were flat and lifeless.

Carol shook her head as if unclear about his meaning. She leaned forward and waited.

Walt's tongue felt thick and his throat dry. "I'm ready to sign the papers."

Carol shot up from her chair.

"I'll call Dr. Maguire," she said and scurried off.

The signing of papers, the verbal explanation from the administrator of what could happen became a blur as Walt agreed to everything and signed wherever the worker pointed his finger. They'd been over this before. He knew the consequences. Just get it over. Carol asked if he wanted time alone with her before they began.

No.

Walt cowered in the corner of the room while two nurses and the doctor performed tests and checked Jessie's vital signs. Right before they shut the respirator down, Dr. Maguire glanced over to see how he was doing. Walt wouldn't look back. He wrapped his arms around his waist and braced himself against the wall.

The respirator stopped.

Many nights, the machine gave him comfort as he sat next to her, thinking of their lives and wishing they were walking down the aisle with her in a stunning white gown. The sudden silence in the room pained his ears. Sweat beaded on his forehead and upper lip.

Closing his eyes, he pictured Jessie's smile. The way she'd laugh and take pictures of him with her camera as they lounged in bed. How she'd make breakfast and always burn the eggs.

Walt jumped as a second monitor beeped in one continuous tone. He knew that alarm. She wasn't getting oxygen. The doctor and nurse worked to remove the tube from her mouth, ripping the tape from her face. Another high-pitched tone joined the beeping. Her heart struggled to beat.

Oh, God! Walt sucked in air as if it were his last breath. The blood ran from his head; his face felt cold, and his world turned ash gray.

"What have I done?" He sobbed the words repeatedly in his head as his knees buckled, and he slid to the floor. He promised to take care of her. He promised.

The beeping stopped.

Chapter 1

::: Jessie :::

Chicago, IL

Three Months & 18 Days Earlier

Jessie flipped open her suitcase in a panic. The sexy tone of the saxophone filtered up to the bedroom as the piano played light jazz. The guests continued to arrive downstairs, and an occasional laugh rose above the music and chatter. She knew Mrs. Arbol would be craning her neck, watching for them to make their entrance.

She rummaged through the clothes but couldn't find what she wanted. Why hadn't she packed her outfit on top? Finding her four-inch heels, she tossed them to the plush carpeted floor. She spotted a pair of black pants and pulled them out.

"Not those," Walt called out. "Dressier."

Jessie took a split second to admire him walking across the bedroom toward the closet. He wore only a towel. He had a straight-lined waist, not muscular but not flabby, with black fuzz curling from his chest to underneath the towel. He used to wax his front side, but she convinced him to go au natural. She was glad he did. It made him sexier. She shook her head and turned back to her task.

Their engagement party, the event of the year, given by Mr. and Mrs. Arbol at their estate for their son Walter Edward and his bride-to-be Jessica Sara Rossen, was about to begin. She needed to be dressy for the formal event. If it were up to her, she would have had a barbecue, beer, and a fire on the beach.

She dug deeper and found her simple black dress. "How 'bout this?"

Walt peeked out from the closet to see what she selected. He hung a crisp gray suit on his valet stand and then removed the pants with care. He seemed so calm and in control. "Didn't you pack your blue dress?"

Good idea, she thought. The dress was stretchy and wouldn't show the wrinkles. A large, jeweled brooch would add the elegance it needed.

"Five minutes." Walt looked at his Rolex.

Jessie moaned to protest. The day had been crazy. She arrived from New York after a two-day photo shoot for an article on the newest clothier in the city. Walt, arriving from their branch office in California, met her at the airport. And then there was the Chicago traffic to deal with before arriving at the estate.

She found the blue dress and slipped it on. She skipped the nylons. Mrs. Arbol wouldn't approve but tough shit. Her legs were smooth and tan.

"Perfect." Walt kissed the back of her neck when she held her long, blonde hair to the side so he could zip her up.

The thrill of his touch made her shiver with delight. She loved his butterfly kisses. She would have been perfectly happy staying in his boyhood bedroom, making love instead of mingling with his family and business acquaintances.

"Are you sure we can't elope?" she asked when he stepped away, their moment over.

The wedding was no longer an intimate event. His mother took control and hired a planner after seeing Jessie search for venues that were unsuitable for the Arbols.

"We can," Walt said but shook his head in contradiction as if subliminally telling her no. He struggled with tying his tie and started over.

"This is insane...all the parties." They had three that weekend—the engagement party, a Sunday morning brunch, and then a cocktail party in the afternoon. She couldn't wait to get back to California. Home. She missed her one-bedroom cottage.

"Let's enjoy ourselves tonight. Relax."

Time to zip it. She heard the irritation in his voice. Jessie didn't want to start a fight; however, she hated when he put her in her place. *This is your new life. Get used to it.*

Dress on. Heels on. She stood by the door and waited for her fiancé as he managed his tie. He grabbed his suit coat.

"You look beautiful," he said, joining her.

"Why, thank you, my handsome man." She helped tame the one strand of his black hair that fell across his forehead.

"Let's do it." Walt took her arm. He straightened his shoulders and became the powerhouse that controlled the family business.

Jessie smiled and her lip began to twitch. She was meeting two hundred people and had to uphold the Arbol standards.

She played her part as the night dragged on, and she tried to be upbeat and positive. After all, her engagement party was a time for celebration. Jessie wandered through the foyer, the grand room, and then the conservatory, where she smiled and mingled with the guests. Walt had disappeared some time ago, but she was used to it. Her fiancé was always in demand.

She stayed in the conservatory where she felt the most comfortable with the lush plants and bright flowers. Here she smelled spring on a cold fall day. Walt's mother spent every morning in the room tending to the plants. She meticulously dusted, fluffed, and watered each one. Like her son, they were perfectly groomed.

"Pinot, please," Jessie said to the bartender when she stopped at one of the bars set up for the evening.

An older man approached the bar and ordered a Scotch. Jessie smiled and he completely ignored her. It wasn't a slap in the face but close. The guest received his drink before she did. Why should she be surprised?

With wine finally in hand, Jessie wandered back to the foyer, wanting to take five minutes to herself. She could slip into the library or run upstairs for a break. She was tired of the men staring at her as if she would make a good trophy wife. The women were just as bad, giving her smirky, polite smiles and congratulating her with air kisses as they pretended to be happy for her. Why should she be upset by their reaction? Mrs. Arbol treated her the same way. Jessie didn't fit in their world. A highly in-demand photographer wasn't on their list of desirable friends.

"Darling, how many of those have you enjoyed drinking so far tonight?" Helen Arbol snuck up from behind and put on her Audrey Hepburn smile. She wore a feathered shawl for the evening and had her hair piled high atop her head.

Jessie tightened her lips. She smiled and said, "Not nearly enough."

"Don't be tipsy for the toast." Her future mother-in-law ignored the remark, having her own agenda. "Walt Senior is ordering the champagne to be served." She gave another pleasant smile and then found guests to join.

Walt's mother never admitted she was disappointed in her son's choice of bride. However, she let her future daughter-in-law know how lucky she was to cast a spell on her son. Jessie should feel privileged and honored that he picked her. Sometimes Jessie wondered if it were more of a curse.

"There's the bride-to-be."

Jessie smiled when she saw Sam. Walt's best friend, a reputable lawyer, didn't fit the mold of the Arbol circle, yet, being Walt's long-time and only pal, he was accepted.

"You're a welcome sight," she said and gave him a hug. He smelled of Old Spice, which reminded her of her grandpa.

"The crowd too rowdy for you? Gotta be alone?"

Jessie laughed when she gazed across the room. The guests in all their finery seemed to be enjoying themselves. They smiled and hugged in greeting, but they did so with poise and charm in case the photographer happened to snap a shot. God forbid if they were caught laughing too hard and showing their wrinkles. "Yes. I need air. Fresh air."

"Then let's wander outside, but first..." He ordered a rum and coke from the bartender.

With drink in one hand, Sam held out his other arm for her to take. His suit was a little snug, and she saw the white of his shirt as the jacket spread apart. He had gained weight, something he did after going through his divorces.

"How's your lake place?" She referred to his cabin in Wisconsin, thinking it would be nice to be up there right now.

"Great. I fished, walked the woods, and didn't have a raging wife to tell me how to run my life." Sam provided her with a cheesy smile. "You still need to get up there, you know."

"We will." She hugged his arm. "One day we'll take you up on the offer."

They walked into the grand room. The three crystal chandeliers and the shimmery gold drapes were like jewelry adorning a queen. The musicians played a waltz but no one danced. What a shame, she thought.

Jessie's parents had loved waltzing around the living room, whether listening to the stereo or humming their own classical masterpiece. They'd make her join them, and they'd dance together without a care in the world.

A lump grew in Jessie's throat. Her cheery façade saddened for a moment. How she wished her parents or even her grandpa, the one who raised her, could be there to see her marry. All three were gone.

"You okay?"

"I'm fine." Jessie smiled, bringing herself back to being the honored guest.

Walt found her from across the room, and she waved to him. He saw Sam with her and walked over to greet him.

"Are you harassing my bride-to-be?" Walt shook his friend's hand.

"Why would I harass her over you?"

Walt laughed.

"We were heading outside for some fresh air," Sam said in an English old lady's voice.

Walt raised his eyebrows and played along. "'Tis a good e'ening for it. But I must steal my bride-to-be for a moment. Would you mind?"

"Carry on." Sam bowed out. "Go find some crumpets or something."

***

Walt wanted Jessie to himself, and the opportunities to be alone were limited. During the three hours since joining the party, he snuck in two quick hugs and a kiss. This was his turn to have her. They could spend time with Sam later.

"Come, follow me. I have something for you," he said and took her hand. He pulled her away from the party while waving or greeting people as they made their way to the patio. They left the music and guests for the quiet October evening.

The fresh air cleared his senses. His parents' friends must own controlling stock in perfume because the concoction of scents filled the room as if it were money. He learned to wear little aftershave after throwing Jessie into a coughing fit when he doused himself on their first date.

From the patio, Walt guided her around to the hedge garden beyond the pool.

"I wouldn't go too far," Jessie warned. "We don't want to disappoint your mother by being late for the toast."

"She'll be fine," he said and patted the stone bench for her to sit. Normally, the fountain was drained for the winter, but his parents kept the water flowing for the guests to enjoy.

Walt took in the moment, listening to the water as it rained into the pool from an ornate spigot. He loved the hedge garden, his favorite place to hide when he needed to be alone.

"Fresh air," Jessie said after taking a deep breath. He knew she referred to the quiet. Inside, she used her polite smile. Outside, with only him, she closed her eyes in relief.

"A beautiful night." Walt looked up to the sky. The stars weren't as bright with the house lit up, but they were still pretty. He turned to face Jessie. Her blonde hair layered down her back as she tilted her head to reveal a slender neck needing to be kissed.

Walt resisted his urge to devour her. The party continued in the background, and the guests must be wondering where they were hiding. He didn't have much time. His hand went to his coat pocket, and he pulled out a velvet box.

"This is for you. I meant to give them to you earlier, but with all the rush..."

He sat down next to her on the bench and held out the present. Jessie opened her eyes and they widened when she saw the box. He cleared his throat. "The day I purchased your diamond ring, I ordered these as well. Cut from the same rock."

Her blue eyes fluttered at him with curiosity and then went to the box when she took it from him. She gasped after opening the top. A pair of earrings, a carat each, sparkled at her.

Walt smiled, pleased with her reaction.

Even in the dark the stones lit up like fire. Each cut released brilliant reds, yellows, and even blues. The gems came to life when he held up her ring finger to show her how they matched.

"They're beautiful." She moved the box around to admire the changing colors.

"And special. They lock."

Jessie laughed with some embarrassment.

She had lost a pair of ruby earrings, a present from him on her last birthday. With the diamonds being rare, he had the jeweler custom-fit the locks to keep them on her ears.

"How do they work?" Jessie couldn't figure out the mechanism.

"Like this." He used his fingernail to push on the edge of the post, which popped a spring. It opened the lock.

Jessie removed the pearls from her ears and placed them in the box. Walt helped her put the diamonds in and locked them in place.

"How do they look?" She placed her hair behind her ears to model them.

Walt smiled. He leaned in and kissed her, first gently and then with solid desire. He moaned, "I could lose myself in you. Right now."

"I wish you could too," she said, kissing him back.

Her hand went to his thigh and her touch triggered a reaction between his legs. He wanted in. They made the perfect couple. She was beautiful inside and out. He had the power and money. They could go a long way together.

"Mrs. Jessica Arbol-to-be, you make me complete."

"And I have no idea why."

"You may not think you fit in, but you do. You're the only woman for my heart."

Jessie laughed and wrinkled her perfect little nose at his corniness.

"I know you're nervous about the wedding and my mother getting in the way. Trust me, it'll be fine."

"I know." She tilted her head upward and welcomed the breeze as it blew against her face. The smile she gave didn't reach her eyes.

Walt ignored it. She had jetlag. Besides, his instincts were never wrong. They were meant to be together.

Chapter 2

::: Jessie :::

Chicago, IL

Jessie flipped the comforter over her head. Birds sang and the sun shined through the window. Neither would let her sleep. She peeked out of her cocoon and over at Walt as he lay by her side, snaked within the sheets. He left her a small wedge of the king-sized bed and claimed the rest for his domain.

She thought about pushing him over a few times during the night, but his snoring, muffled against the white fluffy pillow, made her think twice. Why disturb the vibrant baritones? This was quieter than the bear he became if he didn't get sleep.

Jessie wished the party hadn't overwhelmed her so much. A night filled with too many people and too many ass-kissers. More than enough plastic smiles masked what a true celebration should be. She thought back to the over-friendly reminders of how lucky she was to nab the heir to Arbol Publishing Company as her fiancé.

Walt lived Rolls Royce. She lived Ford. Even when they said their goodnights to the last guests at two in the morning, his mother managed to remind her of it.

Replaying the night or having a vision of his mother in her head was the last thing she wanted now. She remembered Walt's words. "Trust me, it'll be okay." Being the one used to power, he had no idea the pressure she was under.

She stared at the wall shelving Walt's collection of old rare coins, handed down to him from his grandfather. She felt as flat and lifeless as the little treasures. A strong cup of coffee and a jog would get her brain and body functioning again.

Jessie slithered off the mattress to the floor. She crawled to her bra and panties across the velvety blue carpet, where her open suitcase had been tossed off the bed before she went to sleep. She found her yoga pants tucked in one of the side pockets.

A yellow envelope fell to the floor, and she picked it up. Two wrinkled photos slipped out. The first one was of her parents. The couple, with their arms wrapped around each other, gazed into the other's eyes. They posed like Clark Gable and Carole Lombard as they stood in front of a borrowed two-seater plane. Jessie let out a soft, sad sigh. She wondered if they would be proud of her—photographer, traveler, homeowner, and soon to be married. They always told her to go with her heart. Her parents' connection for each other had been deep, and they wanted their only child to find the same type of love.

Jessie switched pictures. The second one was of her and Grandpa. Her rock. His expression was mean, as was his usual stance, but that was only a front. Many didn't like him, but he treated her with a kind heart. She doubted if he'd like Walt. Grandpa Rossen was practical and didn't like all the flash. She placed both photos back into the envelope and tucked it next to her passport.

She grabbed a white, long-sleeved shirt and slipped it on over her bra, both smelling like stale perfume. Next she struggled with the yoga pants. The leggings weren't working to her advantage as she tried sticking her feet into them.

As she danced to get her pants on, Walt sprang up. "Hey!"

Jessie jumped at the sound of his voice and almost fell backward. "Go back to sleep."

"What time is it?" He played with his mouth, and she knew it was dry from the alcohol and snoring. He rubbed his eyes.

"Too early for you to get up," she said.

He flopped back down into the pillows. Soon he was back into a routine snore. Poor guy. He was going to be hurting today. After the toast, she had no idea how many shots of vodka and whiskey were passed his way.

Jessie tiptoed to the bathroom and shut the door. She turned on the ornate silver handle for Hot and waited for the water to turn warm. She washed her face. A shower would be better—wake her up more—but she'd wait until after her jog.

The only towels in the bathroom were thick like pillows and embroidered with Walt's initials. She used a corner of one to pat her face dry. Seeing the mess in the sink, Jessie grabbed a tissue to wipe down the powder-blue scalloped bowl.

She never liked visiting Walt's parents. The house was too stiff and formal. Jessie wondered how Walt had survived their pickiness.

Creeping back into the bedroom, she grabbed her phone and checked for messages. The airline company changed her flight number for her next photo shoot in New York. A new client wanted brochures and a web ad with her photos. Another wanted her to review a contract. All could wait.

"Why aren't you here in bed with me?" Walt's deep voice shot out from the bed. He peeked over the comforter. His black hair spiked in every direction, while dark shadows and saggy skin beat out his good looks and strong appearance.

"You need sleep. I need a good run." She found a binder and used it to put her thick, wavy hair into a messy bun.

"You don't want to stay here with me?" His lips formed a pout. His head came up too fast and he winced.

"I need some fresh air. Get rid of my headache."

"I can get rid of your headache..." He opened the comforter for her to join him.

She laughed. "You're in no shape to please me or us."

"Ahhh, I'm worth it. Honest." He patted the empty space next to him.

Jessie grabbed her jogging shoes and a light jacket before walking over to the bed. Careful, so he couldn't pull her in, she held his chiseled chin upward and gave him a hard, quick kiss on his lips. "I need some coffee. You sleep. We'll see how you're doing when I return."

Walt sighed. "Be careful. Wear your good running shoes so you don't trip."

"They're the only ones I brought with me," she said and rolled her eyes.

"And your reflective shirt."

"It's daylight." She wasn't going to wear bright neon green. Her eyes wouldn't take it.

His phone buzzed, which reminded him. "You have your cell?"

"No. I won't be out for too long." She put on her Nikes while he checked his message.

Walt tossed his phone to the side of the bed. He gave up and dropped his head to the pillow. The phone went off again so she reached over and turned the volume to vibrate. She wondered if his texts were the culprit that kept her up throughout the night.

Jessie closed the door and then walked down the elegant hallway that opened to the grand foyer below. She stopped for a moment to admire the crystal chandelier as it dripped like sparkling rain from the ceiling. She smiled, remembering her earrings. Walt loved showering her with jewelry. The customized locks for the diamond posts were a little over the top but understandably so. The clarity and color were rare, as he stated. She wouldn't forgive herself if she lost the earrings. Or her ring.

At the bottom stair, Jessie stopped to listen to the activity. The sound of shuffling chairs, the faint clinking of glass, and Spanish whispers came from the other room. The hired help were cleaning the mess from the party, and they seemed relaxed as they chatted back and forth. A definite sign Mrs. Arbol wasn't around.

Jessie escaped out the front door. The crisp morning air sent goose bumps across her arms. She was glad she brought a jacket and put it on. She rotated her shoulders, shook out her legs to get the blood flowing, and then walked down the long circular driveway. At the road, she turned left and started her jog. She passed the perfectly manicured lawns, the trophy houses, and the sidewalks so white they shined like marble. Even the leaves on the ground seemed to be in perfect piles after falling from the trees.

Jessie came to an intersection and jogged in place. She decided to turn left to leave the pristine neighborhood and slid through the back gate that secluded the rich from the everyday souls. The smaller, quaint homes fit her comfort zone.

Her side started to hurt. Jessie slowed to a walk. For the first time, she noticed the weathered farmhouse tucked away from the street. The place seemed as if it had been grand in its day, and she wondered if the house would be worth renovating. The shabby white paint, the boarded windows, and the black, crooked shutters were all fixable. She loved the large porch gracing the front and imagined entertaining guests as they sat in white rockers, sipping strawberry margaritas and enjoying the summer day. If the farmhouse weren't so close to the Arbols' estate, she would consider buying it, if for sale. Now, the home stood abandoned, stripped of life.

A group of younger kids ran out from the backyard. They played with a huge, bright blue ball, kicking it back and forth to each other. She counted four boys and one girl, who was younger and maybe tagging along after her brother. Jessie wished she had her camera. The kids were using the yard as their playground, and she envisioned a black and white photo with only the ball colored blue.

The little girl screamed in pretend agony when a redheaded boy around eight years old picked up the ball so the girl couldn't reach it. He tossed it to another boy, who ran and disappeared around the farmhouse. The rest followed.

The moment over, Jessie continued her walk to a busier street. She spotted a coffee shop a few blocks away and increased her pace, the focus on caffeine.

The place was on the corner of two streets and reminded her of a little shack with gray wood siding and a matching door. A whiff of strong, black coffee greeted her even before she entered the shop. A wooden counter, made from an old saloon bar, lined one side of the shop. The other side had a row of tables with chairs for customers to enjoy their fresh lattes and cappuccinos. The chairs were empty.

The lights were on, the door unlocked. They had to be open. Jessie waited at the counter. She traced the gouges in the wood with her finger and wondered how many old-time brawls and beer bottles had passed over the bar.

"How may I help you this morning?" A thick, Jamaican voice sang out to her.

"Oh!" Jessie jumped. Her hands popped away from the counter. She turned to see the woman saunter toward her. *Where did she come from?*

She chuckled. "I'm so sorry. I didn't mean to startle you."

Jessie shook her head, embarrassed. "I should have been paying attention." She was still perplexed by the woman's sudden appearance. Had she come from the back? "I guess I'm a little out of it this morning."

"I can help you with that." She lifted part of the counter top and stepped behind it. "My coffee can be customized with just the right potion."

The woman held her head high like a queen, a Jamaican queen. She had smooth dark-chocolate skin, and her eyes were exotic and deep. Most people would shy away from the intensity of the woman's stare, but Jessie found her intriguing. Something about her made Jessie think of good and evil combined. Again, she wished she had her camera.

The ding of a timer sounded from the back of the coffee shop.

"Excuse me,"—the Jamaican queen bowed her head—"I have scones in the oven."

"Of course," Jessie said.

"Here is the list of my specialties." She pointed to the board on the wall before disappearing.

Jessie studied the specials. Some blends had herbs or powders with unfamiliar names. She tapped her fingernails against her lips while attempting to decipher the different creations. Giving up, she placed her hands on the bar and waited.

The Jamaican queen appeared again. She studied her for a moment and then pointed one of her long, red fingernails toward Jessie's hand. "This is your first time here."

"Yes, it is." Jessie wondered if she had something on her hand. She had her engagement ring on, but the woman wasn't focused on the rock. Instead, she seemed to be reading her fingers like a fortuneteller reading a palm.

Jessie became curious as the Jamaican queen closed her eyes, swayed, and then reopened them. She said, "It's good you finally came to my shop. Maybe a stronger brew for you today?"

"Is it that noticeable?" Jessie wondered if the woman sensed something was wrong or if it was the effects from the night before sending some offbeat vibe.

"Hmmmmm," the woman said and smiled. "I believe I have the right potion for you."

Jessie nodded, unable to speak. This was getting a little creepy.

As the woman made the coffee, Jessie stepped back to get some breathing room between her and the queen. She went to study the painting on the wall above one of the tables. The oil was of a trail within the woods. The forest bed, covered in ferns and speckled with pink flowers, seemed peaceful. She was amazed by the detail and vibrant hues.

"Where is this place?" Jessie asked as the woman placed her coffee on the counter.

"A land that is very special to my heart."

"Jamaica?"

"No, not my island," she said and smiled. "You like the forest?"

Jessie nodded. The way the artist painted the canvas—it drew her in, especially how the sun beamed down between the trees. "It's mystical yet beautiful."

"A sanctuary."

"Yes, exactly." Jessie agreed and then turned back to the bar. The coffee was in a small, dainty black cup with a silver rim. She looked at the size, hoping for a larger version. "Can I get my coffee to go please?"

The Jamaican woman pointed to the cup. "You drink this one here. I will make you another."

Jessie hesitated. The word "potion" from earlier in the conversation had her worried. She wasn't sure why the woman was making her another cup.

"First one is to help erase your troubles. The second is to give you strength."

Two blends. Okay.

Wait—did she just read my mind?

The coffee did smell delicious. As she drank, Jessie kept her eye on the Jamaican queen as she made the next one. She poured the steaming brew into a sixteen-ounce Styrofoam cup and then added a yellowish powder to the liquid. Next she pulled a dark red vial from the back shelf and put two drops of oil into the mix. Once stirred and ready, she handed Jessie the cup.

"Thank you." The second blend smelled even better than the first. Jessie closed her eyes as she inhaled the rich, sweet aroma. After the first sip, she had a new favorite coffee shop.

"This is really good," she said and opened her eyes again.

The Jamaican queen smiled, again like good and evil combined. "I'm glad you like it." She pointed one of her fingers toward Jessie's ear. "You have beautiful diamonds."

Unconsciously, Jessie raised her hand and played with one of the posts. She felt the special locks keeping the diamonds in place. Yep, still there. "They were a gift from my fiancé."

"The one you are troubled by."

Jessie frowned. How did she know? Her nerves must be transparent, she decided. "I'm fine."

"Hmmm." The Jamaican queen seemed to think differently.

Time to leave. Jessie pulled out cash from her jacket pocket. The woman held out her hand to stop her. "You were meant to have both. To you, from me."

"Really? I can pay."

The woman shook her head. "Sometimes you have to end to start. A calling if you will."

"Why, thank you." Jessie fumbled for words. Again, the queen seemed to know something she did not.

"Make sure you drink it all," the woman warned.

"I promise, I will." Jessie raised the cup in thanks and pushed the door open with her back. She had every intention of drinking the liquid gold.

Chapter 3

::: Jessie :::

Chicago, IL

Jessie wanted to remember the name of the coffee shop. *Secret Endeavors*. How fitting. At least now she had a place to visit when staying at Walt's folks' place. The Jamaican queen warned her to drink the entire cup. No issues on her part since she liked the buttery-caramel flavor. She would return for another visit. Somehow, she felt the woman was smiling at her as if to say, "Good girl."

A wisp of smoke filled the air as she neared the farmhouse. Odd that someone built a fire so early in the morning. She threw the empty cup into the stone trash barrel located at the bus stop. She stretched her back, ready to jog back to the Arbols' estate.

The sky was hazier than before. It seemed to be coming from the wooded area where the kids were playing earlier. Nothing out of the norm, she thought.

Nearing the property, the boy who caught the kickball shot across the street without looking. His eyes were two wide orbs and his mouth was closed tight as if running away from something bad.

Jessie's suspicion grew. She slowed her pace near the end of the driveway. Where were the other kids?

What did he do?

A tumbling of nerves began to ball up inside her. The air seemed too thick, the morning too still.

A faint shrill cry, like a bird in distress, came from the side of the house. Jessie's instincts took over. She jumped into action and cut across the uneven yard. She turned around the corner. Black smoke billowed from a broken window on the first floor. She didn't see the other kids, but a girl with red hair and pigtails stood in the yard. Her body seemed frozen in place as she stared at the house.

Jessie's ball of nerves doubled in size. She ran toward the girl. "What happened?"

Only short gasps hiccupped from her mouth. She continued to be transfixed on the house.

Jessie assessed. A shadow passed by one of the windows on the second floor. It could've been smoke. Let it be smoke, she thought. She grabbed the girl's arm. "Who's inside?"

"Aaar...Arr" she stuttered and pointed.

"Shit!" Jessie didn't have time to find out. She shooed the girl away. "Go get help."

The girl didn't move.

"Now!" Jessie yelled like a drill sergeant.

The girl jumped as if reacting to a slap on the rear and ran toward the street. Jessie sprinted up the porch stairs. She expected to find the door locked and wrenched her back when it flew open with a bang.

A wall of smoke jerked her back. Jessie gasped for air and coughed hard. She raised the front of her jacket to cover her mouth and nose. She ducked low and darted inside.

To the right was the living area with torn curtains, an old couch, and scattered newspapers. To the left was a dining room with ripped, pale yellow wallpaper where the smoke seemed heavier. She peeked inside. Light flickered from a back room. She inched forward to find the kitchen. A wood table in the center of the room was on fire. Her first reaction was to drag the table out to the yard. Common sense said that the table wouldn't fit through the doors. Nor could she grab it with the flames turning the wood into burning logs.

The kids.

Jessie backed out of the dining room. She glanced up a staircase and then down a main hallway that led toward the back of the house. Her pulse quickened not knowing what to do. Which way? She chose the hall. The first room was a bathroom: broken tile, rusted fixtures, and a cracked mirror. No kids.

Jessie tried the door on her right, but it was locked... or maybe jammed. Her eyes stung as the smoke filtered into the hall. Was anyone even there? Was she endangering her own life for nothing?

A faint cough came from the other side of the door.

Her head went up to listen. "Hello?"

She took too deep a breath and the smoke filled her lungs. Jessie placed her hands over her mouth and coughed. Her eyes watered. She couldn't let it get to her—had to get the kid.

The door wouldn't open. Jiggling the knob again, she noticed the bottom corner of the door was wedged into the floor. She pulled hard until the door opened an inch wider. Using both hands, she curved her fingers through the opening. A shadow appeared, blocking the light from inside the room.

"Help me!" A small voice pleaded.

"Push on the door!" Jessie yelled as the adrenaline pumped through her.

The kid slammed his shoulder into the door. The gap widened.

"Harder!" She put her foot against the wall for support, leaned back, and grabbed hold of the door. When the boy slammed into the door again, she pulled back, using her full arm and leg strength.

The door flew open. Two boys toppled her over as they fell into the hall. Jessie grabbed both by their jackets.

"Stay down!"

They did as told and scrambled on all fours toward the front door. The taller of the two tripped on the threshold as he rose to bolt outside. He picked himself up and ran down the stairs to the yard. Jessie hooked her arm around the other boy and carried him. She let him go when she fell to her knees and hit the lawn.

Jessie gasped for air. Her lungs burned. She tried short breaths, not wanting to cough because of the pain. She focused on the bright yellow dandelion near her face as she regained normal breathing. The boy next to her coughed a few times and then scrambled to his feet. He went to be with the other boy, and they huddled together near a tree.

They were safe.

She remembered a little girl. *Where's the girl?*

Jessie leaned back on her knees and scanned the yard as she thought back to how many kids had been playing. One of the boys had run across the street and two she found. She spotted the girl who was now next to the boys. All accounted for but one. The boy with red hair.

The pigtailed girl appeared from behind the house. Tears streamed down her face as she sprinted over to the huddled group. Jessie got to her feet. The missing boy must be her brother. Pigtail girl sprang back.

"Aaron's not here." The girl's voice rose an octave as she ran toward Jessie. She pointed toward the house. "He's in there. I...they think he's upstairs."

"What?" Jessie coughed. She remembered the shadow in the window. She forgot. *She forgot!*

No sirens. No police. No fire trucks.

"Aaron?" Jessie choked.

"He has red hair." She tugged on one of her pigtails, and she hopped in place.

Instinct told Jessie not to go back in. But how could she tell the girl no. Or live with herself if she didn't? She had seen the shadow and should have checked.

"It'll be okay," she said. "Make sure help is coming."

Jessie ran up the porch steps for the second time. She took a deep breath and shielded her face before entering the front door. Her tennis shoe caught on the threshold.

Bam!

Down she went. Her head, like a basketball, smacked against the edge of the first step of the staircase and then bounced back up. The blow stunned her. Blood appeared on the stair and the bottom of the rails. She touched her forehead and winced. Her neck tingled.

"Fuck." Her eyes blurred. Jessie blinked hard as she rose to a sitting position. With the palm of her hand, she wiped away the blood that trickled down the side of her face.

The burning heat against her back was a reminder to keep going. The fire lit up the dining room and spread like waves across the ceiling and walls. Soon those flames would be entering the hall.

Aaron. Upstairs. Focus.

The quicker she found him, the faster they'd be out. Safe.

Jessie climbed the stairs on her hands and feet. The wooden steps were old and worn in the middle. She kept her rhythm—hand, foot, hand, foot. Almost to the top.

A loud snap cracked the air as the stair buckled from her weight and then broke loose. Jessie fell backward as her leg went through the board, jolting her to a stop.

Dazed, she hung on to the stair in front of her, digging in with her lower arms to keep balanced. Her fallen-through leg dangled like a lead weight. Jessie hated to think where she'd have landed if she went all the way through. She tried pulling up. The wood snapped again. She froze, not knowing what to do.

A loud whoosh came from behind her. The curtains in the dining room ignited, and the heat ran up the stairs. A rush of panic swept through her as she cried out, "Help!"

Her voice was useless against the crackling of the fire. If the stairs broke and she went down, would they find her? Would it matter? Jessie had to get out. She again tried to free herself. Every time she tried, her leg remained stuck. When a stream of smoke blew upward, she gasped for breath. She tucked her head into the nook of the stair to breathe in a small pocket of air. *I am not going to die!*

Not like this. She managed to turn her leg, hoping the different angle would help. Jessie leaned forward, placed her elbows on the next stair, and then put all her weight on her arms as she raised her body. She had enough pull to make the next step. One arm at a time. The wood around her leg gave a little. Almost. She rocked her body to gain momentum. The wood splintered. She twisted her leg again to break free from whatever it was that got in her way. She found the edge of a stair with her other foot. One additional thrust and her leg came up.

Jessie scrambled to the second floor landing. She crawled down the hallway, making sure she was a safe distance away from the staircase. Her leg felt hot and stiff. She stopped to examine it. A jagged piece of wood stuck out of her thigh. Her head rolled back and her stomach turned woozy.

Don't faint. Do not faint.

Jessie closed her eyes and covered her face with her hands. She couldn't move her leg without the wood stabbing at her from underneath the skin. She reopened her eyes and peeked between her fingers. Her torn yoga pants were stained with blood but still intact. The wood sticking out leaned like the Tower of Pisa. She was thankful her pants were stretchy as the fabric hid the damage to her leg.

After a spasm of coughing, Jessie grabbed her thigh with one hand and the exposed wood with the other. In her head, she counted to three. The splinter tore her skin as she pulled upward. She cried out. The stain on her pants spread like spilled ink as more blood seeped out of the wound. She tossed the wood aside and pressed her hand down on her thigh to stop the bleeding.

She needed help. What the hell was she doing?

The boy.

"Aaron!"

The hallway was long and narrow. Three doors. One closed.

"Aaron!" Her throat burned.

Pulling up to her feet, Jessie limped down the hall with her bloodstained hand still covering her wound. She glanced into the two open rooms. No sign of the boy.

She grabbed the handle on the closed door and turned the knob, but it stuck against the frame. This door opened into the room, not into the hall like the one downstairs. Jessie pushed with her shoulder. Another jammed door. Three hard slams and the door gave way. Once inside, she closed it again to keep the smoke out.

"Aaron?" Her lungs wheezed. The room was empty. She headed for the closet. The door flew open as she reached it. The bottom edge slammed into Jessie's foot.

"Shit!"

She fell backward and landed on the floor. The boy from the closet tripped over her when he ran to get out. Jessie grabbed his leg and corralled him before he could dart out of the room.

Red hair. She pulled his bangs back to make sure he was okay. The freckled face had to be Aaron. He didn't seem to be hurt, only scared.

"Go to the window," Jessie ordered. Her thoughts clouded. Did he hear her? She wasn't sure. She helped him stand. "Go."

He did as told.

She was relieved to see the porch roof on the other side of the window. Their escape. Like the doors, the window wouldn't open. Jessie scanned the room. A few scattered papers, nothing hard or solid. She didn't have the energy to search any further. They needed out.

After pushing Aaron away to keep him at a safe distance, Jessie used her elbow to bust the glass. She removed a shard sticking out from her jacket, not caring if it cut her. Most of the other glass shattered to the ground. Jessie picked at the sharp pieces that remained in the window frame, not wanting the boy to be cut. She worked with speed to brush the glass away and then motioned for him to come closer. She half guided and half pushed him through the window. He fell to the porch roof.

Jessie was soon next to him. She climbed out the window without realizing it. She wheezed in fresh air, but it hurt. Her lungs wanted air but none would enter.

Aaron nearly lost his grip when a shingle loosened under his knee. Jessie grabbed the windowsill with one hand and used her other to pull him close to her. The boy clung to her as they listened to the house shift and groan. She flattened her hand against the shingles for balance.

Above, black smoke poured into the sky. Sirens blared from down the street. Everyone gathered in the front. She and Aaron faced the backyard. No one was there to help them.

"We have to get down. We can't wait."

Aaron squeezed her arm tighter and buried his head in her side. He hadn't said a word since she found him.

"Hang over the edge first," she said and her voice rattled like a smoker's. An odd calm kept her steady, in control. "Slide down the post. You'll be fine."

Aaron hesitated. She helped him turn around so he was on his hands and knees. He crept to the corner of the overhang where he could slide down the post. Jessie flattened on her stomach and spread her legs to brace her feet against the shingles. She kept a firm grip on Aaron's arms.

"Wrap your legs around the post," she said as he dangled his feet over the edge.

He struggled, his legs too short. Jessie helped him scoot further down. His waist disappeared over the side while his hands had a tight grip around her forearms.

"Keep your head up!" Jessie warned when he turned to see where he was going.

She locked eyes with him. Like her, he didn't seem scared but not fine either. More than likely, he was in shock. She mustered a smile and nodded for him to shimmy all the way down until only his head and arms were in view.

A large crack snapped from within the house and the porch jolted. Jessie almost lost him. She hung on to one of his arms, while he used the other to grip the post.

"When you're down, run away from the house. Go to the front." She let go.

Aaron yelled out. She couldn't tell if he fell or was able to slide down the post.

Jessie inched forward. He was nowhere in sight.

The house let out a bellow and a low rumble shook the underside of the house. The roof shifted underneath her, and she lost her grip. Jessie cried out as she scraped against the shingles and tumbled over the edge. She tried grabbing for the corner post but found only air.

Chapter 4

::: Jezamina :::

A Different World
Morlorn Territory

Jezero was nothing but tired.

The storm raged above them. The rain fell with such intensity not even the forest offered protection to the four men traveling there. The cold dulled Jezero's senses, putting him and his men at risk. They had traveled across the clearing before, but this time the danger was too great. He kept them to the perimeter within the trees.

Wiping his face and beard with his hand, Jezero scanned the opening in the woods for any sign of the Morlorns. He waited for his men to climb the path as the storm drummed thunderously against the trees, drowning all sounds. He wasn't sure if he agreed with the blessing or not. If he couldn't hear the dangers ahead, neither could the Morlorns. Jezero assumed their worst enemy hid from the storm. However, the price upon his head was worth it for those wanting the reward of a thick purse.

He turned to his men. They struggled with their footing as they moved away from the clearing toward the valley. The torrents of rain continued and turned the trail into layers of muck. Their saturated tunics and leggings weighed heavily against them, and the added weight made it hard to travel. Their haggard faces showed the chill penetrating their bones. They would have to stop before night fell to pure darkness.

Jezero nodded to Zarac as the man closed the gap between them. He was the largest of the four, and his barrel chest expanded twice the normal size when he took in a long drawn-out breath. Aresen followed close behind. His crystal blue eyes fluttered like a moth's wings to keep the rain from obstructing his view. The three waited for the tail, the straggler.

Raine had fallen behind. The medicine man was frail in comparison to the others, and he labored up the path. His thin frame wobbled from side to side.

"Jezero!"

Jezero's head shot up. He heard the cry; a desperate voice ran through him. The call hadn't come from his men.

"The sea," it called again, vibrating through his soul.

The spell was on him. One he didn't want to follow yet knew he had to. This wasn't the time.

Jezero raised his hand to get the medicine man's attention. "How's the path 'round the rocks?"

"The shore?" Raine twitched. His protruding eyes peered out from under thin, long hair. He nodded. "I remember the way."

Jezero lowered his head. Night was coming and the storm would have no mercy. Listening to his instincts, he made the decision. "We'll follow the sea."

"The water's edge?" Aresen's head jerked. "A danger, wouldn't ye say?"

"Not as bad as the clearing," Jezero responded.

They nodded in agreement and waited for Raine to lead them off the path. One by one, they placed their arrows against their bows and used the points to clear the brush in front of them.

When the terrain turned rocky and the trees melted into sand, the storm lightened to a fine mist. As dusk darkened the skies, they tightened the space between them as they maneuvered their way around the slippery rocks. They used the sound of the waves to pull them closer to the sea, while the fog swallowed them into its fold.

At the water's edge, the shoreline became their guide to take them around the bay. Salt lined the inside of Jezero's mouth, and he grabbed for his depleted flask. He took the last swallow and hoped to find fresh water by morn. The dense white fog shifted, making him stop.

The cliff came out to meet the sea, blocking their path. The rocks were too high and dangerous to climb, nor did they have the time. Raine paid no attention as the shoreline turned from white sand to brown wall. He kept walking into the swirling fog.

Jezero made a noise, a short growl, to catch the medicine man's attention. If they continued, the cliff would separate them from the forest and the other side of the bay, a trap if the Morlorns had followed.

"See here." The frail man stretched his arm and pointed the arrow held in his hand toward the cliff. "We will get through."

Jezero followed and saw a slight indent within the rocks. He squinted and guessed where the passage began.

"I know the way," Raine said with well-deserved smugness.

"I will take your word for it." Jezero motioned for the medicine man to keep going.

The passage was there, underneath an overhang that towered above their heads. The path between the rocks was narrow. Jagged pieces of rock formations jutted out from the walls. Zarac rubbed his chest as if feeling the points piercing his skin. "Am I going to fit through this opening?"

Raine scratched his head as if not remembering.

Jezero tucked his bow and arrow into his sash, pulled out his knife, and placed it between his teeth. He would find out. He leaned, curving sideways, to avoid one of the sharp protrusions guarding the opening as the passage swallowed him.

Foaming white water whipped at his knees, and the force broke his balance. He hit the side of the rock wall and pain shot through his shoulder. He moved on, this time grabbing the jagged edge for support.

"*Jezero!*" the rushed whisper called again.

He lifted his head. Zarac followed behind him, but the man kept his focus on his girth and the rocks. Aresen and Raine still waited to enter.

The waves splashed against the rocks. A cool, salty breeze mixed with the scent of the algae-covered walls, making his nose twitch. He waited for the calling.

"*The sea.*"

Jezero stopped before he left the passage. He scanned the waiting shoreline. The fog wasn't as thick. A lone bird struggled to span its wings to the wind and had to turn back, finding safety on a tree perched halfway up the cliff. The calling offered no inkling of what it wanted besides the desperate need for his attention.

One by one, the others emerged from the passage and readied their bows. They spread out with their backs to the rocks as they took guard. Raine stepped in front of them and raised his nose to sniff the salty air, catching the wind as it passed. He said with graininess in his voice, "There's seaweed on the shore."

Jezero waited as the medicine man again tilted his protruding nose upward and inhaled a sharp, deep breath. He motioned with his head for the rest to follow as the medicine man walked with his head high.

"The seaweed ne'er comes to shore." Raine frowned.

The men continued along the water's edge. The cold spray splashed against their legs and washed away their tracks almost as soon as the prints had formed.

"*Hurry*!" the whisper called again.

Jezero gripped his bow. With the fog lifting, they were vulnerable to the Morlorns and needed to move inland. He had put them all in danger by staying in the open, but he couldn't ignore the calling.

"Lead me..." he told the whispers. Had they gone too far?

"There!" Aresen pointed down the shore to a dark patch dancing on the crest of the water.

"What is it?" Zarac strained to see.

"Seaweed." Raine sniffed again.

Jezero knew better. He thrust his bow and arrows over to Raine. He ran in the direction where the seaweed would wash to shore. Aresen followed. A delicate arm fell away from the long, green tendrils. Jezero's heart beat faster, now understanding the urgency. He pointed.

"What the..." Aresen squinted.

The power of the current rushed across Jezero's legs as he ran into the sea. The cold water sucked the breath out of him. He kept going. Waist deep, the force of the current made him slow down. He leaned forward and tightened his stance to keep from tumbling under as the next wave crashed against him.

Jezero shook his head from side to side to rid his face of the water. He ignored the sting from the salt when he opened his eyes. The seaweed was about to crest over the next wave. Part of a woman's face had turned toward the sky.

Jezero cursed.

The seaweed disappeared on the other side of the wave, threatening to pull the woman back to the open water. He dove forward, determined not to lose her.

He swam hard and fast, stretching his hand to grab a strand of seaweed. He missed and tried again, reaching for her arm. The swell of the water overpowered him.

Jezero tucked his head as the wave crashed against him. The veins on his neck thickened as he defied the current and came up on the other side. A larger wave broke toward him.

As it was about to crash, he dove for the seaweed. He caught one of the tubes tangled around the woman. He pulled her toward him, securing his grip before cresting with the wave. Jezero went under as the water sprayed white. For a moment all sound dissipated with the density of the sea enclosing him. His sense of balance was off, but he kept hold of the woman. He stretched his legs to find the sandy floor and then pushed himself upward.

When he surfaced, Jezero gasped for air. He pulled the seaweed closer to his chest and dug through the fine leaves and slippery tubes until he found the woman's wrist. He held tight while Aresen helped pull them both to shore.

"Is she a Morlorn?" Raine grabbed a handful of weeds and helped move her to the drier sand.

Jezero cut through a tube snagged around her neck. As he pulled it away, her lips quivered. He muttered, "Holy Mother..."

"What's wrong?" Zarac looked down at the woman to see for himself. "She's alive?"

Jezero pressed his fingers against the woman's neck and leaned forward to hear her breath. He glanced toward the bushy-haired man. "Indeed. We need to get her warmed."

Raine dropped his bow and went into action. "Keep the seaweed wrapped around her for protection."

He fluttered his hands about to move Jezero and Aresen out of the way. The men stepped aside, giving him leeway as he hovered over the limp form.

She was naked underneath the layers of seaweed, and her skin was translucent from the cold sea. Luck was on her side when Raine confirmed all her bones were intact. He pulled away pieces of the algae stained with blood. He revealed a deep gash, open and raw, on her thigh. The medicine man clicked his tongue. The wrinkles across his forehead deepened. He showed Jezero the bruises covering her right shoulder and the cut near her temple.

"Is she a Morlorn?" Aresen asked as he tried looking over Raine.

"Maybe a prisoner," Zarac suggested.

"Nay," Raine mumbled as he pulled away the seaweed from her face. "No prisoner would have long hair. Hair is a sign of strength. No marks brand her arms. This woman is—"

Raine jumped backward and his mouth gaped open.

Aresen and Zarac widened their circle as their bows came up, ready to protect Jezero, their doyen.

"What?" Jezero went on high alert. His hands rose to provide protection, but he didn't know what to protect. He glanced toward the cliffs but saw no sign of the Morlorns. He looked back to his medicine man in silent question.

Raine pointed from his ear to her ear. He whispered as if the gods could hear. "She has fire growing from her ears."

Aresen and Zarac moved closer, forgetting their duty to guard against the enemy.

Jezero frowned and bent down to see. He pulled away a lock of her hair to reveal the fiery diamond. Her other ear had the same. The men stepped back.

"She's been called to us." Jezero confirmed what he already knew. The open water seemed calmer as if the urge to push her to shore had been satisfied. The sky wasn't as calm. Another burst of rain threatened the horizon and was heading toward land. They had stayed too long in Morlorn territory.

"We need to leave," Aresen said as if reciting his doyen's thoughts.

"Raine." Jezero gathered the woman into his arms. "Where to?"

The frail man thought for a moment while looking toward the cliffs. "A cave is near. We'll be protected."

With Aresen's help, Jezero lifted the woman to his right shoulder and curled his arm across her backside to keep her snug against him. Raine arranged the seaweed to keep the cold air from hitting her bare skin. They made their trek further inland where the woods would protect them.

The rain hit hard as they left the shore, making it difficult for Jezero to travel across the rocky terrain. His muscles strained as the woman bounced across his shoulder. The gash on her leg opened when his bow snapped against her after being caught on a branch. A red ribbon trailed down the seaweed to the path. The blood vanished as the rain swept it away.

Turning into the forest, they continued onward. The blood from her wound smeared against the leaves along the path. With the trees, the rain didn't have the force to clear the marks, leaving an easy trail for the Morlorns to locate them. They had to stop, being open prey with the markings. He should leave her. Let the Morlorns find her. Vyrone, their doyen, would be pleased with this finding.

Jezero spat. Even as the thought entered his mind, he knew he couldn't leave her to the devil.

Raine caught his attention. He had found a flat patch of moss between two rocks suitable for Jezero to lower the woman to the ground. Aresen swung the leather sack off his shoulder and grabbed a shirt. He gave it to Raine, who wrapped the cloth around her thigh to cover the gash. He tied the sleeves together to cinch the bandage.

When the bleeding stopped, Jezero lifted her again to his shoulder, and they continued on their journey. His movements were short and crisp as he strained to keep himself balanced while glancing about for danger. The spindled trees were no protection from the Morlorns. The path was rocky and turned in sharp switchbacks. When the woman nearly fell off his shoulder, he asked Raine, "How much longer?"

"I thought ye said of a place close by?" Aresen showed his impatience as well.

"We're almost there." Raine clicked his tongue.

Jezero kept his faith in the medicine man as he led them down a ravine. At midpoint, he motioned for them to follow him off the path. They stopped near a cove.

"In here." The medicine man pointed between two large boulders lodged in the steep hill. He smiled as if patting his own back.

"Humpf," Jezero said in amazement.

"How did ye know 'bout the cave?" Aresen shook his head in disbelief.

"I escaped the Morlorns, didn't I?" He let out a squeak of a laugh. "They never found me, even when they stood right here." He stomped the ground.

"Ye be lucky," Zarac said and brushed the rain from his face with one swoop of his wide, thick hand.

The narrow entrance was enough for a man to squeeze through. Raine went in first to check the cave. When he signaled all was clear, Aresen entered next. He waited on the other side for Jezero to pass the woman to him. They slid her between the rocks.

Jezero let Zarac through before entering himself. Raine had lit a torch to let them explore the cave. Their hideout had smaller alcoves off to the side and ample room for them to move around in.

"Exact to how I left the place." Raine beamed as he presented the place to Jezero. "No one's set foot in here since."

"You did good." He surveyed the area.

"Ahem," Aresen said as he struggled to keep the woman upright.

Jezero took her from him. She seemed heavier. The seaweed was cold and damp. It may have been wise to keep her covered for traveling, but now he saw the algae as a threat. He looked to Raine who was busy grabbing stones from the side and placing them in a circle. "Where should I put her?"

Raine tapped his fingers together while he thought. Then he motioned for his doyen to lay her down in a specific area between the stones and wall. After he helped position her, the medicine man went over to select a few pieces of wood stored in one of the alcoves. "We must bring in some heat."

"We can't have a fire in here!" Zarac placed his hand in front of Raine as if to stop his antics.

"'Tis safe." Raine piled the wood inside the stones and then poked at a rock above him with his finger. He put his hand inside a crevice and punched a clump of mud with his fist until it gave away. Fresh air filtered into the cave and swirled with the staleness inside. "The smoke leaves through the other caves under the land. I had many fires and was never found."

The big man looked as if he were trying to figure out Raine's logic but gave up. He turned to Jezero. "I'll have a look around outside."

The doyen nodded as he removed the seaweed from around the woman's face. "Take Aresen."

"Head away from the ravine, to where the trees are gray and short. Good hunting ground. Ye can find fresh water in the area as well. A small spring near the clearing," Raine instructed before the men left.

Jezero switched places with Raine and took over tending the fire, while the medicine man cut the tangled seaweed with his knife. "She is beautiful but frail."

Jezero glanced over. Her skin was blue and beaten by the sea. Even so he had seen her soft features—the curve to her cheeks and the slant to her small nose. He tried not to think how she was going to react when she woke. How he would react to her. She was dangerous for him to protect, and yet more dangerous to leave behind.

Chapter 5

::: Jezamina :::

Morlorn Territory

Jezero stayed back while Raine took care of the woman. The medicine man removed the seaweed from her arms and chest. Once she was bare, he placed one hand across her exposed breasts and started in a slow, circular motion to warm her heart. As her skin turned rosy, he widened the circle. Jezero wished he were in the medicine man's shoes. No, he thought and turned away. *Don't get attached.*

"I need a shirt."

Jezero was happy to oblige. He found one in his sack and handed it to Raine.

"A little help here," Raine said when he couldn't hold her up and pull the shirt over her head.

With hesitancy, Jezero walked over and wrapped his arm around the woman's shoulders to lift her. She smelled of the sea. And of being a woman. He closed his eyes to enjoy the sweetness.

"The sea was her friend," Raine said as he guided one of her arms into a sleeve. "The cold kept the swelling down."

"Aye," Jezero agreed. He helped pull the shirt down. The length was enough to cover all womanly parts. A good thing since they were all men.

Raine went to his pouch of medicines and emptied the contents. As he decided what to concoct he said, "Stay by the woman."

Sitting back, Jezero cradled her in his arms in hopes the heat from his body would help to warm her. Her lips were still blue and her face pale even with the fire warming the cave. He picked at the dried seaweed near the wound on her forehead.

"Make sure to give her something for the pain," he said to the medicine man. "She will have a nasty headache when she wakes."

Raine huffed a few times before mumbling to himself. He selected a long stem with yellow-striped leaves from his sack. He shredded the stem with his fingernails to extract the medicine, letting the sap drip into the woman's mouth.

"What's the matter?" Jezero didn't like how the medicine man's brows wove together in a frown.

Raine stopped what he was doing to listen. A shuffling noise came from above the cave. Clumps of dirt fell from the ceiling. One landed on the woman's arm. Next was a loud thump.

Jezero rose and removed his knife from the sheath. He stepped over the woman and went to stand near one side of the entrance. The noise stopped. Raine's hands trembled as he stared at the opening.

The fire crackled. If the enemy was nearby, they'd hear the continuous snap of the bark separating from the wood. Jezero wanted to kick the flames out but knew the woman needed the heat, and he trusted Raine. Instead, he waited. Only one could enter at a time.

A shadow danced across the rocks. A scrapping noise, the swishing of leather, along with the sloshing of rain-drenched clothes sounded familiar. Jezero put his knife down and let out his breath.

Zarac re-entered the cave. He held their flasks, fat with water. Aresen followed. He held two skewers of raw meat. Raine went back to preparing the medicine.

"Did she wake?" Aresen asked and squatted with his arms resting on his legs. He held their meal over the fire. Soon the red chunks turned brown. The juice sizzled as it dripped against the burning logs.

Jezero gave Aresen a pat on the back for finding their meal for the night. His stomach growled with anticipation. "No. Not of yet."

"She hit her head hard," Raine said. His boney fingers pressed against the skin near the wound. "I may not have the medicine she needs."

"Why waste the time?" Zarac sat near the fire. "If she is no use..."

"She could be a bargaining chip," Aresen said. "She belongs to the Morlorns, to Vyrone."

"Enough," Jezero growled at his men. "I have answered the calling. She is mine to protect."

All three turned to stare at him. They kept their silence. He knew his words had been sharp, but the thought of them speaking as if she were dead or a pawn infuriated him.

Yes, she would live. He was too stubborn to think differently. The calling was strong and powerful. She had a reason for being there and for him finding her.

"Awff," Zarac raised his hand to his nose.

Raine had opened a vial from his pile of medicine, and the stench leaked out. Jezero turned his head away as the pungent odor, a smell like rotted leaves, burned through the air. His eyes watered from the bitterness as Raine dabbed the oil on the wound.

"This should draw the poison out." Raine pressed a leaf over the wound. Next, he worked on her thigh.

Zarac unsheathed his knife and helped remove the strips of blood-soaked cloth from around her thigh. He left to bury the seaweed and bandages outside. Raine grabbed one of the flasks next to the fire and poured warm water on her leg to wash the dirt and blood away.

"The sea was an angry one," Raine said and showed Jezero how the gash hooked around her upper thigh.

"More than the sea," Jezero said when he spotted a dark splinter inside her thigh. He crouched down.

"'Tis a piece of wood?" Raine touched the jagged edge with his gnarled finger. He tugged to pull it out, but his fingers kept slipping. "What happens if we can't?"

"We need to take the wood out." Jezero wasn't a medicine man, but he knew she wouldn't heal if they left the wood inside her. He pulled out the knife hidden in his boot. The blade was long, narrow, and pointed.

Raine leaned back, letting Jezero have room to work.

The first attempt failed; Jezero had been too cautious. The woman hadn't flinched. He looked to Raine for approval.

The medicine man nodded.

Holding his breath, Jezero dug his blade in again, this time cutting in to find the end of the sliver. He twisted the blade until the piece came out. Blood pooled around the wound as the piece broke free. Raine pressed the medicine into the area and wrapped it with clean strips of cloth. He clicked his tongue.

"How does wood like that get in yer leg?" Aresen asked while turning the meat.

Jezero ignored the question and said, "Not just one."

Raine peered down to see the other pieces where Jezero pointed. They worked diligently to remove what they could. "The small ones should come out with the paste after the leaves dry. Otherwise..." He shook his head.

The two finished bandaging her wounds when Zarac rejoined them. He checked on the meat cooking over the fire, then glanced toward the woman. "How is she?"

"We found this in her leg." Raine held up the jagged piece of wood. He showed it to Zarac and then Aresen before tucking the sliver back into his sack.

Jezero noted the water dripping from Zarac's beard as the man cut a slice of meat from the skewer. "I see the rain hasn't let up."

"Daylight will see the higher clouds again," the big man grunted.

Jezero nodded. "We'll stay here for the night."

"And what about the woman?" Aresen asked as he grabbed a slice of meat.

"She will be known as Jezamina," Jezero announced, giving her a name similar to his to give her strength. "She will be a warrior."

He looked to Raine. The man was good with medicine. Jezero could never fault him for that, but her wounds were too deep. Jezamina was going to need the medicine woman, the one who healed him in his time of need.

"She needs Veita."

"We'll head to the village?" Zarac cut another chunk of meat and handed it to Raine.

"Nay," Jezero said and their eyes turned to him. "We'll take her to Dusken. Veita will come to us."

Aresen choked on the water he drank. Raine's eyebrows twitched. Zarac grunted. No one said a word and Jezero understood. Never before had any woman set foot in Dusken.

Chapter 6

::: Jessie :::

Chicago, IL

Present Day

Jessie thrashed across the bed. Walt covered his ears. The sound of her in agony was unbearable. He imagined her lungs trying to breathe in air, her brain screaming for oxygen. She was supposed to die quietly.

"She's breathing."

Walt heard the doctor's muffled words. He opened his eyes and shot his head upward. Dr. Maguire rattled orders to Carol. As she left her spot near the bed, the nurse glanced toward him. Her face showed signs of hope.

Could it be?

Walt stood up and sprang over to the bed. Another nurse came in. Another doctor. They pushed Walt out of the way.

His heart pounded hard, and he put his hand to his chest as if to slow it down. He didn't like being pushed aside. This was his Jessie. Walt had every right to be next to her when she woke. He should be the first person she saw when her eyes opened.

He moved back to the bed. Walt tried holding her hand, but she fought it. The nurse latched constraints around her wrists and ankles. He cursed. "What are you doing?"

"Temporary. We don't want her to harm herself," Carol said.

Jessie's eyes fluttered open.

Walt's heart jumped when she winced in pain. He laughed with joy. Finally, an emotion. Her head moved from side to side. She didn't seem to recognize him. "Jessie."

"No!" she cried out. Her eyes continued to flutter. She seemed confused, as if trying to find someone or something.

Walt leaned in closer, befuddled. "Jessie. It's me. Walt."

Jessie stopped thrashing. Yes, she recognized his voice. This was a good sign.

"Jessie, you're here with me. You're okay."

Her head went down toward her shoulder, and she started to cry. She whimpered and then whispered a word...a name?

"Jezero. Jezero. Jezero."

Walt shook his head. "Who? What?"

He couldn't place the name. *Why isn't she recognizing me?*

The doctor leaned over to check her eyes. "Jessie, this is Dr. Maguire." He placed his stethoscope on her chest. "Do you know where you are?"

She didn't respond.

"What's your name?"

She formed her lips as if ready to tell them, but the words wouldn't come out. The doctor used a sponge to wet her mouth. He waited before repeating his question. "What is your name?"

She swallowed hard. "Jezamina."

The doctor looked up at the nurse and then back to Jessie. "Where do you live?"

"Dusken," she barely whispered. Her voice was raspy.

"Why does she keep moving her head back and forth?" Walt asked. She wouldn't focus on any of them.

"She's fine," Carol said to stop his worries. "This is normal."

Jessie raised her head and forced her eyes open again. She blinked repeatedly.

Walt moved closer. Her head jerked back, startled.

He smiled with anticipation. "I'm here for you, Jessie. I'm here."

She glanced over to the doctor and then back to Walt. Her eyes spoke fear, sadness, and panic mixed into one. Not love, relief, or happiness.

Walt's heart fell to the floor. This wasn't how he thought it would be. He envisioned her waking while he slept near her bedside. She'd caress his hair, gently waking him. They'd both smile. They'd laugh with joy, finally together again.

Give her time.

The rejection still hurt. She turned away from him to stare at Dr. Maguire and then at Carol, as if trying to remember them. Walt wasn't ready to lose her. He took her hand and wrapped his fingers around hers like he always did when they woke in the morning. "I'm here, Jessie. You're okay."

"No!" Jessie jerked her hand away. Even in the constraints she managed to squeeze her hand into a fist. "Please. Leave me alone."

Walt felt like he'd been slapped in the face. He held the cold steel bedrail, and his knuckles turned white.

Carol moved toward him and sympathized with his hurt. She patted his hand. "Let her come around. Jessie's not fully awake. She may be confused."

"Do you remember our engagement party?" Walt asked his fiancée, ignoring the nurse. He hoped the memory would trigger something. He leaned down as if being closer to her would help. "You were in a coma. We thought we lost you."

"Don't do this," Jessie pleaded and turned her head the other way. She stared into the air. "Oh my god, what happened? Where are you, Jezero?"

"I'm right here," Walt said. His tone was harsh. Why couldn't she remember his name?

Carol intervened, guiding him back a few steps. Walt tried to step around her, but she blocked him. "Let's give Dr. Maguire room to work."

Walt leaned his body sideways to see her. He said again, "I'm right here."

The doctor had been monitoring her heart rate. He moved back to the bed. While her eyes were closed, he explained how she ran into a burning house. How she saved the kids playing inside.

Walt steamed. He should be the one telling her what happened. The doctor asked questions. She answered.

Jessie didn't seem confused. The blueness in her eyes was sharp and clear. She knew what was happening. Walt stumbled back. This wasn't the cheery awakening he expected. They should be crying and laughing with joy. Instead, Carol made him sit on the couch, away from the bed.

"You didn't get the reaction you wanted," she said and sat down next to him. "I should have warned you. I was anxious about her waking as well." She gave him a sad face. "These things happen. Patients can say the oddest things. You have to remember what she went through. Trauma can do a lot to a person."

Walt nodded but her words fell off. They gave no comfort. Jessie's plea burned in his brain. Her look was clear and to the point. She didn't want him.

"Do you recognize the name she called out?" Carol asked.

"Huh?"

"Who was Jessie asking for?"

Walt rubbed his face. He felt a headache coming on. He shook his head. "I have no fucking clue."

Chapter 7

::: Jessie :::

Chicago, IL

The ties around Jessie's wrists tightened when she tried moving. The room was dark and quiet when she opened her eyes again. An IV towered at her side, and the machine attached to it made clicking noises, while the clear liquid ran from the pouch down to her arm.

This can't be happening to me.

She still felt drugged.

Jessie squeezed her eyes shut. Before she woke, her last memory was of Jezero's deep brown eyes. The look of fear and desperation that passed across his face when he faded into the smoke branded her thoughts. Did he know she was leaving him? All of it was so confusing.

She tried clearing her parched throat. Water sounded so good right now. She opened her eyes. The room, cast in shadows, turned quiet and cold. How long had she been in Dusken? How long had she been in the hospital?

For the past few days the doctors and nurses probed her. They questioned her about Dusken and why she thought her name was Jezamina. She learned to keep her mouth shut. Her cries for Jezero went silent. Her life with him and his men became nonexistent to the outside world. The staff at the hospital looked at her as if she were crazy. They couldn't understand her condition or why her body violently jerked at random points of time.

Walt never left her side. Each time she woke, he was there. *Right there in her face.*

Jessie tried bringing her hand up but the constraints stopped her again.

A prisoner.

She was held against her will, both body and soul. She wanted to go back to Dusken where life meant survival.

An abrupt snort from the corner of the room made Jessie jump. She had fallen asleep while letting the tears fall. Another snort.

Walt sat in the recliner near her bed with his legs stretched out. His head rested against his open hand. With disheveled hair and a two-day beard shadowing his face, it was so unlike him. The nurse said he stayed with her, day and night. He waited for her to wake.

She let out a long breath. All that and he was the last person she wanted to see right now. How could she face him when he woke? How could she explain what happened to her?

None of it made sense. The coma didn't make sense. Would it be wrong to want to leave her life here? If she died would she go back to Dusken? *Will I ever see Jezero again?*

Jessie's heart beat faster. She stared at the monitor and focused on her breathing. She lay still to keep herself steady and watched her heart rate lower. The shadows in the room blended into one as night fell. Outside the window, a bright star appeared in the sky. She wondered if it were Jezero's. Did it belong to him? Did he grieve for her? She bit her lip to keep from crying. This was so unfair.

"Jessie!"

She jumped again.

Walt leaned over the bed. His face beamed as if he viewed a newborn baby. His lips widened in a smile. The dip in his chin deepened.

She had loved him. No, she still loved him. Only in a different way. For this she said, "I'm sorry."

"It's not your fault."

Her throat hurt from being dry. She nodded toward the cup of water near her bed.

Walt understood her request. He leaned over and grabbed the cup, putting the straw to her mouth. "It doesn't matter. You're here now. You're awake."

It did matter. She had lived in a different world and learned a new way of life. How could she tell him about Jezero? About Dusken?

The water tasted good even at room temperature. She let the liquid swirl around her mouth and then trickle down her throat. When she had her fill of water, she pulled away. He set the cup back on the table. She asked, "You stayed here every night?"

"You went through hell. It's the least I could do."

Jessie winced as a pain ran down her side. She needed to run, to let her arms and legs stretch out. Her muscles were tight like a bowstring, ready to spring forward.

"What do you need? More water? Medicine? You want me to call the nurse?"

"No." She didn't want the nurse. "Let me loose. I don't want to be tied down."

Walt hesitated.

It was just like him—always by the book and obeying orders. "I won't run, if that's what you're thinking."

"Run?" Walt seemed surprised. "Why would you run?"

"Isn't that why I'm bound?"

"It's so you won't hurt yourself."

"Why would I hurt myself?"

"You thrashed a lot when you woke. You're having these...seizures."

"How many have I had?" She didn't remember any of them.

"You had a few bad ones when you first woke. Now they seem to come on at night, but they are fewer and farther apart. You're getting better."

"Better for whom?" Jessie said, then clamped her mouth shut. The words came out with unexpected force.

"What do you mean by that? Don't you want to be here?" By his expression, she had touched a sore spot.

Jessie changed the conversation. "Can you please call the nurse? I hate being tied up."

Walt nodded his head and stepped away from the bed. He walked, his frame tall and lean, with purpose. People looked up to him. He was a powerhouse in the publishing industry. Women wanted him. She should feel honored that he dedicated his time to her.

Jessie closed her eyes to remember the two of them in happier times. She opened them again when Walt re-entered the room with Carol, on call for the evening.

The nurse took her vitals.

She asked Jessie questions. Did she feel faint? Did her heart flutter? Headaches? Pain? She made Jessie wait until the doctor arrived. He repeated the nurse's questions and asked more.

Jessie lay still. She kept calm and said what she needed to say, what they wanted to hear. She played the game well and won. The constraints came off.

"Thank you," Jessie told Carol with relief. She rubbed her wrists and raised her knees up, enjoying the freedom to move about. She remembered being in shackles, chained to the floor. The bed wasn't as torturous as the dungeon, but freedom was freedom.

"You be a good girl," the nurse warned and raised her finger. "Don't go thinking you can walk around on your own. Remember, you just came out of a coma."

"Got it." Jessie wasn't going to argue.

Carol turned to Walt, who stood by the window. "You seem pretty quiet, over there. Are you all right?"

"I'm not your patient," he reminded her.

"You could be, for as long as you've hung around here," she said while helping Jessie sit up in bed. "Is that love or what?"

Jessie made the effort to smile.

"He's a special guy. Not many would stick around like he did."

Carol was right. Jessie had something special with Walt. She remembered the way they played on the beach, took naps on the porch, traveled to different countries. At one time they had a life together. The nurse left the room, offering a perfect time for Jessie to test the waters.

"I remember the events before the fire, but they are vague." She grabbed the cup of water and took another drink. Between sips she said, "Our engagement party was the night before at your parents' estate. We were late. I remember sneaking in the back and running upstairs to get ready. Your mother kept hounding us, irked at how we delayed the party. I remember the toast at midnight, and you holding my waist. You drank like a fish, if I remember correctly, and I had to hold you up."

"Not that drunk," Walt said. His body relaxed when he leaned against the wall.

"The next morning, I went for a run. You wanted me to stay in bed, but I couldn't sleep. I figured a good run would help get rid of my headache."

"I should've kept you in bed."

Jessie nodded. If she'd stayed, she wouldn't be struggling with Walt or her feelings. With a quick shake of her head, she answered her own question. She wouldn't have met Jezero and she wouldn't understand the power of love and courage. To Walt she said, "Those kids wouldn't have survived the fire if I hadn't found them."

He stared at the ceiling as they drifted into another silent moment. Walt bit his lip. Something troubled him.

"This wasn't what you expected, was it?" She knew him well enough to know that he wanted their reunion to be joyous; they'd both cry and kiss each other, professing endless love. They'd leave the hospital and head to the courtroom to get married, not wanting to wait a second longer.

Walt let out a half-laugh but didn't answer. A sign she was on the right track.

"I'm not the same person, Walt."

He looked up, confused.

"I don't know what or how to explain this." Jessie took a deep breath to gather enough will to tell him. "I wasn't here."

He seemed hesitant. "Yes, you were. I've been here the entire time."

"But I haven't."

Walt set his jaw. "You were here in a coma. You were barely alive."

"Physically, yes."

"You had an out-of-body experience?" he half-joked.

Jessie closed her eyes. This was going to be tough. He wouldn't understand, but how could he when she didn't get it herself. The gods were crazy. She was crazy for trying to explain and second-guessed herself about telling him. If she didn't tell anyone, it wouldn't be real.

"I lived another life." There, she said it.

Walt smiled as if ready to laugh in her face but knew better than to do it.

His reaction stung, but she remembered this was new to him. "I lived in a forest, on a ledge. I still remember the striking greens and browns saturating the valley. The flowers were amazing, beautiful, and fragrant. Nothing like I'd ever seen here." Her spirits lifted as her mind wandered back. "You would have loved the tiered waterfall—crystal blue pools of water where I could see to the bottom. The water was fresh and pure to drink."

"Sounds like Oz to me," Walt huffed.

"This wasn't a dream. I was physically there."

"Where?"

"Dusken."

Walt flinched. His mood darkened. He asked, "Who is Jerizo?"

"Jezero," she corrected him, "the one who found me."

"I see," he said as if to appease her. Walt moved from the wall to the chair near her bed. He sat down and leaned forward so both elbows rested on top of his knees. He rubbed his hands together.

"He found me in the sea and took me to Dusken to heal me."

Walt's upper lip twitched. "The paramedics found you on the ground in the backyard of the farmhouse. The doctors healed you."

"Jezero saved me. I was kept alive because of him, Veita, and Raine."

Walt jumped up from the chair and cursed. He paced the open area near the window.

"This is difficult." Jessie sat up more in her bed. "But I need you to understand where I've been. Why I feel different."

"You're not Dorothy," Walt snapped. His upper lip curled in anger or frustration. "At least she had the sense to know it was only a dream."

The tone in his voice was sharp and left no doubt he thought she was being ridiculous. Jessie brought her legs up and hugged her knees. She put her head down, unsure what to do. He wasn't supposed to react as he did, but she had to expect it. She got why he felt the way he did, but not to say he was right. He didn't need to come at her with such anger. If he were telling her, she'd have listened.

"I'm sorry." His arms flapped near his side. "I just..."

"What?" Jessie raised her head and her voice. "You of all people should know I'm not one to be flippant. I don't make up stories. I never lied to you before."

"I've never seen you act out before either."

Jessie frowned, unsure what he meant.

"You cried out for him." Walt's voice choked. "Not me!"

The hurt resonated in his voice. Now she understood why he acted so strange and distant. She vaguely remembered crying out when she first woke. The doctors kept asking her about Jezero and Dusken. What did she confess to them?

"I'm sorry." She didn't know what else to say.

Jessie lay back down. She stared at the tiny holes in the yellow ceiling tiles and followed the swirled pattern that flowed from one square to the other. She wasn't in a position to argue.

Walt stood near the end of her bed. His hands were on his hips. She wondered if he could survive where she had been. He had a lean, fit physique but lacked the muscles or agility needed to fight the Morlorns.

"Okay." She tried a different approach. "Let me tell my story, then you can decide for yourself. You can justify what I say as a dream or an effect from the drugs. But for now, the least you can do is hear me out."

"Why? If it's fictitious, then isn't it wrong to let you continue believing it's real?" Walt moved to the side of the bed and clenched his hands around the protective side bar. His knuckles turned white. The lines around his mouth tightened when he said, "I sat and waited here for you to wake. I touched you. I held your hand. You were here."

"Maybe so. Maybe not." Her head pounded above her temples. She tried rubbing the pain away. Was it so important to tell him? Should she continue to keep her other life buried inside her head?

"You need your rest, Jessie."

He turned away from the bed and grabbed his jacket from the chair.

"Walt, I went to a different place in time. I woke with no memory and discovered a different me. This place flows in my blood now. I can't forget it."

He shook his head as if tired of her ranting.

"I need to tell you what happened to me. What I went through." She didn't want to keep it a secret. The guilt would haunt her. Falling in love with Jezero was wrong. Jessie knew she'd been unfaithful to Walt, but not until she woke. All of it was beyond her control. With no memory, she had to survive in their world and not think about how it would affect her previous life.

Walt's upper lip turned upward in a growl. His eyes narrowed. "What *you* went through?" He put on his jacket with short, jerky movements. "How about what I went through? The nights I slept in this chair." He pointed to the chair next to her bed. "I waited for you to wake. Each day I wondered if it'd be your last or if I'd be able to enjoy your smile again."

The last words caught in his throat, and he was visibly shaking. He pushed the chair back with his foot.

"Walt," she said to settle him down. "I get that this is hard to hear."

He ignored her, too consumed by his own anger. "Who the hell do you think you are? Telling me how you've been in some paradise while I planted my ass here for weeks, praying you'd awaken. I stayed with you as much as I could. I didn't go to work like I should have."

This was big. Walt loved his job, loved the family business.

"Please," Jessie pleaded with him when he headed for the door. She didn't want their conversation to end in hostility. She only wanted him to understand.

He paused when he got to the door. He bowed his head and put his hand on the doorframe.

"I'm sorry. I shouldn't have..." Jessie said and shook her head. This was all wrong. Why did this happen to her? Why did she have to wake?

Walt knocked on the frame as if thinking about it. Without a word, he disappeared into the hall.

Jessie buried her face in her hands. Nothing would ever be the same again.

Chapter 8

::: Jessie :::

Chicago, IL

Every muscle in Walt's body tightened like a piano string. Each word Jessie spoke, the way her eyes lit up when she talked of that place and Jezero, sent him reeling in anger and frustration. He didn't give a damn about where she'd been. He didn't need to understand. She was infatuated with a dream. *A fucking dream.*

The hard stomp of his heels hammered the tile floor when he headed for the elevator. He didn't bother acknowledging the night nurse. So many times before, he had leaned over the station counter and struck up a conversation. They liked hearing how Jessie and he met. How he proposed to her, and their plans for the wedding. This time, he was like a horse with blinders. His only goal was to leave.

Walt hit his fist against the down button.

Son-of-a-bitch!

He paced. The elevator was taking too long. He jabbed his fingers at the word "Down." Nothing. He walked away and found the stairs instead. His polished brown shoes beat against the cement steps like a machine pounding in a factory. The rhythm only stopped when he rounded the corners to take the next flight down.

At the main level, Walt burst through the door to the hallway and almost knocked over a man in a long, brown coat.

"Sorry," he apologized, out of breath.

"Walt!" The man was Sam.

"Sorry, bud." Walt kept going. He turned to the main entrance and headed for the doors.

"Hey, what's going on?" Sam caught up with him.

Walt stopped and turned to his friend. They'd been best buds since ninth grade when they moved into the same neighborhood on the north side of Chicago. Walt took his side when the kids bullied Sam in school. In return, Sam used his charm and rationalization to get the two of them out of trouble. Back then, Sam knew he was going to be a lawyer just as Walt knew he was going to take over his father's publishing company.

"Is Jessie all right?"

"She's fine. Just fine," Walt snapped as if it were a curse.

"But you're not."

Walt didn't trust himself yet. He turned and pushed his way through the door. A burst of crisp Chicago air caught his breath and tousled his hair. He walked to the street. The traffic was loud, and he watched the vehicles pass until a break allowed him to cross over to the park. Again, Sam followed.

"What happened?" His friend nudged him.

Walt passed it off. "We had some words."

"You two fought?" Sam sounded surprised as they walked the shoveled path.

"Not one of my better days."

"Not that you've had many of those lately," his friend commented.

Walt kept his head down. How could he explain the look in Jessie's eyes? The way she smiled or how she spoke this guy's name? With his hands crammed into his jacket pockets, Walt hesitated in his step. His friend could help. "She told me about a dream. Remember when I said she called out names when she first woke?"

Sam nodded. He flipped up the collar to his coat to ward off the cold. "I remember."

"Well, she thinks she's been to another place. I think she said Dusken. A man named Jerizo...Jeziro...saved her life. Anyway, I lost it. I couldn't handle her telling me. Not after what I'd been through." Not after feeling so alone, he thought, but didn't say.

"I don't get it." Sam seemed confused. "What's the big deal?"

Walt felt his upper back constrict. The tightness ran down his entire body. "She told me how she's changed. I sense it, Sam. I can see it in her eyes."

"Of course she's changed. She's also probably scared. Think of the trauma she's been through."

Walt nodded. It made sense.

"People do weird stuff after events like this. Give her time to understand what's happened. Maybe she did have a dream."

"But she swears it's real."

"So what? Maybe she has to believe the dream in order to get over the shock. How about one of those out-of-body experiences? Don't rule that out either."

Walt lifted his head. Sam may have a point. The doctor said only the strong survive the type of situation she'd been through. Could this be her way of coping?

Sam continued. "The way I see it, she wants to share her experience with you. Hear her out. If you don't, she'll shut you out. Is that what you want? Let her tell you her side of the story."

"What about my side of the story?"

"We know what you did."

Chapter 9

::: Jessie :::

Chicago, IL

Walt peeked inside the hospital room. He had his act together. After sleep, a shower, and a change of clothes, he was ready to face Jessie with a new outlook. As Sam said, he needed to hear her out. She would tell him her dream, realize how crazy she sounded, and then come to her senses.

Jessie sat on the bed with her legs crossed and her head down. Her long, sandy blonde hair hid her face as she combed through the locks with her fingers. She appeared solemn but not upset. Seeing her in that moment was like having the old reflective Jessie back. He loved watching her in those moments.

She flicked her hair back, eyes full and alert as if knowing someone watched her.

He knocked on the door, pretending he just arrived. "Mind if I come in?"

"Please do." She stretched her legs out and pulled the covers over her, tucking the edges near her hips. The spark wasn't in her eyes. The smile seemed sad.

"I'm hoping you'll forgive me." He ventured farther into the room., Walt kept his hands in his pockets. Normally he had the confidence of a lion—not today. He let out a breath and said, "I owe you an apology for my behavior."

"You don't owe me anything."

Her words were simple but powerful in the way she spoke them. The pull of her separating from him, being independent, made him realize that he needed a change of attitude—and fast. Walt swallowed hard, feeling the anxiety.

The arms on her bed were down so he couldn't wrap his hands around the steel side rail like he did almost every day when talking to her. They had many conversations over the weeks, him telling her about his day, while she stayed in a coma. Time to suck it up, be open, and win her trust back by having the two-way discussion she wanted.

"This whole..." He waved his arm as he tried finding the words. "This whole ordeal is beyond anything I'd ever imagine. Or what I want to go through again."

She raised her eyebrows as if agreeing with him.

Walt grabbed the smaller chair and pulled it closer to her. He sat with his shoulders square and his back straight. He owed her.

"Ehh...I'm ready."

"Ready?" Jessie seemed confused.

"I want you to tell me what happened."

She turned slightly and tried to decipher if he was telling the truth.

"I didn't give you a chance." He leaned forward, like a catcher ready for the ball. "I was quick to criticize you. I thought only about me and the days I spent waiting for you to wake. I want us to get on with our lives again. I didn't think about what you went through, being in a coma and healing from your injuries. You should be able to tell me how you were affected by the events that took place."

"You pretty much told me what you thought." Jessie's voice had a hard edge to it. "Why change now?"

"You scared me. You wanting someone else didn't make sense to me." In truth, damage control was in order. He had to keep his opinion to himself and keep the focus on her. "I finally figured it out. Your...your experience is important so both of us can understand and move on."

Jessie pushed her hair behind her ears. Her one remaining diamond stud sparkled back at him.

"I contacted the jeweler to see if we can buy you another earring," Walt said to ease their conversation. "I complained that the lock didn't work."

"The lock worked. The earring isn't lost."

Walt frowned. "You know where the other diamond is?"

***

Jessie didn't want to tell Walt about the "lost" diamond earring—not yet, anyway. If he wasn't ready to hear how she woke in Dusken, he couldn't handle hearing about the earring either. She wondered what made him change his mind now.

Did he want to hear how crazy she'd become? Walt could decide to tell the doctors and demand she get proper treatment. Dr. Maguire or the shrink who kept coming in may have asked him to probe her for the information since they couldn't pull it from her.

No, he wouldn't do that to her. She still had to ask to appease her curiosity. "Why this sudden change of heart?"

"I didn't give you a fair chance."

"That doesn't tell me anything."

Walt let out a puff of air. He looked away. "Sam thought I should."

Jessie nodded. Sam reasoning with him made sense. She could see his friend scolding him. There had to be conditions. "I want to tell you, Walt, but I do fear you'll shut me down again. You may not like what I tell you."

Walt paled as if he wondered what he was getting himself into. He held up his hand. "I will do my best."

Jessie laughed. "I know if I confided in someone else, I bet they'd lock me up in a nut house." She then spoke slowly to make sure her words held meaning. "I will not become one of those zombies, medicated on drugs to keep me normal." Now she refused to take any addictive medicine at the hospital. If committed, she may not have a choice. Her hopes to find Jezero would be forever lost. "I trust you, Walt."

He used his finger to cross his heart. "I will not have you checked into a psychiatric hospital. I will not make you go to my therapist. I will not tell my therapist or the doctors here. This will be between you and me."

She chewed on her lower lip. He stared into her eyes. Normally when he became uncomfortable, the lines around his jaw deepened. He seemed genuine with no lines or tightness in his face.

Walt moved closer and grabbed her hand. "I want us back, Jessie. I miss us being together."

This time his eyes seemed to plead with her. Jessie nodded her head before realizing she caved to him. While Walt thought it would bring the two of them back together, her intent was to understand what happened to her. If she kept her life in Dusken to herself, she feared it would be lost. She needed Jezero to be real.

Jessie started with a slight tremble in her voice. "When I first woke to Dusken, I remember tremendous pain pounding in my head."

"What is Dusken?"

She eyed him with care, waiting to see how he handled it. "Jezero's home."

Walt blinked hard but contained his emotions. His nostrils didn't flare. His lips didn't tighten. He was there to hear her out.

Chapter 10

::: Jezamina :::

Dusken

Jezero stood on the ledge jutting out from the base of the cliff and scanned the forest before him. The woods, peaceful and covered in a bluish-gray haze, announced the onset of night. Another day gone and still no sign of the woman waking.

She had opened her eyes once since they arrived in Dusken. The woman found in the sea stared at him as if looking into his soul, blue eyes searching for a new life. And then an infection had set in, and she burned with fever. The woman named Jezamina pulled at his heart, and he needed to resist. She would have to prove she could survive.

A slight brush against the leaves caught his attention. He raised his bow with arrow in place and aimed toward the path leading up to the ledge.

The soft cooing of night birds rose from the trees. A red-bellied skiet roamed the forest floor below him. The animal trotted in a skittish pattern as if moving away from potential danger. Jezero waited to see what caused its angst.

The answer came in the way of a low threshing noise, barely audible to most humans. Jezero lowered his bow. Zarac announced his return and soon trudged up the path near the rocks. The burly man's step seemed quicker. Jezero offered his hand to help him to the ledge after the man jumped on to a lower rock.

"Any sign?"

Zarac nodded. "Aresen is on his way."

Jezero's breath came out in a puff of steam. He swung his bow across his shoulder. "How far out?"

"They crossed the river and crested the bank."

"Tell Raine to prepare food for the travelers."

Zarac tipped his head in acknowledgement. He picked up one of the smaller torches near the rock and tossed it to his doyen. "Ye need this."

"Aye." Jezero jumped the six feet to the ground and headed down the path into the valley.

Night hadn't reached them yet. The woods were thick and the trees towered above him. Ferns covered the ground in a blanket and drooped as if ready for sleep. Jezero walked the path and thanked the spirits for the rich hues and the beauty of his home. He picked his forest well, and not many were welcome. Veita, like Jezamina, was another exception.

The medicine woman swayed back and forth as she walked the path. Her breaths were short puffs and her head down to track her footing. She struggled as the incline steepened. He guessed Aresen had traveled an extra two days because of the medicine woman's age.

Nevertheless, she had come.

He met them as they reached the peak. The plump woman's face brightened when she saw him. Jezero doubted her joy had anything to do with him but more with her journey ending. He bowed in appreciation when she stopped in front of him.

"Jezero," she said. Even though tired and flushed from walking, the medicine woman managed a smile. "A long time has passed."

"Too long," he agreed. "I am honored you came to visit us based on our circumstance."

"Always a pleasure to be in your company," she said and took his arm for support. Dark circles shadowed her eyes. She had grown deep wrinkles and a thicker jawline since the last time they met. She used a cloth to wipe the sweat from her face. "However, I'm more interested in meeting this woman. Aresen told me what he knew."

"She needs your help." Jezero handed the torch to Aresen.

Veita's eyebrows rose in curiosity as if encouraging him to continue.

"Her name is Jezamina."

"Naming her is a good sign and brings hope." She leaned in. "Aresen said she was called to you?"

"Aye. The whispers led me to her."

Aresen lit the torch and held it high to help light the path as blackness swallowed the forest.

"No concerns, I'm assuming?" Jezero asked Aresen.

"We've been seen but no approach."

Jezero pressed his lips together. The Morlorns would catch on.

"My fault I'm sure," Veita said. "I do not travel with the agility I once had."

"'Tis no fault of anyone's," Jezero assured her as they continued their way to the ledge.

Raine waited near the steep rocks. He had lit several torches up on the ledge. Jezero didn't like the way the light called extra attention to their home, but he understood the purpose.

"Raine!" Veita raised her arms to greet the frail man. "The last leg of my journey is complete."

"Welcome to Dusken," Raine said and flinched when she hugged him. He stepped aside the moment she released him and then looked to his doyen for approval.

Jezero nodded, pleased with his action, knowing that the medicine man didn't like to be touched.

Veita stumbled up the stairs. Zarac appeared and offered his hand from the top. Once on the ledge, the medicine woman seemed confused as to where to go. The clearing in the middle held the fire pit, a few logs used for sitting, and a table with eating utensils surrounded by trees, rocks, and small foliage. She walked to the back where the steep, rock wall contained small caves that held their supplies.

"We live here on this platform," Jezero explained as she peaked inside one of the alcoves hidden behind a strategically placed rock.

"This is the most unusual place for a home," Veita said while taking in her first glimpse of their dwelling. She returned to the center near the fire. "You don't live in shays?"

"We find no need for them," Jezero said to her reference to the mud and hay dwellings built in the villages. "The rocks and trees provide ample space for our privacy and shelter."

"Interesting..." Her voice trailed off as she walked around the perimeter of the common area again. Jezero and his men gave her space to explore. She stepped up to the fire, small in comparison to the one she had left behind, the one that continually burned in the village's center place for any villager to use. The medicine woman raised her hands to warm them. She also scanned the shadows. Befuddled, she asked, "And where is this woman...hiding?"

Jezero pointed beyond the common area and toward the shadows where Raine stood guard.

Veita tilted her head and frowned as if she didn't understand. "You point to trees and rocks?"

He motioned to Raine, who removed the torch from the stand and held it closer to the shelter where the woman slept. The medicine woman lifted her skirt as she walked over to him.

"We covered her with ferns," Raine explained. "The coolness helps keep the fever down."

"She must breathe!" Veita scolded as she fell to her knees and began removing the thick leaves, tossing them behind her.

Raine's face dropped. He balled his hands into fists and held them close to his chest, crushed by her words.

"And so it begins," Jezero mumbled under his breath. He shook his head and waved his hand to tell Raine to let it go.

"Ye need me for anything?" Aresen asked as he came up behind him.

"Go eat and sleep."

"Aye," Aresen said while watching Veita. "I've had my fill."

Jezero chuckled knowingly. The medicine woman must have given him an earful when traveling, which neither he nor his men were used to. The tall, thin man helped himself to a prepared bowl of food then disappeared between the rocks to the long side of the ledge where they made their beds.

"Her face is so pale and drawn." Veita clicked her tongue. She moved her hand over the woman as if feeling her energy. "Oh dear," she said when discovering the gash in her leg.

"An infection has set in," Raine said.

"I can tell," she muttered. "You were right to bring me here. We will need to start right away."

Jezero took it as his cue to leave. He was better at protecting his forest than fighting fate.

"Raine," he called out while gathering his bow and arrows. "Make sure Veita has the necessary comforts she needs. Show her where she'll sleep."

They had made a bed for their guest, private like a shay, yet the shelter fit their surroundings. It was the best he could do to make her feel comfortable without jeopardizing their home.

The medicine man nodded but shifted his focus back to Veita when she gave her first order. Somehow Jezero knew the woman wouldn't be using her bed too soon.

The morning light streamed through the trees and warmed the earth when Jezero returned to the ledge. His sanctuary bustled with activity as Veita hustled Aresen to fetch water and Zarac to build a low-burning fire. She pulled a plant from her medicine pouch and handed it to Raine when he went to check on their progress.

"Do you grow this plant here in Dusken?" Veita asked. Her long gray hair was coming undone from the braid. The circles underneath her eyes had grown in size and her skin sagged, obvious signs she hadn't slept.

Raine wrinkled his nose and took the plant to examine it. "What is it called?"

"The queeno plant. See how the leaves curl upward?"

Raine studied the detail and then sniffed the leaf. "I'm not familiar."

The frail man passed it to Jezero, and he rubbed the plant between his fingers. The stem had soft, long hairs, while the leaf had a waxy sheen. The leaf emitted a bitter yet earthy scent—one familiar to him. He tried remembering why. Was this what she used on him after one of his battles? He handed it back to Raine. "I would try along the river."

"I will need you to find as many of these as possible," Veita said. "This woman's life may depend on the strength of those leaves."

"Come. I will help," Aresen said to Raine. His lean, muscular frame towered over the medicine man. He held two casks of water, one in each hand. Raine motioned for him to set them near Veita's staging area where she had her bag of potions and plants out for selection.

"The fire is ready," Zarac, the next one to finish his orders from Veita, called out. "The coals are hot, and they be spread out across the pit. The fire's low-burning."

Veita rubbed her hands on her dress and walked over to check on his work. She smiled. "Perfect to what I need. Thank you."

"Anything else?" Zarac asked. When she shook her head, he turned to Jezero. "I'll finish the spears now."

Jezero nodded. He grabbed a piece of dried meat from storage and ate his meal while he watched Veita fret over the woman. When he finished, he took a swig of water from his flask, brushed his hands on his leggings, and then went to stand behind her. "How is she?"

He couldn't see the new woman with Veita hovering over her.

"I'm concerned about the pieces of wood in her leg. And these..." She sat up and raised her open hand to show him the clear, flat rock. "I've found a few in her hand and up her arm."

Jezero picked up the piece and the sharp edge cut into his finger. A dot of blood appeared where it had pierced his skin. Blue-green glass. "I remember this from many years ago."

He gave the piece back to Veita, and she said, "I thought so too. Such a rare find." She put the glass into a small, square pouch. A little disappointed, she said, "Aresen didn't tell me about the stones in her ears."

"The diamonds? There will be a heavy reward for them."

"So you can imagine what the Morlorns will be like. Can you remove them?"

"No," Jezero said. Not for lack of trying. He couldn't figure out how they locked in place and ripping them off her ears wasn't an option.

"Do they know about her?"

"I scanned the shore before we left, and I found no sign of them. She was naked and her skin showed no marks of being a Morlorn. But it doesn't mean they aren't aware of her." He thought of the remark from Aresen and how they had seen Veita traveling with him. They would continue their efforts to find out why.

The medicine woman's face softened as she brushed away a strand of hair from Jezamina's face. "She is a special gift."

"Indeed." Jezero wasn't quite sure of the lifeless and pale gift. To him, her presence meant putting his men in danger. The Morlorns would not ignore this one. Even in her state, he saw beauty. The color of her pale skin and the finer lines in her face showed her unique difference from the villagers. They would notice her curved hips and defined slender waist. Most women in the villages had harsh straight lines with darker features. Jezamina would be hard to disguise as one of them.

Jezero stepped aside to give the medicine woman room to work as she moved to Jezamina's leg. He tended the fire and kept the coals glowing. He wasn't sure why Veita needed the embers, but he wasn't going to let Zarac's work go to waste.

The day passed slowly as the medicine woman continued to work. The blood pooled in the dirt beside the woman. Too much blood. She wouldn't survive.

Jezero began to pace. He scanned the area, looking for movement or a shadow. His forest was quiet except for the occasional rustle of leaves when the wind caught the tops of the trees. The birds sang and flew from branch to branch. No cause for alarm. Except for the pool of blood as it continued to grow. He wiped the sweat from his forehead.

The woman was weak enough. Losing blood wouldn't help.

"Would you be still?" Veita snapped with exasperation. She leaned back on her feet to glare at him.

Jezero jerked his attention back to her, unaware of why she was so angry. He opened his arms, flipping his hands up to ask why.

"First you're in my light, then you're out, then you're back."

Jezero opened his mouth and then stopped. He didn't know what to say. He turned and then came back. She glared at him again. This time he said, "There's a lot of blood."

"I know."

She knows. Of course she knows. Jezero felt his own blood boil.

"Go!" Veita shot her arm out and pointed a finger toward the forest.

Jezero's fists slammed on to his hips. This was his territory.

"Go!" she repeated. "There's nothing you can do right now. If you want her to live, you have to let me do what I do best."

She was right, but he didn't like it.

Her face was set and determined as she looked at him. "I...will...not...lose...her."

Jezero stared at her for a moment, taking in her words. Veita knew the importance of the calling. Without another word, he snatched his bow and a quiver full of arrows, then left the ledge.

His head continued to fill with thoughts of the woman as he walked the main path into the valley. She needed protection, and his job was to provide it. But he needed her well, on her feet. He struggled with his own decision to bring her to Dusken. His men would've been fine leaving her on the shore. They were surprised when he didn't take her to the nearest village. They showed concern when he carried her to their home. This was his choice.

"How is she?"

Startled, Jezero looked up when he heard Zarac's voice behind him. Realizing he missed the path to the clearing, he cursed. The woman was clouding his senses. He turned and walked back.

"We won't know until Veita is finished," he replied and then mumbled with some contempt, "She has banned me from the ledge until she is done."

Zarac looked at him in disbelief. He chuckled as if finding the situation humorous. "'Tis what happens when ye let a woman into yer forest."

"Two women for that matter." He shook his head.

"I found it!" Raine came sprinting across the clearing, displaying the plant held in his fist. He giggled with delight and then sang, "We have a whole patch!"

They watched as he disappeared again among the trees toward the ledge. Their heads were still turned and watching Raine when Aresen came up from behind.

"I've never seen Raine get so excited over a plant," he said between breaths. He wiped the sweat from his forehead with his arm.

"Where'd you find it?" Jezero asked.

"Right on the edge, where the river splits. They were growing in a rotted tree stump." He set down his bow and removed the pouch hanging from his shoulder. "How is she?"

Zarac chuckled, the sound coming from deep inside. "Veita has banned Jezero from the ledge."

"Banned?" Aresen's expression turned from being stunned to amused.

"Enough." Jezero huffed but cracked a smile. "Let's work on the skins."

Aresen stayed in the clearing to help. They took two skins out of the big vat filled with cool water to soften the skins. They worked the skins over a board to break up and remove the tight layer of tissue. On occasion they glanced toward the ledge as they waited for a sign that they'd been approved to return. As the sun passed beyond the trees, their glances became more frequent; their concentration on the skins lessened.

"It's getting late." Aresen scanned the forest. He worked one of the skins with the back edge of a knife to fine-clean all the flesh and tissue from the skin.

"What do you think is going on?" Zarac asked. "What happens if she doesn't survive?"

"Veita knows what she's doing," Jezero said. He remembered the determination on her face. She would not lose the woman.

With the skins cleaned, they carefully placed them in another larger vat to soak. They poked the skins with a stick to make sure all parts were immersed in the liquid mixture that would loosen the hair.

"Look." Aresen pointed toward the path and accidently smacked the stick against the vat, making the liquid splash upward. He jumped away before getting it on his skin.

Jezero's attention turned to Veita after making sure Aresen was safe. She was carrying a small torch to guide her down the path. Even in the faint light, he saw the blood covering her skirt.

Her feet swayed heavily as she made her way toward them. For the moment, Jezero was more concerned for the medicine woman than for Jezamina. He leaned his stick against the nearest tree and quickly met up with her.

"Raine could've come to bring us back."

"I needed the walk to loosen my legs." She smiled with weariness. The deep wrinkles around her eyes and mouth showed the strain. The medicine woman used the back of her hand to push her hair away from her face.

The others came to circle around Veita. She turned her head, looking at each one of them. "Aye, she is out of danger."

Jezero let the air out of his lungs, not realizing he had been holding his breath. Aresen let out a whoop, while Zarac puckered his mouth as if satisfied with the news.

"Your service is appreciated." Jezero bowed to her.

"Lucky for her, Raine found the plant with the strong medicine," she replied as if not wanting to take all the credit. "We caught the infection in time. Her leg should heal with no complications. Her other cuts and marks will heal with time. I wrapped her ribs as well. Two of them were cracked."

Jezero remembered how she had bounced against his shoulder as he carried her through the Morlorn Territory. He didn't have time to worry about comfort.

"Is that food I smell?" Aresen's nose went up.

"Aye, your meal should be ready," Veita said.

"What are we waiting for?" Zarac was ready for a meal. He smacked his lips.

"Wait." Veita held up her hand. "Remember. This is only the beginning for the one you call Jezamina. Try to understand how she is going to feel waking up to four unknown men."

Aresen's hand went to his heart. "We're not mean. We're the most civilized men around."

"We may be too rough in her eyes," Jezero said, knowing what Veita meant. Jezamina was different. He was anxious to see her reaction. The beginning of her new life.

Chapter 11

::: Jezamina :::

Dusken

The birds chirped overhead, causing her to wake. The flapping of wings, a rustling of leaves, and fire crackling made her come out of a deep sleep. Jezamina listened to a muttered conversation—too far away to comprehend the words spoken. Two, three voices? None were familiar.

A warm breeze stirred the air and blew across her face. She breathed in the fragrance of flowers, and the outdoor woodsy scent of being in the forest. *Why am I outside?*

The voices stopped. Jezamina opened her eyes and stared at a leather canvas. The ends, tied together on a wooden frame, hung between two large trees. Again the flapping noise. One of the ends of the canvas appeared to be looser than the others, and the tie was coming undone.

A hand slipped underneath her neck to tilt her head up. She winced as a sharp pain ran like lightning across the top of her forehead. Hold steady, no sudden movements, she thought.

"Drink this," a woman said.

She placed a cup to her swollen lips. The water tasted like heaven against her thick tongue and parched throat.

"Welcome, Jezamina," the woman said. "You've been on a rough journey."

She called her by a name that didn't sound right. The woman kneeled next to her, ready with the cup if she wanted more. Jezamina did. As she drank, she opened her eyes and studied the hazel eyes, the gray hair, and the wrinkled, motherly face of the person before her.

"You are safe here with us."

Jezamina tried getting up. She didn't like the woman telling her she was safe, and it set off all kinds of alarms. What did she mean? Had she been in danger?

"Relax. You need time to heal." The woman gently pushed her down.

"Why...what happened?" Her voice failed. Jezamina wasn't sure if the words came out.

"We can't tell you at the moment. Jezero found you unconscious in the sea." The woman removed her hand and sat back. "My name is Veita. I am the medicine woman from the village nearby. Jezero asked me to come here and heal you. He is the doyen here in Dusken."

None of the names sounded familiar. The sea? Why would she be in the sea?

"Drink more of this," Veita told her. "The medicine will help ease your pain."

This time a small spoon pressed against her lips and tipped upward. The thick liquid burned when it poured into her mouth. Minty.

"Swish it around your mouth before swallowing."

Jezamina did as told. The medicine woman hummed a tune to distract her from the throbbing that danced in her head. In time, both went away. When she opened her eyes again, she was alone and still groggy. She must have slept for quite some time as the sky glowed from the setting sun. Her head hurt but not as bad as the first time she woke. The woman wasn't in front of her any more to block her view, which gave her a chance to take in her surroundings.

A cup, hammered out of pewter, rested on top of a flat rock. She assumed this held the water she drank earlier. The grass-woven mat Veita sat on was next to her bed.

A sweet scent came from underneath her. Jezamina picked at the grass she laid on. Thick blankets—furs—kept her warm. Was this her bed? Outside?

Jezamina tried shifting her legs but the pain stopped her. She touched her thigh to find it wrapped in heavy cloth. She remembered the medicine given to her by the woman named Veita—the mint flavor lingered in her mouth. Potent stuff, she thought as her body sank into the grass bed.

She went through waves of falling asleep and waking. The woman named Veita stayed nearby and continued to give her water and the thick, minty liquid. Each time she woke, her headache lightened and her thoughts became clearer.

***

Jezero froze with knife in hand when Jezamina jumped from inside her bed area. She made a gasping noise as she flicked an insect off her shoulder.

The woman was awake, this time more alert than the last few days.

He waited for Veita, who always listened for Jezamina to stir, to come to her aid. However, the medicine woman kept stirring whatever was in the pot over the fire. She had her back turned away from them as she focused on her task.

Jezero continued holding his knife up in the air. He feared if he set it down, the sun would reflect off the blade and cause attention. Nor could he disappear off the ledge or wait near the other shelters. If he moved, she'd see him.

Veita asked for them to have patience and let Jezamina get familiar with her setting before meeting them. Jezero respected the medicine woman's request, but now he might not be able to grant her wish. He waited until the new woman seemed occupied with her furs. He stepped back at the right opportunity to lean against the rock behind him. With his knife in the shadows, he lowered his arm.

He wondered what she thought as she ran her hands against the soft fur keeping her warm. She glanced from the fur to the leather shelter, and then over to Veita. She seemed curious but not afraid. How different if she'd been captured by the Morlorns. Jezero turned bitter thinking of the cold, damp dungeon meant for him to die in. Fate was on Jezamina's side when they—not Vyrone—found her.

Aresen's laugh broke the silence. He came up the path from the forest. Jezero straightened, on high alert. He had to warn his men to stay away. He cursed under his breath when Zarac's deep voice caused Jezamina to gasp again. She drew the fur up to her neck and her eyes widened. Signs she wasn't ready to meet anyone.

Cupping his hands over his mouth, Jezero made a ruffling noise. A sharper tone would mean danger. His new call tried buffering the warning in hopes his men would proceed with caution. He wasn't sure if they'd catch on but Veita did. She stood as if to stretch and then glanced his way. Jezero nodded toward Jezamina. He pointed to the woods. The men's voices grew louder. The medicine woman raised her chin up in response. She understood.

Veita wiped off her hands on her skirt. She stepped down from the ledge to barricade the men from their home. She did it without causing a stir.

Soon, the voices in the forest faded. The fur came down, away from her face, as Jezamina relaxed. Jezero let out his breath.

An insect buzzed near his face. He swished it away. The annoying pest continued to fly nearby, creating more of a distraction than it was worth. Time to move on. He stepped away from the rock. As he decided the best route to take without Jezamina discovering him, a sharp bite stung his back and made him react. Without thinking, Jezero raised his hand with the knife and slapped the flat side of his blade against his shoulder.

***

A loud snap cracked the air and caused Jezamina to jump. A shadow, like a bird, flew across the top of her shelter. She rose to one side, leaning against her elbow to find where the noise came from. She stretched her neck and almost fell back. A man stood less than ten feet from her. He held a knife. Her eyes widened when the big, shiny blade loomed in front of her. She jerked back to hide deeper into her shelter. Pain seared her side and sucked the air from her lungs.

Don't faint.

He must have seen the fear in her eyes for he flung the knife behind him. He opened his hands to her, as if showing he meant no harm. The man stayed still, giving her time to recover.

Jezamina assessed whether or not she was in danger. He had a rugged and confident appearance, yet his dark, sharp eyes seemed watchful and concerned. The man wore leather leggings with no shirt. His tanned, muscular chest and hard stomach glistened in the sun. Veita had talked about the one who sent for her. This had to be him.

"You must be Jezero," she said, her concern at being in danger now vanished.

"I am." He ran his fingers through his wavy, black hair to pull it away from his face. "Veita has told you about me?"

"Only that you found me. She explained how you brought me here, to your home."

The unfamiliar dialect was similar to Veita's when he said, "Welcome to Dusken. We found you in the sea, in Morlorn Territory."

He seemed to be testing her, but Jezamina wasn't sure why. Should she know what he meant?

The man stepped toward her. His closeness, or his half-naked body, made her pull back. She used the blanket as a shield to protect herself.

He smiled and seemed amused. "If I were to hurt you, I would have done so already."

"You could've caused my injuries."

"I assure you, I did not cause your injuries."

For a split second, he turned his eyes, telling her different. She wasn't sure if she could trust him yet. Jezero picked up the mug from the rock and sat down. He sniffed the contents and then offered her a drink.

She hesitated, not wanting to be drugged again. She asked, "Minty?"

"No, more grassy with a touch of lemon."

Jezamina nodded. She'd tasted the beverage before. She reached out to take it from him. The liquid spilled out, the mug heavier than she realized. Jezero slid from the rock and helped keep the drink upright by holding the mug to her lips. His touch ignited a spark between them. She blushed. *Where did that come from?*

Jezero coughed. He must have felt the connection as well. "Do you remember what happened?"

He moved back, to her relief, and set the mug down on the rock. He stayed, crouched on one knee, next to her bed. When she didn't respond, he asked again.

How many times had the same question run through her head? Each time she woke, she wished for only one dream, one word, one smell, one anything, to trigger her memory. Instead, a white void passed through her like fog on a cool night. Her stomach tightened with unease. She whispered, "I don't remember."

"And your name?"

She remembered Veita saying her name. "Jezamina."

"Yes, I gave you the name. Do you recall anything before your injuries? Why we found you in the sea?"

Jezamina turned away, not knowing how to respond. She hated saying she didn't remember. It left her vulnerable, exposed. She thought back and pictured herself on a boat in a storm or swimming in the sea. Nothing came to her, not one clue to remember anyone close to her or to know where she had come from. Jezamina squeezed her eyes shut, forcing herself to think harder.

Still nothing. A tear rolled from her eye. She brushed it away before he could see it.

"You had a blow to your head. In time your memory will return."

She could only hope. Maybe in a few days it would return. The head injury explained why her head continued to throb.

"What else is wrong with me?" She knew of the bandage on her thigh. Her ribs hurt. Her body ached.

He pointed his finger to her leg. "You have a gash running from your knee to your upper thigh. An infection set in. Veita was able to save your leg."

Jezamina's eyes popped. Was he serious? Her leg? She stared at him. The bright sun made it hard to see his face, but he didn't seem to be teasing. She wiggled her toes and sighed with relief.

"Oh, yes. You also have cracked ribs. The reason why you couldn't sit up like you wanted." He rubbed the growth on his chin as if there were more meaning behind the words than what he told her.

"How did my ribs crack?" She studied him as he continued to rub his stubble. For a person living in the forest, he did seem somewhat groomed and clean. He took care of himself, so he wasn't quite the savage she thought.

Jezero stood. "Perhaps I should leave you alone now. I'm sure you're tired."

Jezamina cleared her throat. "It's not a tough question."

He stopped but kept his gaze toward the trees. "I had to carry you through rugged territory. I may have cracked them."

"*What?*"

He was gone before the word left her mouth.

The next morning, Jezamina snuggled into the furs to keep warm. The dew covering the leaves sparkled as the sun peaked through the trees. The fresh air smelled like water with a slight flowery fragrance. The area was beautiful with the agate blue sky and the emerald green trees standing tall and majestic. The smaller trees surrounding her had huge roots growing around the rocks like fingers and even made up her bed to keep the grass contained. She liked the comfort and safety of her shelter.

All was quiet, neither Veita nor Jezero in sight. She wondered how many times he had watched her as she weaved in and out of sleep. And for how long was she out? One day? Two days?

Finally her head didn't hurt as much. Her body wasn't as achy. She inched up to her elbows, taking care as to how she moved with cracked ribs.

Jezero's home, Dusken, was larger than what she had thought. She was on the edge of an open area where the fire still burned in the center. A pot hung above the flames and the smell of stew wafted through the air. They used rough-cut logs scattered around the fire to sit on. Beyond the ledge, a vast forest held the unknown. The unknown seemed amazing. The bright green leaves covered the trees like a canopy and the black-to-brown bark made the other colors of the forest pop. She wished she could see more. Instead, Jezamina satisfied her time by studying the steep cliff protecting the backside of the ledge. Interesting, how the gray rock speckled with gold danced when the sun hit the side. The palette of colors seemed new to her.

All day she stayed awake with little to do. Jezamina wanted to explore, go for a walk, and to touch the leaves and texture on the bark. Most of all, she wanted to be out in the warm sun instead of lying in the shadows under the makeshift roof made of leather.

A critter moved to her side, making her jump. A sharp pain stabbed her side. As she waited for it to subside, she wondered what else crawled around her while she slept. This wasn't normal, sleeping outside, but what was different about it?

What happened to her? Why couldn't the simplest things come to her? Where did she live? Who was her family? All questions but no answers.

Jezamina went to scratch her forehead but stopped where the tender new skin was too sore to touch. She patted it with her finger to estimate the size. The wound had been pretty large. Jezero didn't mention her head. Wait, he did. She had a blow to her head. The days blurred together, including what she had done while awake. She tried scratching around the scab.

"Here." A boney hand held out a wooden spoon in front of her. "This will help."

Startled, Jezamina turned to find a thin man sitting where Veita and Jezero sat before, near the rock. He wasn't there a few seconds ago. The mixture, cradled in the spoon, was a white lumpy glob. He continued to hold it in front of her.

The man scooted forward and said, "Put this on your wound, and the itching will stop."

Jezamina brought her finger up, not sure if she wanted to touch the goo. The frail man lowered the spoon and nodded his head to encourage her. The mixture was cold. She had to use more than one finger to scoop out the balm as it was harder than she expected.

"Crush the balm in your hand to break it down."

She did as told and then applied a dab of the mixture to her forehead. The man scooted back. He held the spoon and waited while Jezamina applied more of the medicine near the center of the wound. Her skin absorbed the balm and tingled, giving her instant relief from the itching.

He motioned for her to add more.

"Thank you," she said, finishing the task. She was curious about the man. He seemed afraid of her as his one eye twitched and his legs were ready to spring up and run at a moment's notice—very skittish. He reminded her of a troll, the way his skin hung from his face and body and how large and round his eyes were. His long, brown hair was thin and stringy, like his beard. His oversized clothes—leather leggings and a white tunic—draped his body, but at least he was more clothed than Jezero had been when she met him.

"Raine," he said, bringing her thoughts back.

She looked up at the sky. There wasn't a cloud in sight. She raised her eyebrows in question.

"I am Raine."

"Your name is Raine?"

He bowed his head to her before disappearing into the bushes.

Jezamina nestled back into the fur. What an odd man.

Another voice, somewhere in the distance, broke the quiet. "I met with two villagers near the crossing."

"Did they bring a message?"

She recognized Jezero's voice.

"There's word on the woman." The new voice was deeper, more like gravel. "They want to know more about her."

The woman.

Jezamina caught her breath. She perked up to hear more.

"How could they possibly know we have her here?" Another, lighter voice joined the mix.

"I assume from my village," Veita responded. "They were the only ones to know where I travelled and why."

"Word was bound to get out." Jezero sighed loudly enough for her to hear. "At least now we're aware of it."

"The Morlorns will know." Raine's voice? "They will come for her."

"We'll need to stay on alert," the lighter voice spoke again.

"She needs time to heal," Veita said.

"If attacked—" The deep voice stopped midsentence. Feet shuffled about.

Jezamina rose to her elbows and ignored the pain. They were talking about her, but the sudden break made her nerves pop. Were they being attacked? She couldn't see anyone or anything. Her heart pounded faster. "Veita?"

"You're awake!"

She jumped when the medicine woman's voice came from a different direction. The woman appeared in front of her, flustering Jezamina.

"Oh dear, are you all right?" Her skirt swished as she rushed to lean toward the bed.

"Are we being attacked?" Jezamina's voice shook.

"No, no," Veita said. "You're safe. No worries."

"But I heard..."

"We're well-protected here. Jezero brought you here for that very reason and to see to your health," Veita said. She switched subjects. "Let's check your leg."

Jezamina frowned at the change in focus. The furs had come off and exposed her legs. A greenish-brown stain covered the bandage on her thigh. The day wasn't going well. Her stomach flipped at the sight of the mess.

"I need to change the dressing on your leg." Veita began to unwrap the cloth. "The medicine has dried."

"My leg is okay, right?" Jezamina wished for a simple yes or no response so she could ask about the men and their discussion.

"This may hurt a bit." The medicine woman pecked at the wound.

Jezamina felt the tug on her skin. She remembered Jezero saying how they had saved her leg. Veita's expression seemed more important now than the other conversation.

"Did the infection come back?" she asked.

"The paste carries the infection. We need to remove it so not to infect your leg again."

A little more relieved, Jezamina helped by bending her knee to add space between her leg and the bed. If the infection was coming out, it had to be a good sign.

Raine placed a bowl with steaming water on the ground near Veita along with some clean strips of cloth. Next, he placed a rougher pelt underneath her thigh and butt after the medicine woman lifted her hip.

Jezamina pictured her leg all mangled. Her stomach turned queasy. It couldn't be too bad. Veita commented the other day on her progress and how she was healing.

"The bandages are off," the medicine woman said. She handed the pile of cloth to Raine. He carried the tangled, spindled mess over to the fire and dropped it in. A big whoosh of flame towered above the pit, and then it burned to nothing.

The air was cold, almost like ice, against Jezamina's exposed skin. She didn't dare look at her leg, afraid she'd panic or pass out. Her anxiety accelerated.

"Don't you worry," Veita said as if reading her mind. "The worst is over. Each day forward, you will get stronger." She dipped a piece of cloth into the bowl of steaming water and then placed it on her thigh.

Jezamina jerked her leg. It didn't hurt. She just wasn't prepared. Stop being a baby, she thought. As Veita confirmed, the worst was over.

She tried to relax when Veita dabbed at the dried medicine stuck to her skin. The larger flakes were tossed into a wooden bowl, while the smaller ones fell on the rough pelt underneath her. The process continued with the medicine woman skillfully using a knife to rid her of the paste.

At first the tugging at her skin was bearable. Veita worked on the outer edge of her leg and then moved closer to the wound. As she continued, the pulling began to sting. Jezamina clenched her toes together. She tried keeping her leg still to help the process, but each time the pain grew.

The medicine woman hummed a tune while she worked. She glanced up on occasion to see how her patient was doing. Jezamina thought she handled the procedure well until the pulling moved to the tender skin.

"Ohh, okay..." she cried out when her skin felt like it were on fire. She twisted about and Raine had to help hold her leg down.

Veita worked with speed. Her hands and the knife moved faster, and she didn't look at Jezamina anymore. Now she knew the pain point.

Jezamina's thigh throbbed. Every inch of muscle, skin, and even bone hurt. The pain ran down to her toes and up to her side. She stared at one branch hanging overhead. The leaves reflected gold as they shimmered from the wind. Stay focused. Don't think about the pain. She let out a cry, swearing her skin had been ripped away from her thigh.

"Stop!" She grabbed for Veita's arm when a hand came out and prevented her from interfering. Jezero's grip tightened. His other hand came out to hold hers and she squeezed tight. He didn't flinch.

"I know this hurts," Veita said and she seemed sympathetic. "We have to get all the paste out. You're doing good."

Easy for her to say, Jezamina thought as sweat trickled down her face.

Jezero gave her hand a reassuring squeeze when the flicking of the knife continued. Jezamina held her breath. She bit her lip to keep from crying out. The medicine woman had to be working on raw flesh. Jezamina tried withdrawing her hand from Jezero's grip, but he held tight.

"Stop! Stop!" she pleaded. Her head spun. Her stomach tightened and twisted in knots.

Raine kept her legs trapped by pressing against them with both hands and his full weight. Surprisingly the boney man had strength. She couldn't wiggle her way out of his grip.

"Keep steady," Jezero warned her. "Veita can't finish if you're moving about."

"Wait," she panted. "Let me take a break."

"I'm almost done." Veita kept working with her head down. The humming stopped.

"You're doing fine," Jezero said without sympathy or any feeling.

"I'm fine?" Jezamina screeched at him. Both Veita and Raine jumped at her sudden outburst.

Another pull. Definitely muscle. Raw. Unprotected.

The tears rolled from her eyes. Maybe cutting her leg off wasn't such a bad idea. She did short, quick breaths.

"A little more," Jezero said. "This is nothing compared to what you've been through."

"Fuck you!" Jezamina sobbed. Everything about her was on fire. She was burning in hell as the sweat poured from her. She wanted nothing to do with Jezero, Veita, or Raine. She buried her head into her arm. "Fuck all of you. I want to go home."

"This is your home now," Jezero snapped.

Chapter 12

::: Jessie :::

Chicago, IL

The rattling cart outside the hospital room brought Walt back to the present. Jessie took a sip of water as the aide appeared with her lunch tray. As she conversed with the young woman about her meal, he got up to stretch.

So far her story didn't seem so bad. What she said made sense. Dusken was her safe haven. The place she stayed while in her coma, a way to handle the trauma and heal. Dr. Angela Landreau cleaned and stitched her leg at the hospital. She could've been Veita to Jessie.

He knew his fiancée must have been subconsciously trying to handle the pain. What better way than through a dream. The idea of a beautiful forest fit her style. She loved the outdoors, and she was always aware of her surroundings, whether vibrant or drab.

Walt hoped to share his explanation with Jessie after the aide left, but the room became busy. The social worker came in. No one gave them time for privacy. When Carol came in the second time, to give her a sponge bath, he left for the diner down the street. He learned hospital food was just that—hospital food. Nothing edible to excite the palette.

When he returned, the physical therapist occupied the room, making his regular stop to work with his patient. Jessie stood next to the bed with the big guy leaning down to bend her leg. Walt stopped in the doorway.

Jessie leaned to see him over the wide girth of the therapist. "He says I have great muscle tone."

Walt raised his eyebrows and smiled. How many weeks passed where she was flat on her back? Now she stood on her feet. He could actually hug her. But he didn't. It took all his willpower to stay back and let the therapist do his job.

When she turned, her long blonde hair fell over her shoulders and down her back. He loved how the thick layers curled in soft waves, now almost to her lower back. He remembered how he'd pull the strands into a ponytail, lean her back, and then give her a long kiss. One day he would do it again, once she was ready. At a distance, he fantasized about pulling off her gown, untying the back to reveal her perfect, round ass.

"Your balance is excellent," the therapist said.

"Did you hear that?" Jessie smiled. Her face lit up.

"You'll be out of here in no time," Walt said and shared in her excitement. He tossed his sport coat over to the couch.

Forget the wedding. They could elope like she wanted to do when he proposed. He longed to keep her to himself. Vegas? Bahamas? Paris? He'd have to think about it. His mother would be pissed, but she'd get over it. She could still plan the big wedding celebration, but Walt didn't want to wait. He wanted Jessie as his wife. He craved the reassurance, not wanting to lose her again.

The therapist continued to test her while Walt daydreamed about taking her away. When the guy helped Jessie back into bed and left, they had a little over an hour before the next rounds began. Two and a half hours before his mother came for a visit.

Walt pulled his chair closer to the bed. He hated when the staff moved it, but he understood. They needed access to their patient from all sides.

"Are you comfortable?" He helped Jessie adjust the pillow between her back and the bed before sitting.

She nodded.

Good. He sat on the edge of the seat and leaned forward so his arms rested on the side rail. "Do you remember being in surgery? The doctors fixed your leg."

Jessie hesitated as if about to say something then stopped.

"The doctor, Angela Landreau, worked on your leg. She is female, like Veita."

Her lips thinned as she closed her mouth, but Walt ignored the sign. He was on to something.

"Even Dr. Maguire said she had done wonders on your leg." He changed the subject, knowing she was about to argue that it was Veita. Walt didn't want her to bring up the medicine woman again. "Do you remember how you ripped your leg open?"

Jessie turned her gaze to the window. "I remember running into the farmhouse. Everything else is still fuzzy." She closed her eyes as if trying to replay the scene. "I fell. No, I was climbing up the stairs on my hands and feet." She rubbed her temples as if it would help. "No...yes. The stairs." She opened her eyes. "I was on the stairs and then I went down. The wood gave way. I had to pull a large splinter out of my leg." Her face turned pale.

Walt placed his hand on her arm. "You know you saved those kids. Right?"

Jessie's gaze lowered. She nodded her head.

"All that happened is now in the past. You can move on. Feel good about what you did."

Her face fell. She wasn't buying it. Walt knew to be cautious. Instinct told him to wait before explaining what Dusken symbolized. How the place was her buffer zone. He'd get her back into the story and then unravel the pieces. She'd see the similarities.

"So tell me why these people lived in the woods. No houses? No protection?"

"The ledge offered them protection," she said, defending the place. "The high cliff on one side protected them from the enemy.

The rocks and trees on the ledge provided shelter and protection as well. The view into the valley gave them the advantage."

"Who would attack them?" Walt remembered her concern earlier on.

"The Morlorns."

"Okay..." He needed more. Walt wanted to unravel her dream.

Chapter 13

::: Jezamina :::

Dusken

A loud clash of thunder bellowed across the forest. Jezamina woke as the lightning flashed across the sky. She buried herself deeper into the shelter as the ice-cold rain dripped on her face.

Another rumble of thunder rolled above the trees. She counted the seconds until the sky lit again. Three seconds away. Dusken was near the center of the storm.

How long had she been out? The last thing she remembered, Veita had been working on her leg, the pain unbearable. She patted her thigh and let out a sigh of relief. Still attached.

This is your home now. Jezero's words came back.

The wind picked up and tested the covering over her head. The leather snapped and threatened to break loose. She reached up with her hand, but the tie kept flapping about, making it hard to grab.

The rain came down and drummed on to the earth, sending her back in retreat. Looking out, she spotted someone hovering near the stairs that led down from the ledge. She guessed it was Jezero.

This was his home. How dare he think this was her home? She had a place to live. Somewhere. Didn't she? Jezamina sat up and scooted to the corner to lean against the tree trunk. She kept her bad leg straight while raising her other knee toward her chest.

Someone had to be waiting for her. She knew it in her heart.

***

The rain pelted down in sheets. Jezero adjusted the hood on his cape as the wind shifted. Lightning flashed through the sky, giving him a chance to see Jezamina move around in her shelter. He longed to race over and join her, but her last words didn't sit well with him. Life would never be as she once thought. A lesson she'd soon learn.

Her expression, her response, when he told her how this was her home made him realize how far she had to go before accepting her new fate. She had nothing left of her identity to claim, but she would survive. He learned, after his own near kiss with death, to live once again and she would too.

A branch snapped.

He moved with caution toward the edge, behind the tall rock. With his head down, he listened again. Beyond the rain he heard movement. Jezero prepared his bow and arrow. No one in their right mind would be out on such a night. Unless of course Vyrone raised the price on his head—then a few might dare. The Morlorns didn't have the advantage in Dusken, so they might not be out for an attack, not yet. However, a quick glance at the woman would be worth risking the traps set throughout the forest. She would be a prized capture.

Jezero waited for the lightning. With bow up, he aimed in the direction of the noise.

A flash of light.

Movement.

A walato.

Jezero lowered his bow and let out his breath.

He returned his gaze to the shelter. This was not how he wanted to welcome her to his home.

***

Jezamina drifted in and out of sleep as the storm passed. Her comfort came with knowing Jezero braved the storm to guard them. She glanced about. He was no longer at his perch overlooking the ledge. She wondered if his absence was good or bad.

Raine was the only one out, and he crouched near the fire. She waved to him, knowing he'd get her mug of hot herbs ready. True to form, he poured steaming water into a mug and then sprinkled dried leaves into it. Veita always filtered the leaves out; Raine did not. Jezamina preferred filtered. In time, she'd be able to make it herself.

"Are ye cold?" He handed her the mug.

She nodded. The storm left everything damp, including the grass she used for her bed. Jezamina peeked out beyond the shelter and hoped the sun would come out soon. No chance, she decided. The thick gray clouds covering the sky diminished her hope.

Raine wore a fur-lined vest and thicker leggings to keep warm. She wore only a leather tunic, two sizes too big for her frame. Realizing her legs were bare, Jezamina covered them again with the pelt. She shivered.

She took a sip of the herbal brew before asking, "Why did Jezero stay up all night during the storm?"

"He protects his land." Raine dumped the water out of the bowls, the ones Veita used to clean her leg. They must have left them out.

"Isn't standing out in the storm a little extreme?" He did wear raingear and seemed to stay dry.

Raine shrugged, which made her think Jezero's watchfulness was more of the norm than not.

"Good morning." Veita appeared but didn't join them. She began picking up the scattered branches and clumps of leaves that had fallen off the trees. She tossed the larger pieces over the edge, into the woods, while keeping the smaller ones for starting a new fire. Jezamina longed to help her.

Raine dug into the bag attached to his sash. He crouched down next to her and held up a jagged piece of wood between his fingers. "We found this in yer leg."

Jezamina took the long splinter and felt the rough edges.

"This too." He switched hands and held out a shard of glass. "This one cuts. Ye be careful." He pressed the tip against his finger until a perfect dot of ruby-red blood appeared.

"A piece of glass. Why were they in my leg?"

"We hoped ye'd tell us." A voice spoke up.

The man came forward and rested one foot on a tree root. His spiked white hair stood tall, similar to his lean, muscular frame. His smile went from ear to ear. When he turned to eye Veita, as if knowing he shouldn't be imposing, Jezamina noticed the scar running from the corner of his mouth to his jawline. She recognized his voice from the earlier conversation she overheard.

Raine brought her attention back to him. He held up the glass. "This was in yer arm, not yer leg," he corrected her.

The other man stepped to the side and crouched near Raine.

"My name is Aresen." He bowed his head. "I'm pleasured to meet ye, Jezamina. Veita wanted us to wait for a time."

"Didn't want to scare ye," Raine added.

She wasn't sure why. Aresen seemed like the gallant one so far among the men.

Jezamina handed the wood piece back to Raine. "I don't know why they were inside me."

Raine tucked the splinter and the shard back into his sack.

Aresen waved his hand. "All will be resolved in time. We're happy ye decided to wake. Veita says the infection is gone." His accent was similar to Raine's. "Do ye mind if I sit?"

Jezamina granted him permission. She smiled, the first in a long time, liking his positive manners and energy. He reminded her of a Greek god with his chiseled yet handsome features. She opened her mouth to ask if he knew mythology, but he spoke again.

"Did Raine here tell ye how we found ye?"

"I was found in the sea."

"Aye, ye danced upon the waves, a lifeless form." He grabbed a log and used it as a chair. "The weather was similar to last night. Sheets of rain pelted the forest, and the mist clouded our view. We were chilled to the bone as we traveled through the Morlorn territory."

Veita coughed as she hovered nearby like a watchful mother.

Aresen nodded to her and then went back to his story. "Jezero knew the dangers of traveling through the woods. He steered us toward the sea." He tilted his head while chewing on a stem from a plant. Veita kept her stance, as if warning him of something, and he winked at her before continuing. "The fog met up with the sea when we reached the shore. Jezero perked his ears and heard the calling. We fanned out along the coast and there ye were, tumbling in the waves, tangled in seaweed." He gazed off to the woods as if looking out to sea. "Jezero walked waist-deep into the waters as the waves crashed against him." Aresen spread his feet apart. "He braced his legs and held firm to keep from going under. Our doyen ignored the salt stinging his eyes and blurring his vision. He kept steady, waiting for the right moment to grab ye."

Both Jezamina and Raine flinched when he reached out to grab the air in front of him.

"When he realized how the wave swelled like an arm, Jezero feared the sea would take ye back, pull ye under. He dove forward and stretched to reach for a piece of the seaweed wrapped around ye. He missed and tried again, going for yer arm. The current was too strong. Jezero lost his grip, and then he disappeared under the water as another wave came in. We waited." Aresen paused for effect and Jezamina leaned closer. His arm rose again. "Jezero reached out and grabbed yer arm as the next wave crested. He pulled ye toward him, and that's when I came to help. Aye, it took both our efforts to pull ye to shore."

"Seaweed covered me?" Jezamina made a face.

"It protected ye from the cold," Raine said. "Yer wounds too."

"Raine feared infection when he examined ye. He needed to tend ye, but we couldn't stay and be exposed in enemy land. Jezero carried ye to Dusken on his shoulder, while I traveled to request Veita's assistance."

Jezero sat near the fire, and he poked the burning logs with a long stick. He'd been listening to their conversation but didn't join in. Another man with red hair and a bushy beard sat next to him. He used a knife to shave a precise tip on the end of a long stick. His broad shoulders, thick muscular arms, and barrel chest were twice the size of Jezero's. Aresen caught her staring toward the fire and turned.

"Ah," he said and opened his arm as if presenting the two by the fire. "Jezero, our doyen, is highly respected among the lands. Next to him is Zarac. As ye can tell, the man is strong enough to tear a person in half. No one messes with him. He too made sure ye made it here without troubles."

Jezamina had no doubt. The huge man gave her a nod and then continued slicing the blade against the stick. His eye contact with her was brief and only out of politeness. Her instincts said that he didn't agree with her being here, in his home.

The pounding in her head started again. Quick, short bouts of pain darted from her temple to the back of her head. She tried rubbing it away while fighting the confusion and mixed emotions on why she, of all people, survived.

"Child." Veita became alarmed. "Are you all right?"

The medicine woman rushed over and pushed Aresen aside. Even Raine, at his safe distance, stepped back.

"I'm fine," Jezamina said without confidence. She turned to Aresen. "Thank you for sharing with me. I'm surprised I survived. I owe my thanks to you."

"We merely helped. Jezero is the one to find and save ye."

"I'm sure," she replied and glanced over at Jezero. He stared at the fire.

"Go." Veita fluttered her hands. "Jezamina needs rest."

"Until next time," Aresen said with a nod. His blue eyes sparkled even without the sun as he bid farewell.

Jezamina tried to sleep, but she needed activity. She was tired of staying in bed. Her muscles ached from lack of exercise. She needed to walk the woods, to learn her surroundings, and to know why Dusken seemed so special to the men. Veita kept reminding her, saying, "One step at a time, child."

The next few days, Jezamina practiced those steps. She crawled out of her bed and sat on the mat to enjoy the sun. Veita loved having her grind seeds and grain to make their bread. Jezamina liked how the chore shaped her arms.

At one point on a warm afternoon, she became curious when a consistent thump echoed through the forest. She scooted out from her bed to the mat and pulled a large fern aside. Jezero stood near the edge of the ledge, his legs apart in a stance. He held his bow in one hand and with the other he reached for an arrow. He took his time adjusting the tension in his bow. The arrow soon came up and into position. His bare chest heaved upward and his arm flexed as he pulled back on the string.

Jezamina sat mesmerized by his actions. She admired his flat, tight stomach and liked how his hips barely held up his leggings. The hint of his hairline started near his belly and trailed underneath the leather ties. She visualized his full naked body standing before her.

Her chest fluttered. Jezamina pressed her hand to her heart, not sure if it was her health or Jezero causing the reaction. She had no reason to be aroused. He wasn't exactly kind to her. She was a mere woman whom he had to "protect."

Jezero released the arrow, and she heard the ping. She waited for the thump, not being able to see where it landed. He seemed satisfied for his lips curled into a smile.

"He is good." Veita broke Jezamina's thoughts.

"Yes, he seems to be," she said after the medicine woman's words registered. "But I'm still not sure if he's friend or foe."

Veita chuckled. "Give him time. Jezero's heart is made of gold. His honor is true. We are very grateful his determination and faith are strong."

"How do you mean?" Jezamina asked, her eyes staying on the doyen as he removed another arrow from the quiver. This time he turned to display his back. The muscles were as tight and hard as his front but not as smooth. Scars lined both sides of his back, some crisscrossing.

Veita never responded to her question, but Jezamina forgot what she asked. The scars held a story, one not only of hardship but of sacrifice. *Who is this man?*

"Please, Veita. I need context...understanding." Jezamina sat up straighter. She held her ribs as a precaution, knowing the pain would come with movement.

The medicine woman sat on the rock next to her. She carried a bowl of round, purple pods and placed it on her lap. She removed the stringy outer shell until the nuts inside fell out. Jezamina offered to help, so Veita placed the bowl between them.

"Fate smiled when the gods brought us Jezero," Veita said after they settled into a routine. The nuts pinged in different tones when they landed in the bowl, creating a rhythmic beat based on where they hit. "Like you, he came to us wounded and near death. Unfortunately for him, the Morlorns captured him during an attack. Vyrone nursed him back to health and then groomed him to be a Morlorn."

"Vyrone?" Jezamina said to make sure she followed. "He is doyen to the Morlorns?"

"Aye, he rules over the Morlorns but more like a king. He is a man with a black hole through his heart. His wish, or pleasure may it be, is to see the villages suffer under his rage and power."

Jezamina stopped shelling the pods for a moment, surprised by Veita's anger. The medicine woman hadn't shown such strong feelings before. "He sounds like a monster."

"He is," she said and kept her voice low. "Vyrone sends his people out to attack us, to take our lands and murder anyone who stands in his way. He's taken our people as prisoners. He will burn the villages so we lose everything."

"I'm sorry." Now she knew why Veita struggled with her emotions. "I didn't mean to upset you."

Veita shook her head. "I'm fine." She sighed and took a moment to gather herself, then said, "When they first met, Vyrone knew Jezero had a gift. He beat Jezero almost to death. He showed no mercy until the very end when he told Jezero he'd let him live if he trained to be a Morlorn. Jezero agreed so the evil doyen groomed him to fight with rage, to slaughter without care.

"One day Vyrone decided to test his worthiness. He ordered an attack on a village, putting Jezero in charge. Vyrone, however, wasn't a fool. The Morlorns kept a close eye on Jezero, making sure he did as told. Jezero turned out to be the smarter one. He warned the village ahead of time. On the day of the attack, the villagers were ready. And yes, bloodshed occurred. The Morlorns, when they realized what had happened, turned on Jezero. Again, he nearly lost his life, but he saved ours."

"Your village was the one attacked?" Jezamina asked, but she knew the answer.

"Yes. Jezero never intended to be part of the Morlorns, even when he touched the folds of death. Since then, he's saved many lives."

Jezamina thought about the strength needed to survive the attacks. "Were you the one who nursed him back to health?"

"Yes, I cared for him. I and others. We hid him until he gained enough strength to leave our village and heal on his own. I believe he discovered and claimed Dusken during this time."

Jezamina nodded, lost in thought. She admired the courage it took for Jezero to make the decision to live and work with Vyrone until able to betray him. He chose to live to help the villages. She assumed the scars on Jezero's back were from Vyrone's hands. A chill ran through her, thinking about the cruelty.

Aresen leaped onto the ledge, catching her attention. He spoke to Jezero, his face serious. With a nod from his doyen, the agile man jumped off the ledge again.

"How far away are the villages from here?" Jezamina turned back to Veita.

"They are scattered throughout the lands."

"And your village?"

"About two to three days' travel from here."

Jezamina wondered if she'd ever get there. Maybe she would live with Veita in her village. "Where are the Morlorns?"

"A decent three days' travel from here." Veita frowned and her face turned dark again. "But they also hide in the forests."

"That doesn't sound good."

The lines around the medicine woman's mouth deepened. "We fear getting attacked. They want our lands. They want our people. Once, many years ago, we lived peaceful lives. Now we long for those days to return."

Jezero stepped down from the ledge with bow in hand, the show over.

"Why don't all the villages group together and attack the Morlorns?"

Veita sighed. "They have attacked most of the villages within the area, taking the lives of our strongest men. We need to rebuild and learn to fight before conquering evil."

Jezamina rubbed her eyes. She hated being so tired, unable to stay up for the full day. Veita helped her back into bed.

"I still don't understand why I'm here." Jezamina pulled the furs up. She felt cold.

"You needed help."

"There's something else." Jezamina shook her head. She couldn't put her finger on it, but there had to be a purpose and a reason why she had no memory. What tragic event happened to her? Why did Jezero and not the Morlorns find her? Why did she live deep in a forest with no one around? "Jezero said I was called to him. What does he mean?"

"Jezero has these callings. The spirits said you were in trouble, so he found you."

"But why?"

Veita patted her furs. "I don't know."

Jezamina believed differently. The medicine woman's gaze darted to the side. She knew.

Veita confessed. "Aye, you are special, my child."

"Why am I special?" She leaned forward, hoping for any clue.

The medicine woman knit her eyebrows together to think, as if wanting to choose her words carefully. "The rocks in your ears are rare. No one has rocks in their ears."

Rocks. Her earrings. Jezamina raised her hand and touched the hard edge of one of the diamonds. She remembered how Raine had crouched close to her head one morning, trying to examine her ear. He wanted to see the fire.

Jezamina flinched when a drop of rain hit the tip of her nose. Dark clouds moved toward them again.

"Another strong storm is headed our way." Veita gathered the bowls with the shredded pods and nuts.

"Does it always rain so hard?" She didn't like the storms in Dusken. During the last two she had buried herself under the furs until they passed. She feared being struck by lightning or having a tree fall on her.

"No," Veita assured her. "This will end soon. We always have spurts of rain at this time of season to keep the forests nourished."

The rain fell like nuts dropping from a tree. Veita excused herself and went over to the fire where she placed a lid on the pot of stew she had prepared that morning. She then checked on Jezamina one more time before taking cover.

The day dragged on for Jezamina as the storm left her without company. She spotted the men every so often when they approached or disappeared from the ledge. She forced herself to sleep, listening to the rhythm of the rain as it drummed against the leather covering over her bed. When she nodded off, a spray of cold droplets from the wind would shock her awake again.

As evening approached and the rain tapered, the men gathered around the fire to eat without sitting. They didn't linger like they did on most nights to banter in light conversation. Normally Veita joined them. Tonight she stayed dry in her own shelter, somewhere down the path behind Jezamina.

Raine completed the duty of bringing her meal, a bowl of stew. Aresen followed to keep her company while she ate. Jezamina appreciated having him join her, even for the brief time.

"Ye'll be snug and safe," Aresen said in a promise as he sat with the rain beating down on him. He wore the same type of cape as Jezero. The water beaded off the leather. "Ye don't want to get wet."

"I'll be happy to walk again, rain or shine."

Aresen laughed. "I believe ye. But for now ye need rest. Once the storm passes, it'll bring a nice cool breeze to help ye sleep."

When the rain stopped, Jezamina waited for the breeze. She settled into her bed and closed her eyes, looking forward to uninterrupted sleep.

The critters were quieter than usual. She didn't hear their little feet flittering about or their wrestling underneath the ferns and bushes. Even the birds stayed in their nests.

The silence was almost deafening against the night. The air became thick and heavy, making it hard to breathe. Jezamina tossed the furs off and sat up. If only she could walk...

What harm would be done? She'd been exercising. If she was careful, she could scoot her way over to the fire pit.

She peeked out from her bed to survey the sky. Patches of stars appeared between the clouds. Aresen had said the rain would end.

Jezamina turned and swung her legs out. The ledge's floor was still soggy, but she wasn't concerned. Her oversized tunic would keep her dry.

The black dirt stuck to her feet as she patted the ground with her toes. She flicked the dirt with the tip of her toe and smiled. How nice it would be to walk.

The ledge, dark with the fire completely out, seemed eerie in a way. She liked having a small flame or the glow of the coals at night for comfort. Jezamina spotted the larger rock where Veita sat to mend the men's shirts or prepare their food. Ten steps away. The medicine woman had said she liked how the stone molded to her behind, offering some comfort when sitting for long periods. The top curved in, creating a perfect chair. Jezamina knew she could reach the rock.

She braced her hands against one of the roots as she flipped to her side. She couldn't apply pressure to the leg with the wound. *Plan B.* She plotted her route and then crawled like an injured crab with her face to the sky. A drop of rain hit her cheek, and it scared her. She almost lost her balance.

The sky still showed a few stars above her. The water must have fallen from one of the trees. Another drop hit her above the eye and she fell backward. Pain darted up her thigh to her hip. Jezamina stopped to rub her leg.

Rain didn't hurt. She wouldn't melt. She could do this. A few more feet, and Jezamina would be at the rock.

The night air turned cooler as Aresen had promised. Jezamina breathed easier being out in the open. She waited until the pain subsided before moving on again, like a crab, until she reached the stone monument. The chair could be a place to sit during the day instead of staying in bed or on the mat.

She pressed her cheek against the stone and hugged the rock in victory. If any one of the men witnessed her antics, he would have laughed. Jezamina didn't care. This was her accomplishment. She did it without help. Her bed was a shadow in the dark. If she had come upon the place, she wouldn't have known one existed.

Jezamina brushed aside the water pooling in the crevice of the rock. She then used her arms to pull her body up to sit on the flat edge of the seat. The rock molded to her curves and now she understood why Veita liked it so much. To Jezamina, it was freedom. She smiled and held her head high.

The wind blew against her face. She didn't care how her arms became chilled, giving her goosebumps, or how the forest surrounding her was a black void. The independence gave her a euphoric high. Jezamina sat on her perch. She could've stayed there all night, but the air turned colder as the breeze picked up like Aresen had said it would. She didn't have furs or a fire to keep her warm.

She eyed the fire pit. Not one ember glowed within the watery muck.

Jezamina contemplated her next move. Raine would be out in the early morning to start the fire again. She remembered how he struggled to get the flames going after the last heavy rain. If the water was drained, the pit might dry out before morning.

How many times had Veita and the men sat by the fire to enjoy a pleasant night of conversation? Their voices were too low, except for an occasional laugh, to hear what they said. She was an outcast. Maybe now she'd be able to join them.

Jezamina spotted a long spindly stick a few feet away from where she sat. She slid off the rock and reached over to grab the end with her outstretched hand. The length was right and felt solid, sturdy enough to hold her weight. She gave her new cane a test by first pressing the end into the dirt. Satisfied the stick wouldn't break, Jezamina used it to take a step. She teetered but held herself steady. Another step. Her good leg was still too weak to hold her weight. She had been in bed way too long.

A roll of thunder cut across the forest and echoed against the trees—still a distance away. One star peeked out between the clouds. She had some time. Testing her bad leg, she put weight on her foot. The pain was manageable. She took two steps and then had to rest.

"I can do this," Jezamina told herself a few times. "Mind over matter."

She hopped with her good leg and used the cane for balance. Four hops in, she twisted and her leg hit the cane. Jezamina danced about, trying not to fall. The pain shot through her foot when she tried placing weight on it. She quivered like a fawn testing its legs for the first time. She closed her eyes and used short breaths to recover.

Opening her eyes again, she assessed her situation. She turned to the rock. She could go back. Jezamina looked toward the fire pit. Her calculations might have been off. It didn't seem as far when she first started.

Another roll of thunder swept the forest sky. One drop. Two drops. Jezamina bowed her head to keep the water out of her eyes. She had no strength to move. She wanted to, but her legs wouldn't cooperate.

"Fuck," she said under her breath. Her good knee buckled and she fell to the ground. Her hands hit first, one in a puddle. The mud came up and splashed her face. She sat up and wiped her cheek with her arm. It did no good as the rain dropped from the sky, soaking her in an instant.

"Enjoying the evening?" Jezero's voice rose above the thunderous noise.

Jezamina jerked her arm upward to protect herself, startled by his sudden appearance. She almost hit him in the head, but he jerked away in time. She glared at him for scaring her. His shadowed face, tucked inside the hood of his cape, made it impossible for her to know if he saw her anger.

"Decide to go for a walk? Picked the wrong night for it, wouldn't you say?"

She wiped the mud off her cheek with the back of her hand. She wanted to push him over as he leaned toward her with his hands on his thighs.

"I thought the storm had passed," she said to defend her actions.

"The rain will likely stay throughout the night. My advice is to get back to your bed. Stay warm." He stood and stepped away.

Jezamina's mouth gaped open, shocked when he didn't offer a hand. He turned to leave and panic seized her. "*What?* You're not going to help?"

Jezero pointed to her shelter. "This was your choice."

The distance to her bed was too far, the ground too muddy. She didn't trust herself, even with her stick, to walk back. Jezamina wrapped her arms around her body, shaking from the cold. She was beyond showing any type of independence, but she wouldn't beg.

Jezero moved closer. She thought he changed his mind to help, but he tipped his head instead to bow away from her. "I wouldn't stay here too long."

Jezamina's inner pressure rose.

"Argggh!" With all her might, she threw her stick at him, hoping to hit the back of his head. Instead, it bounced off the ground and landed halfway between them. She then raised her middle finger at him, but Jezero never looked back. He disappeared off the ledge.

The rain softened into a steady hum, unlike the earlier pounding. Jezamina sat in the dark. She no longer had her stick to help her walk. Defeated, she dug her hands into the mud and dragged herself toward her bed.

Chapter 14

::: Jezamina :::

Dusken

Jezamina woke to Jezero sitting next to her. His black, wavy hair was pulled back into a ponytail. He stared at her with intense brown eyes—not the face she wanted to see.

Abruptly she turned so her back faced him. He should know he wasn't welcome. What kind of person would leave her out in the open, soaking wet, and unable to walk back to her shelter?

He was being a total asshole. A cold-hearted bastard. More names came to mind and she rattled them off in her head.

Yet, he stayed.

Her attempt to sleep was useless. His energy broke into her space.

"Go away," she snapped at him.

A strand of her hair, cold and still wet, fell across her cheek. Jezamina raised her mud-stained hand to push it away. All night she shivered as if the rain had turned to ice on her skin. She should have taken off her tunic when sliding into bed, but the slow crawl back exhausted her.

Jezero leaned in. His hot breath covered her neck, making it itch.

She tried shooing him away as if he were an annoying insect.

"Lesson number one," he said in a distinct, curt voice. "Learn to take care of yourself."

Just what she wanted to hear. Jezamina pulled the furs over her head.

He tossed them back. "Here. I offer you hot herbs to heat your insides."

"Go away."

The sweet, warm blend of herbs filled the air, emitting comfort.

"Take it," he ordered.

Jezamina sighed. He wasn't going to leave her alone. She sat up without looking at him and took the mug. She knew Veita had made it for her. The medicine woman was proud of her special blends and rightly so.

Forgetting about Jezero, she curled her hands around the mug and let the heat thaw her fingers. She then let the steam warm her cheeks before taking the first sip.

"Survival out here takes strength," Jezero said.

She glared at him for interrupting her ritual. He was looking at her hands and the mud caked to her skin. The whole scenario from the night before made her angry again. She said, "Kindness goes a long way too."

"Not out here." His stare penetrated her. "You have to be strong to make it here. Body, mind, soul."

"Why is that?" she asked. "Because men like you are assholes when it comes to helping a woman out?"

He seemed caught off guard by her sudden outburst but recovered as his lips curled into a slight smile, one she thought was sexy.

"Oh, my goodness!" Veita gasped. She stopped short, throwing her hands up to her chest when she saw Jezamina. Her eyes widened in disbelief, while her voice rose two notches. "Why are you covered in mud?"

Jezamina glared at Jezero.

"She practiced walking last night," he answered.

The medicine woman shot him an accusing look before nudging her way in, making Jezero step back. She turned her attention to Jezamina. "You poor thing. You're shaking!"

Veita stepped forward, then back, flustered about what to do. She opened her mouth as if wanting to lecture Jezero, yet she seemed to know it would do no good.

A twig snapped. Raine was trying to hide in the nearby bush.

"Raine." She fluttered her hands at him. "Hurry now. Go get Jezamina dry clothes."

He obliged, staring at Jezamina with the same disbelief Veita showed minutes before.

"What did you do to her?" The medicine woman glared at Jezero.

"She'll be fine," he said again in the distinct, curt voice.

Jezamina drank her herbs and kept quiet as Veita lectured Jezero indirectly. The medicine woman spoke in a low mumble about how he found her in the sea, brought her to Dusken to heal, and now treated her without respect. Louder, she said, "Jezamina is not one of your men."

Hallelujah.

Veita stopped her lecture when Raine brought clothes. Jezero got up to leave.

"Oh, no," Veita called out to him before he disappeared. "I'm not finished."

This Jezamina had to see. The mighty Jezero being scolded. His shoulders broadened.

Jezero turned back around, giving the medicine woman the attention she demanded. His hands turned to fists as if controlling his anger.

Jezamina smirked. *The doyen doesn't like someone telling him what to do.*

"She needs a bath. The falls are too far for her to walk on her own, and I cannot carry her."

He stood for a moment with a cold, dead stare.

"Shall I find someone else?" she challenged him. "Zarac? Aresen?"

His eyes squinted at the medicine woman as if trying to figure out what she was implying. He then gave her a nod as if understanding what those consequences could be. "I shall take her. Once the sun warms the air."

"Good," the medicine woman snipped. She turned to Jezamina. "When you bathe, Raine and I will re-pack your bed with fresh ferns and grass. This mud will harden like a rock and be uncomfortable as ever."

Jezamina nodded and finished drinking her herbs. She was surprised a scolding on her end wasn't forthcoming. At least Veita knew the mud wasn't entirely her fault.

When Raine returned, he helped her change into a loose tunic. She wondered if her oversized "dress" belonged to Zarac. No matter. Having something clean and dry against her skin lightened her spirits.

And a bath!

How long had it been since she'd taken a bath? Jezamina appreciated Veita's occasional effort to wash her hair and body, but the medicine woman could only do so much. Jezamina sighed. The thought of water surrounding her, scrubbing her scalp, and cleaning every inch of her body lifted her mood.

She waited with extreme patience for the sun to rise above the trees. Jezero had disappeared, but she knew he'd show up. Soon. Today there were no clouds to threaten rain. The wind was mild. She hoped the water wasn't too cold. She still had a chill.

As she nibbled on her midday meal, Jezamina's excitement grew. She was going to see the forest, go beyond the tiny area around her shelter. Now she'd know where the men disappeared to when they left the ledge.

Would any of it trigger her memory? Veita knew she wasn't from their land. The way she talked, the diamonds in her ears, were all signs she wasn't a villager. Or a Morlorn. But maybe one thing she spotted or a familiar scent could jolt a thought or an idea of where she belonged.

True to his word, Jezero reappeared on the ledge when the sun was high above the trees. He set his bow and arrow against a taller rock, grabbed a slice of meat from the rack near the fire, ate his meal, and then headed toward her. His confident sway defined his lean, strong body. He wore fitted leather leggings and a loose white tunic.

He was handsome. Sexy.

She hated to think that way.

A slight smile curled on his lips as he made his way to her bed. Jezamina's breath caught in her throat when his eyes found hers. He seemed happier, or did he have a change of heart? He'd trimmed his beard and moustache as if trying to lessen his ruggedness or to impress her.

Jezamina rubbed her palms on her thighs. Her nerves took over. She was leaving the ledge. Would he leave her in the forest and make her walk back? Or leave her to survive on her own? She bit her lip.

He crouched down next to her. Again, his slight smile captured her. "Do you think you can behave? Keep me out of trouble for the rest of the day?"

Her stomach fluttered. She tried keeping her wits. "That depends. Do you plan on leaving me in the woods to find my way back alone?"

He was about to say something but changed his mind.

Yes, she was scared to be alone with him in a huge forest. Who knows what he might surprise her with?

"I promise. I will behave today." His words were simple, but they carried a softness she hadn't heard before.

She stared for a moment into his eyes. Jezamina cleared her throat before speaking. "Then, please, let's go. I'm anxious to be clean again."

"Aren't we all," Jezero agreed as he reached down to take her hand.

Jezamina's cheeks burned with embarrassment. Did she smell that bad? Now she didn't want to go near him. Jezero's hand stayed, ready for her when she hesitated.

"I will be honored to show you one of my favorite spots in Dusken. If you'll let me."

Knowing the reward and being curious won Jezamina over. She took his hand and let him lift her without effort into his arms. She slid her hand around his neck. His musky scent was pleasant.

"We are leaving, Veita."

The medicine woman appeared with a mug of herbs in her hand. This time, she was the one to enjoy the hot drink. "Be off. Be safe."

Jezamina gripped him tighter when he stepped down from the ledge. The rocks were strategically placed to make stairs going down to the path. So why did they always jump off the edge?

She continued to look behind her. Jezero's home was like a stage against the cliff. The ledge and steps blended with nature. She would never have realized someone lived there. The trees kept them hidden, yet she knew the men were at an advantage when they guarded their place.

Turning forward, Jezamina welcomed the beauty and colors before her. She forgot about Jezero carrying her. The ferns were so green and vibrant. The soil, a rich and rusty black, covered the path. She wished to run with her arms open and gather all the beauty into one big hug.

She caught Jezero staring at her. "What?"

"I'm hoping you're pleased."

Jezamina nodded. "Amazed. It's stunning."

"This is my sanctuary. The place I am the most comfortable."

Her heart softened. She liked the crow's feet near his eyes and the tiny freckles on his cheeks. She also liked how he revealed something personal—not a lesson, not an order.

"I can see why. I feel protected here," she said while looking up. The branches high in the trees intertwined with each other as if to form a friendship, a pact, to keep the forest safe.

"I'm glad. For now, these woods are your protection. Your home."

"For now?" Jezamina repeated. She knew she belonged elsewhere. People were waiting for her. Family. They had to be. But the way he said those words struck her as odd.

Jezero ignored her question while he focused on a rockier part of the path. A slight frown crossed his face. Why did everyone avoid her questions? They were simple questions.

"Tell me what you know about me." This time she tried a different approach and stated rather than asked.

Jezero stopped near a soft patch of grass. "I cannot tell you anything about your life, where you're from, or who you are." He lowered his one arm until her feet touched the soft, long blades. "Nor can I tell you why you're here."

Jezamina couldn't resist brushing the bottoms of her feet against the grass, letting the tips tickle her skin. This was so unfair, to have a serious conversation when she wanted to prance about. She asked, "Will I ever know?"

Jezero had his arm around her waist and he held tight. They seemed closer than when he carried her. He didn't seem so daunting. She liked his possessiveness toward her.

She jerked back, unsure where her reaction came from. One minute she hated him, the next she felt like she belonged with him.

"Careful," he said when she stumbled backward. He pulled away, letting her stand somewhat on her own. He kept his hand out, ready to catch her if she fell.

He didn't answer her last question. In time, she thought. In time. Now she wanted to dig her feet into the dirt on the path. The unusual color led her to believe it was soft and airy.

She looked to Jezero, wanting his approval before attempting to walk. He nodded and held out his arm for her to take. She used him to keep her balance as she hopped over to the path.

"No running. Not yet," he warned her. "Veita would not be happy with me."

Jezamina laughed, picturing Veita's angry face when she scolded him, just as she had earlier.

She was right—the dirt was soft and airy. She curled her toes in and then dug small ditches on the path. If only she could run barefoot. The impact on her feet would be like walking on feathers. Taking a deep breath, she gave Jezero a large smile, one of gratitude. "Thank you. This is beautiful."

Jezero nodded. "I'm glad you like Dusken."

"How did you find the forest?"

He held his hand out for her. This time Jezamina accepted his offer and wrapped her arms around him when he lifted her again.

"I was injured and needed a place to heal. When I came upon this valley, the forest captured my spirit. When I found the ledge and the protection it provided, I knew this would be my home."

"So you just claimed it?"

"Somewhat," he continued. "There are still many undiscovered forests within the lands. Most of Dusken was unclaimed. Part, I took from the Morlorns."

"Veita told me about..." she wasn't quite sure how to say it—"you helping the villages."

He nodded with some caution. "What else did she tell you?"

Jezamina chose her words carefully, remembering that Veita didn't want to give up too much information. Now Jezamina wondered if it was for his privacy or another reason. "She explained how the villages are grateful for you and your men."

He seemed satisfied with her response. His focus turned to the path as the decline became steeper.

Jezamina tightened her grip around his neck. She wished she could help in some way, but he didn't seem to mind holding her; or at least, her weight didn't seem to be an issue.

"Listen," he said. "Do you hear the water?"

The birds chirped as they flew from one tree to the next. The trees swayed with the wind and the leaves fluttered. Animals walked the forest, and the ferns sprang back as they passed. She waited. A few more steps down the path and she picked up the lull of water rushing over the rocks.

"Took you long enough," he teased. "One thing to learn here is to keep your ears and eyes open. Always listen. Always watch for trouble."

Jezamina perked up, not thinking about trouble. She tensed.

"Relax," he said. "We're fine for now."

They turned off the main path to one narrow and steep. Jezero maneuvered around the rocks and trees. The waterfall became louder but was still out of view. She kept looking, knowing it was close.

Finally, they reached a point on the hill where the trees opened and created a path to the waterfall. She and Jezero seemed to be at the midpoint. The rush of water was deafening as it pulsated over the rocks high above and then cascaded down some distance below them.

Jezero stopped for a moment, allowing her to soak in the beauty of the landscape. She lifted her head and the soft spray of water tickled her face. She loved the smell of water, the fresh, clean scent. When they continued on, they followed the waterfall. The path descended to an area where a pool of water swirled off to the side and then cascaded again over another set of rocks.

"This is where we get our drinking water," he said and pointed to a crevice in the rocks. The water was deep and undisturbed by the rushing falls. "Would you like a drink?"

Jezamina nodded, needing to quench her thirst. He set her down on a large, flat rock near the edge of the pool.

"Look down," he told her while grabbing a cup stored off to the side.

She leaned over and placed her hand on the rock for balance. A current swirled downward to keep the pool from stagnating. The clarity was amazing. She could see the stone base at the bottom of the pool. "How far does it go down?"

"About twice your length, I'd say."

"It's so clear!"

Jezero sat next to her and dipped the cup into the pool. He offered her the first drink.

Cold, crisp, and pure. Jezamina smiled as she drank the full cup without stopping for air. He offered her seconds, but she shook her head.

Jezamina wiped her mouth with the tips of her fingers. As Jezero took his drink, she spotted a dark pink flower with a large bell-shaped bottom growing between the rocks nearby. She leaned over and touched the petals, outlining the curve of the bell with her fingertip. "So soft and silky."

"The pentias flower," he said. "They grow throughout the forest. The orange ones over there"—he pointed toward the woods at a cluster of flowers—"are called cyrolus."

The cyroluses had bright orange centers that spread out and turned into red, jagged petals. The flowers stood out against the dark green ferns and the smoky black bark dressing the trees.

"Neither plant has been seen outside of Dusken."

Jezamina leaned closer to the pink flower and inhaled its sweet fragrance. She jerked back when the scent exploded in her nose.

Jezero laughed. "It sneaks up on you, doesn't it?"

She laughed too and then blew out her nose. "Yes, a little strong."

He dipped the cup into the water again and offered her another drink.

"This is the path we normally take." Jezero nodded his head toward the edge of the falls where the thick layer of rocks acted like steps to the river. "But for now, we'll take the safer route—until you can walk on your own."

He picked her up once more after she drank the water and set the cup aside. They headed back into the woods and weaved around and down the hill to an area with a little beach.

"Ohhh my!" Jezamina's eyes widened at the perfect escape. A pool of water nestled in a cove between the waterfall and the river, enticing her to jump in. The trees offered privacy yet allowed the sun to shine through, offering warmth after a long swim.

Jezero let her down so her feet touched the sandy beach. He kept his other arm firmly around her waist while she took in the view. *Stunning. Breathtaking.* Her eyes widened in awe. And the sun...she loved the brightness and the heat against her skin.

"Are you ready for your bath?" He let go of her but stayed close in case she should lose her balance.

She nodded, eager to wade into the turquoise water.

He took off his shirt and dropped it to the sandy beach. Something she wasn't expecting. Jezamina stared at his bare chest—muscular, smooth, and shiny. His hands went to his leggings to untie the front.

"What are you doing?" she shrieked in panic. She almost lost her balance and grabbed for the closest tree branch.

"You want a bath, right?" His arms went out but he didn't have to help her.

She nodded with some reservation.

"You can't go in the water alone."

Jezamina cleared her throat, not thinking about needing help.

He was joining her? The thought never occurred to her. Of course he had to be in the water. Of course he would be naked. How else would you take a bath?

His hand continued to pull on the string to his leggings. She swallowed hard. How easily they fell. His hard stomach, muscled legs, and manhood were all open for view. She already imagined him without leggings. She had seen men before. But he was like a statue—hard and firm.

"Ahem." Jezero made a sound to catch her attention. He raised his hand so her eyes moved away from his lower half to his face.

"Would you like some help?"

Jezamina's cheeks grew hot.

***

Jezero didn't think his undressing would cause a reaction. But then, he wasn't around women much. In fact, he preferred to stay away from them. Most times they were trouble—even this one who blushed in front of him.

He couldn't resist. "I'm glad you like what you see."

"Ohh!" She turned redder and tried hitting him with her fist. He grabbed her hand.

She turned her head down, but he caught the smile. Jezamina had a cute, sexy smile with a full bottom lip. Maybe he had been too hard on her, making her fend for herself during the storm. He treated her no differently than he would have treated one of his men.

But then...she wasn't one of his men.

"Come on," he said. "The water is waiting."

Jezamina composed herself. Her eyes darted away when she held the two sides of her tunic. She played with the end of the fabric as if modesty kept her from doing what she wanted. The temptation of water won out. She lifted the fabric over her hips. The soft patch between her legs, golden curly hair, formed a perfect V. Jezero bit his lip.

Not bothering to ask again if she needed help, he pulled the tunic over her head. The back of his fingers brushed against the side of her breast. Her soft, womanly sides.

Jezero caught his breath. He turned away for a moment, while the tunic was still over her head, to stay in control. She was overpowering his senses. He thought of Veita scolding him, giving him an incentive to refocus. Her tunic came off, and he dropped it to the ground. He then lifted her into his arms and carried her to the pool.

The water was cool and refreshing, which helped ease his reaction to her nakedness. His lower half was shocked into behaving.

Jezamina let go of him and moved into the water when he released her legs. "The bottom is sandy."

"You're surprised?"

"I thought it would be rocky." She nodded toward the waterfall where the rocks protruded out.

"The riverbed is filled with rocks," he said, half listening. She strategically placed her hair to cover her breasts. Not that it mattered. One nipple peeked out between the clumps of dirt-filled hair. She did need a bath. It would do her good to feel clean and get some sun on her skin. Her body was still stick thin, but she'd get there. Jezero was satisfied with her progress and how—

"You're staring at me," Jezamina said and broke into his thoughts.

"Admiring," he corrected and she blushed again. He moved closer and hooked his arm around her waist. He guided her to deeper water and toward the bank near the waterfall.

Jezamina placed her hand on his shoulder. She braced herself, before going under. He watched as she stayed below the surface. When she was ready, he helped pull her up.

"That felt so good," she said while pulling her hair away from her face.

The water glistened on her hard nipples. He yearned to lick the drops away and to roll his thumb over her breasts. This would be a perfect scenario to hold her close. Skin on skin.

Jezero shook his head. He remembered the reason for taking her to the waterfall. Why she was in Dusken. He protected her because of the calling. Nothing more. Jezero turned from her and dived into the water.

The cold cleared his senses. He took two long arm strokes before surfacing again. This time he was near the edge of the bank where three flat rocks jutted out. He reached over and took three of the crystals cradled in a nook. He offered them to Jezamina, who swam toward him.

She opened her palm, and he dropped the translucent blue stones into her hand. She questioned him again, unsure what to do with them. Jezero took another three crystals for himself and showed her how to rub them together until a thick lather foamed. He then rolled them around on his head to wash his hair. The lather sprayed around him as he scrubbed with vigor.

Jezamina was still rubbing the crystals together when he finished his hair with a rinse. He went to help but she backed away, wanting to do it herself. Slowly the lather began to bubble up in her hands. Triumph showed on her face. A good sign. He remembered when he woke to the life before him. How he learned new ways of doing things. Jezamina had the same curiosity.

She tried rubbing the crystals against her scalp, like he had. One of the blue stones fell out of her hand. Jezamina tried catching the stone by batting it up in the air to catch it again. Instead, Jezero caught the crystal right before it hit the water. She wrinkled her nose and expressed a silent apology.

"Would you like help?"

"Only because my ribs still hurt," she said and gave him one crystal.

He refrained from saying anything, but he noted one stone was missing.

Jezamina rolled her eyes when he kept his palm out. "Okay. It fell into the water."

Jezero would find the stone later. The crystals weren't easy to come by.

He moved around to her backside, feeling he'd be safer based on proximity to her nakedness. He began with a strong lather before rolling the crystals around her scalp. The more he massaged, the more she relaxed. Jezero took his time. The dirt and grime ran from her hair into the water. He needed to rinse the top of her head so he leaned her back. Her hair tickled his chest as it floated across the surface. She closed her eyes to enjoy the sun on her face.

Jezero kept one hand under her shoulders and used his other hand as a cup to pour water over her head. Having her tilt back more, he became distracted when her breasts popped up like islands in the sea. The lather and water danced around the soft, rosy peaks. It took all his willpower to keep from sliding his hand across her side, bringing her in, and then cupping one of the mounds with his lips.

"Ohh!" Jezamina shot upward as water poured over her face and into her mouth.

"Sorry!" Jezero brushed off her face as she coughed out the water.

She glared at him, but he ignored her, maintaining his innocence. He had her turn again, while he washed the rest of her hair. She kept silent, her mouth closed.

"You seem deep in thought," he said, deciding it was best to strike up a conversation to keep his mind from what he desired to do.

She half nodded. "I was thinking about Dusken."

"What were you thinking?"

"Why do you have to guard this land if it's yours? Every night you or one of your men keeps watch."

"We still need to protect it."

"From the Morlorns?"

"Yes, from the Morlorns." He finished with her hair and dunked her head into the water.

"Do they want the land back?" she asked when resurfacing. She held out her hand for the crystals and took over washing the rest of her body.

"One reason." He felt slight disappointment in not being able to help her.

"And another reason?"

He went over to grab more crystals and then rejoined her. "Another is because I fight for the villages. The same reason why I have a price upon my head."

"I don't understand why they want to attack the villages." She had trouble bringing her foot up to wash it. Jezero forced himself to stay back.

"Greed. Revenge. Sometimes for the land and other times to show their power. They are fighting people, not peaceful in nature. They attack without reason."

She turned to him, showing concern. Jezero realized the anger had come out in his voice. Maybe it was best. She needed to know how dangerous they were.

"Have they tried attacking Dusken?"

"They have. I am not kind to trespassers. Only a few are allowed to make it out alive—for the sole purpose of warning others of the dire consequences."

"So you use the same tactic on them as they do with the villages."

Jezero's eyes narrowed. "A little different, but yes. I'm defending my land."

She swam toward him again and gave him the crystals. He caught her smirk and waited, wondering what went on in her head.

"Sooo," she said as if plotting. "Is the price upon your head for being dead or alive?"

Jezero chuckled. "Capturing me alive has a higher price than bringing me in dead."

The shades of blue in her eyes came back to life. They sparkled underneath dark lashes as she circled around him. "Is that so?"

He played along. "Are you planning to trade me in for a higher purse?"

She smiled coyly, not answering.

Taking her time, Jezamina dipped her head in the water, then came up close to his front side. "Maybe not. But I am curious as to why I sense no fear in you."

"You sense no fear," he said, grabbing her waist, "because I'm not afraid. If I die for a cause, I will be honored to have fought for as long as I have."

He pulled her toward him and took the crystals from her. She had missed a few spots on the soft sides of her neck. He rolled the stones across her skin from her ears to the front of her chest.

Jezero stopped when her eyes penetrated his. She opened her mouth seductively and asked, "Should I be afraid of you?"

"Oh, yes, you should," he thought but didn't say.

Chapter 15

::: Jessie :::

Chicago, IL

Jessie smiled, remembering the thrill of Jezero washing her hair. She shivered with pleasure. This had been the first time, bathing in the pool, she felt close to him, or at least, since he'd become more human than savage. She saw his gentleness toward her. His determination to help the villages. His full male figure. Her heart fluttered. He almost kissed her. She was the one to pull away, hesitant because of guilt.

Now Walt, the underlying reason for her guilt, sat frozen to his chair in front of her. His hand rested on his chin and covered his mouth. He bit his fingernails, something he did when irritated. He showed little emotion when she told him about her bath with Jezero, but then she was reminiscing more than telling. For Walt, she toned it down and kept out the sexual tension between Jezero and her. How they both could've taken it farther.

Walt frowned. "What do you think Veita meant by the other guys' intention? Why didn't she want them taking you for a bath? Did they want to harm you? Rape you?" Walt removed his hand from his face.

Really? That was what he got out of it? She didn't like Walt's wrong impression about the men, and she set him straight. "They're my protectors. Aresen is the ardent one, yes, but he knew his place. He is the sharpshooter and hunter of food. Also, a gentleman. Zarac didn't want me there in the first place. After the bath, new clothes waited for me on the beach. Zarac made me leggings, a skirt, a halter top, tunic, and footwear. All fit perfectly. Even though he wasn't happy I lived in Dusken, he treated me with respect."

Without warning, Walt leaped from his chair and swooped down to give her a hug.

Jessie froze. He emitted warmth but was so different from Jezero. She slid her arms around him and patted his back.

"I'm sorry," he said. He took two sharp breaths through his nose. "God, you smell so good."

"Walt..." Jessie's mind raced, searching for what to say, what to do. He seemed to need forgiveness, but she didn't understand why. No one was at fault. They lived in an odd, tangled mess of emotions. So many unknowns controlled their lives. Neither one knew the outcome. She wanted to help yet feared if she gave in, he'd take it the wrong way.

Walt started caressing her hair. His breathing became heavier. Jessie needed him to back away. He wanted more than she could give, but he held on so tight.

A cough saved her.

Mrs. Arbol stood in the doorway. She pursed her lips together and tapped her foot.

"Hello, Mother."

Jessie breathed a sigh of relief when Walt let go of her.

"Walt." His mother took off her gloves. "Jessica."

"Mrs. Arbol." She would never call the woman "Mother." Ever.

"Has the doctor made his rounds?" Helen looked toward her son and ignored Jessie.

"Not yet. Why?" Walt walked around the bed and gave his mother a hug and an air kiss.

Jessie wondered the same. Mrs. Arbol hesitated as if she didn't want to say anything in front of her future daughter-in-law. What did she have up her sleeve?

"Are we meeting with him?" Walt checked his watch.

She lowered her voice. "I'm here to discuss the release date with Dr. Maguire."

"Why?" Jessie frowned as she leaned to see Mrs. Arbol beyond Walt's frame. He blocked her view as if to separate them. His mother had no business discussing her release date or talking to the doctor.

"Why, darling, we must make plans." Mrs. Arbol stepped out from Walt's shadow. She expressed her fake smile, the one saying "I'll be polite because I have to tolerate you."

"What do you mean by making plans?" Jessie asked again. This was her life they were talking about. Her plan included leaving the hospital and getting back to California to hibernate at home. Her home.

Jessie blew out a puff of air and her bangs flew up. Dusken. What she really wanted was to return to Dusken. The tension moved into her back, and she rolled her shoulders, hoping to ease the tightness.

"We made arrangements. You'll still need care," Mrs. Arbol said, keeping her voice in control and pleasant. "We prepared a room, next to Walt's, and we've hired a nurse."

"Wonderful news, Mother," Walt piped in while he tried scooting her out the door. "Why don't you find Dr. Maguire."

Jessie's blood pressure shot up. She gave Walt a killer glare. He'd never said anything about living at his parents' estate. Not one word. Her throat constricted as she tried keeping her emotions steady.

When his mother left, she let loose. "I'm not staying at your mother's."

"You'll be fine," Walt said and motioned for her to keep her voice down.

Jessie steamed. He'd never cut her off or dismissed her words before. Now he was acting like a parent telling a child "enough."

Carol walked into the room. She smiled and sang hello, her usual greeting. She added, "I'm told you had a restless night, missy."

"I slept some." She longed for one night, out in the open, with the stars high above her head, and with Jezero sleeping by her side. Then she'd get a good night's sleep.

The nurse stepped to the side of the bed to check the monitors and the tube going into her patient's arm. She glanced over to Walt. "I see you went home for a change. Good for you."

"I cleaned up before you could throw me out."

She looked from him to Jessie at his poor attempt to joke with her. Carol's radar seemed to go off, aware of the thickness to the air. "Well, I won't be too long."

"Take your time," Walt said. "I'll find out what my mother is up to."

"Mrs. Arbol is here?"

Jessie raised her eyebrows in surprise. "You didn't hear her?"

Walt made a noise to show he disapproved of her comment but otherwise kept quiet.

"I must have just missed her." The nurse stayed neutral, making a show of checking Jessie's pulse.

"I'll be back," he said, fumbling for his phone to make a call.

Jessie waited until he left before asking, "Carol, when can I go home?"

"I'm not the one to ask. Dr. Maguire gets to decide your release." She matched the tone of Jessie's voice as if they were telling secrets. She wrapped the blood pressure cuff around Jessie's arm. "However, rumor has it you'll be out of here in a couple of days."

"I'm fine. Why not today?"

"Ask Dr. Maguire when he checks on you this afternoon. He's the boss."

"And you're the nurse. What's preventing me from leaving?"

Carol made a noise in her throat at Jessie's persistence. She caved. "Your vitals haven't stabilized yet. We've had problems reading your kidney levels and regulating your heart rate."

Jessie lowered her eyes at the not-so-promising news.

Carol patted Jessie's arm. "Be patient. We don't need you rushed back to the emergency room because we didn't do our job."

Jessie nodded in surrender. Her shoulders dropped and her head went down.

"Besides, I don't think Walt could handle coming back here if you were admitted again. He's been an angel, staying by your side."

"And why, I have no idea." Jessie wished he didn't care so much.

Walt wasn't the type to sit for long periods of time. He kept busy, whereas Jezero found the downtime to enjoy the day or to relax at night, even when he protected his land. The simplicity of life versus running crazy played to the extremes. Walt's life was too structured. Her life before the fire had been too busy. She preferred simplicity.

A soft movement, the swish of cloth, caught her attention. Walt stood in the doorway with his shoulder leaning against the frame. His expression was blank, similar to what she'd seen before he left for work to contemplate the next crisis.

"Is that for me?" She referred to the two milkshakes he held in his hands.

"Chocolate. Your favorite."

Jessie smiled. "I won't pass up chocolate."

"Now, don't spoil your dinner," Carol teased. She did one final check, taking Jessie's temperature, before saying goodbye and leaving the room for her next patient.

Walt handed her the chocolate milkshake while he kept the strawberry. He plopped down into his chair and took a long sip from the straw. He seemed fine, the irritation gone. She had to admit he did well, not losing his cool when she told him about the bath scene.

"Would you like me to continue?" she asked.

"Please do," he said.

Jessie frowned, wondering why he seemed so businesslike. "No, we can wait."

"Please continue."

Again the attitude. He acted like a therapist, very professional except for having the milkshake in his hand. Jessie didn't want a confrontation with him, but she didn't want to waste her breath either if he didn't plan to listen. "I'm not getting a warm, fuzzy feeling."

Walt leaned forward. His lip curled into a snarl. "Would you like me to give you a bath? Make you feel warm and fuzzy?"

Jessie squeezed the cup holding her milkshake. She refrained from throwing it at him. "And here I thought you meant what you said. That you were here for me. You wanted to understand what I went through."

She took a long draw from the straw. Her cheeks sucked in. The cold ice cream tasted good. Cooled her down. She was angry. No. Hurt.

He sighed, letting all the air release from his lungs. "I'm sorry." He scooted his chair closer to the bed. "Jessie, I'm sorry. Yes, I want to hear what you have to say. Another man was giving you a bath. It wasn't me." He leaned forward and put his chin on the edge of her bed. "Do you know how much I'd give to be him? To be the one giving you a bath?"

Walt looked like a puppy that'd been caught being naughty. His eyes drooped. He gave her a timid smile, but it didn't reach his eyes. He was livid inside. His ears were red. The bath must have bugged him more than he let on.

Jessie decided to continue. The more he heard about her life in Dusken, the better chance of him understanding why she was in love with another man.

Chapter 16

::: Jezamina :::

Dusken

Jezamina smoothed her hands across the soft leather skirt. She admired the consistent and tightly stitched seams and how the skins draped so she had room to move. Zarac's talent surprised her. He even burned a leaf design along the hem and in the waistband. The same design carried through to the halter top. They both fit perfectly.

She waited that evening for his return to the ledge. When he did, she let him settle down near the fire before approaching him.

Jezamina tightened her grip on the long, thick stick Jezero found on their way back from the waterfall. With a few adjustments, he made the crutch to help her walk. Now she used it to hobble toward the burliest of the men.

"Zarac," she said with hesitation. He didn't turn, so she called his name again.

The man frowned. He had been staring into the fire, lost in thought. He took a swig from his mug and then wiped the froth from his moustache and beard.

She took another few steps forward to stand in front of him. "Thank you for the clothes. They're beautiful." She opened her arms, moving the crutch to display his handiwork.

Zarac grunted as if dismissing the appreciation. He did eye his handiwork to see how the clothes fit.

"Your kindness means more than you can imagine."

He took another swig of his ale and stared at the fire again. She reminded herself that he wasn't an ogre. Veita had a lot of respect for him. There was no concern for her to be afraid.

With a genuine smile, she said, "You made me feel good about myself again." She hoped never to wear the huge tunics again.

"You needed clothing," he mumbled.

"Yes, I did, among other things" she said, thinking about her other wants or needs as the list increased. She longed for friendship, a family, and most of all her memory. She understood the men in Dusken came from different backgrounds. They found a common bond and blended into a solid family. They made it work. She was an outcast. Without realizing it, she spoke her thoughts. "What I would really like is to find a place where I could belong, be of some importance."

Zarac continued to stare at the fire. His face, underneath the bushy beard, seemed to soften, but he wasn't in the mood for conversation. A man of few words.

Disheartened, she turned and placed the crutch under her arm. She hopped, using her good leg, to change directions before heading toward her shelter. First step forward, a rock caught under her crutch. The bottom of the crutch swung behind her while she continued forward. Jezamina would have fallen flat on her face if two strong hands hadn't swept her into an upright position again. Zarac stood at her side. With little effort, he lifted her up by the waist and carried her the rest of the way to her shelter.

He placed her so her feet landed on the mat in front of her bed. He tipped his head and said, "Ye have a home."

The burly man turned around and went back to the fire as if nothing had happened.

Veita's voice woke Jezamina. She came out of a heavy sleep and had to gain her bearings. The sun crested the treetops. Birds chirped, flying from branch to branch. The day started without her. *I slept that long?*

Jezamina sat up and stretched. The scent of fresh fern leaves, grass, and flower petals rose from her newly made bed when she moved. She smiled and stretched again, this time raising her arms and circling them around. She put her head back and her hair bounced, no longer weighted by the mud stuck to the strands. Shaking her head, the layers brushed across her bare back and gave her a slight shiver. She ran her fingers through the waves, wanting to add shine and control the strays.

Once her fingers ran through her hair without catching, she focused on her new clothing. Jezamina played with the decorative strips on the halter-top. Her breasts swelled under the fabric and showed more cleavage than she realized. If she kept her back straight, it helped keep her from being overexposed. She wouldn't complain. Zarac gave her a wonderful present.

His last words filled her head. *Ye have a home.* Jezero always said the words with authority, not giving her a choice. Zarac said them in a manner to welcome her with acceptance. The big oaf caught her heart.

Veita's voice drew her attention over to the fire. The medicine woman gave a handful of dried medicinal plants to Raine. Her mouth sagged as if sad or tired. Jezero went over and placed his hands on her shoulder.

Jezamina swung to her side and rose to her hands. She found her crutch and used it to help stand. She didn't like how the medicine woman seemed upset.

"You saved many more lives than I have. I'm just an old, gray-haired woman," Veita replied to whatever Jezero had said.

"I beg to differ. Your skills are more important. I cannot heal, only fight. You saved Jezamina's life. Think about all those lives you saved, including mine." He moved to give her a hug. When he did, Jezero caught Jezamina watching them. He stepped back, causing both Raine and Veita to turn.

"You're awake," the medicine woman said as if surprised and relieved. "We were getting worried."

"I slept for a long time, didn't I?" Jezamina struggled to keep her balance, only having the crutch to hold her up. She determined the crutch wasn't so easy to manage.

Veita took a few steps to come to her aid, but Jezero threw out his arm as a barrier to stop the medicine woman. He frowned and seemed irritated.

"I'm sorry." Jezamina blushed, realizing her rudeness. She'd disrupted their conversation. "Please, don't let me stop what you were doing. I can stay here. Give you privacy."

"No, please join us." Veita motioned for her to join them. "We're fine."

Jezero turned to pick up a log near the fire. He grabbed the end and set it against another log covered in flames. He glanced over to the medicine woman. "Are we set?"

"Yes, I have done what I came here to do," Veita said and her eyes looked downward as if sad. She recovered within seconds and turned to pay attention to her patient.

Jezamina approached slowly, using the crutch.

The medicine woman waited like a proud mother. She clasped her hands together and placed them near her heart as she smiled.

Jezamina held the crutch away from her and leaned toward Veita to give her a hug. Many times the medicine woman had stayed with her, being there when she cried in pain. Veita had patted her on the shoulder or leg and hummed under her breath to help comfort her. Never had they hugged. "I am so thankful for you, Veita."

The medicine woman's lip trembled as if her words had struck a nerve. She struggled to keep her emotions intact. "Let's get you sitting, child."

Jezamina chose the log with the carved-out seat. She let her crutch fall to the ground and awkwardly sat down, keeping her bad leg straight. Veita helped to make sure she was comfortable before walking over to Jezero. She whispered something in his ear. Whatever she said made him scowl. The way they stood, Jezero's distance—Jezamina detected tension. "What's going on? Are we in danger?"

Jezero brushed off his hands. He glanced to Veita and then back to the fire. "Veita is ready to return to the village."

The words didn't make sense. "Leave here?"

"Her work is done."

Shock sucked the air out of Jezamina's lungs. She couldn't breathe or talk. She looked at Veita, horrified.

"I need to return home, to my village." Veita poured a mug of steaming herbs and then offered it to her.

Jezamina took the mug without thinking. Her hand began to shake, and she had to set the mug on the ground to avoid spilling the hot liquid. Her insides turned numb. "You're leaving me?"

"I must go. Raine will take care of your needs. He knows his medicine."

Jezamina bit her lower lip to keep from crying. She would be at Jezero's mercy. Left to rot on her own if she didn't earn his approval. If it weren't for Veita scolding him and making him take her for a bath, she would still be caked in mud. Who was going to protect her? The other men? Her hand shot out and grabbed Veita by the arm. She whispered, not wanting Jezero to hear. "Take me with you."

He heard and his one eyebrow went up but Jezero refrained from saying anything. He stoked the fire with a long, pointed stick, and she swallowed hard.

"Jezero will take care of you. This is the way it's supposed to be."

"I still need you, Veita," Jezamina pleaded. She turned away from Jezero, not wanting him to think she didn't like Dusken. She loved the forest. But Veita had to be there, like a mother, to protect her.

"The calling came to Jezero. Not me." The medicine shot a look toward the doyen, as he finished stoking the fire and set the stick down.

Why did they always bring up the calling? Jezamina scowled, her bad mood turning worse. "Who makes the rules? Is it written in stone somewhere?"

Jezero stepped toward them. He crouched down to her level. His elbows rested on his legs. A hint of irritation twitched his lip. "This is Veita's choice to leave. Not mine."

His intense stare drew Jezamina in and she recognized he seemed upset by the decision as well. She turned back to the medicine woman. Why would she want to leave? Her voice shook. "Is this your choice?"

Veita's head dropped for a moment. She raised it again with determination. "Yes, I made the decision yesterday."

Hurt pierced Jezamina's heart. The tremor in her lip doubled in size.

Veita brushed her hands against her hips. "I came on Jezero's request. When I first arrived, you were near death. Now you are walking. Healthy. I did as he asked."

A cry of protest escaped Jezamina. She shook her head, not wanting the medicine woman to leave. She looked up to plead with Jezero but he had left.

"My village needs me," Veita explained. "You are one. There are many others who need my help."

Of course, Jezamina thought. How stupid to be so selfish. She covered her face with her hands. "I'm sorry. I wasn't thinking."

"Trust me. You are in good hands here. Jezero will take care of you."

"Like a lion circling his prey."

***

"She is scared," Veita warned Jezero as they stopped to say their goodbyes. "Her heart is in your hands."

"There is more at stake here," he said and handed Aresen the medicine woman's bag. They stood near the edge of Dusken where the trees grew like soldiers, tall and straight, as if protecting his land.

"Which is reason for you to show her how to survive. The Morlorns will find out about her."

Jezero refrained from telling the medicine woman about the Morlorns entering Dusken two nights beforehand. Three entered, based on the footprints—one fell into a trap, the other two escaped. Instead he said, "My concern now is getting you back to your village."

Veita's smile held sadness and worry. "I shall miss you. I wish you well."

Jezero hugged her tight. He breathed in clove and spice near the crook of her neck. The medicine woman, like a mother to him, always kept him grounded. Whenever he needed advice, he sought her wisdom. He wouldn't disappoint her. "Jezamina will be fine."

"Do you promise?"

"I promise. She will learn. One day, she will understand as well."

She nodded, accepting his word.

Jezero let go of Veita and stepped away. Aresen took over and helped the medicine woman down the bank where Zarac waited. She raised her arms, placing them around the burly man's neck as he pulled her across his back. She turned her head to look at Jezero again.

"Be kind," she warned. "She is still fragile."

"I will."

He waited until they crossed the river before heading back through the valley. If the Morlorns knew only he and Raine remained to protect Dusken and the woman, Jezero would have more trouble than they could handle.

He ran across the meadow, staying close to the trees. He followed the trail into the valley, checking each trap and searching for evidence—a footprint, a broken twig, droppings, or soiled plants. So far, the Morlorns stayed close to the river and did not come into the forest beyond the riverbank.

She is fragile.

Veita's words echoed in his head. Fragile for now. Determination burned in Jezamina's eyes; she would survive. She would be fine. Fighting the infection took strength. Seeing her curiosity with Dusken showed her willingness to adapt.

He thought of their day at the water pool when she hesitated to undress in front of him. The vision of her naked body stirred his parts again. The way she smiled, her cobalt blue eyes sparkling like the sun hitting the pool. How the water found its way down her breasts and gleamed across the curve of her hips when she walked toward shore. Her beauty affected him in ways he tried to forget.

Jezero's steps quickened as he approached the ledge. He didn't intend to scare her, but Jezamina almost spilled her herbs when he jumped up to the landing. He thought to apologize but decided against it. She needed to be aware of her surroundings, know when outsiders approached.

She kept her head down, her face solemn, as she sat on what seemed to be her favorite chair near the fire. She drank her herbs in silence. Jezero didn't like how ghostly white she had become.

"You need to eat," he said and motioned for Raine to get her food.

Veita had made them bread, a stockpile of loaves, to keep them fed for a few days. The medicine man broke one of the loaves into thirds. Jezero pulled out two strips of the meat simmering over the fire. He placed them in a bowl and handed it to Jezamina. She took her meal without saying a word.

Jezero didn't waste any time eating his. The morning trek left him hungry. He glanced toward the woman as she picked at the food. At least she ate something. They needed to keep her distracted and her thoughts away from missing Veita.

"Raine, show her the different plants today. Let her know which ones are poisonous," Jezero said after finishing his meal.

Jezamina perked up. "Poisonous plants?"

He cocked an eyebrow, amused at what caught her interest.

***

Jezamina cried after Veita left for her village, traveling with Jezero, Aresen, and Zarac. She watched as the woman who healed her became smaller and smaller, descending the path, until all four disappeared. What was she going to do without her? Who would protect her from the men she lived with? Her leaving was like a bad storm. A big, black cloud sweeping across the forest, showing no mercy to the life left behind.

The fire became her new friend. Occasionally she added another piece of wood to keep the flames going for the meat to cook. Raine offered her ale, but Jezamina preferred a strong mug of herbs. Bless his soul, he tried staying close to her side, hoping to give her comfort, but she only wanted to be alone.

Jezero returned as she started her third mug of herbs. She hated how he scared her, making her jump when he popped up on the ledge. She rolled her eyes when he ordered her to eat. He brought the food over and her stomach growled. Maybe she could eat a little.

While Jezero wolfed his food down, she nibbled. Jezamina loved the bread. The crust had a sweet taste with a warm and doughy inside. Raine made his bread with few ingredients and baked it until hard. The first task on her list was to make decent bread. She figured Jezero wanted her around to cook for them and keep the ledge in order. Hearing him mention the plants caught her interest. And poison? What did they do with the poisonous plants? Or was it more to warn her of their dangers if she wandered about? One thing, a must, is she had to learn how to survive on her own.

When they finished eating, Jezero grabbed his bow and quiver full of arrows. He tightened the strings on his leggings. No show tonight, she thought. His tunic covered his stomach. He stopped before leaving.

"Raine," he called out.

"Aye," the medicine man said. The two seemed to communicate without words.

Jezero turned to her. "Until tonight."

A man of simple words. She figured he left to make his rounds through Dusken. Waiting until he disappeared, she turned to Raine. "What was that all about?"

"What?"

"You and Jezero." She motioned back and forth with her hands to describe their silent communication.

"I am to watch you."

"Babysit me?"

Raine's expression turned blank as if not understanding.

"Hold my hand, take care of me."

"Jezero is in the woods. He will watch the forest. I will watch you and the ledge."

"You mean watch for Morlorns?"

"Morlorns," Raine grunted.

"I thought we are safe here. From them."

"We are safe."

She frowned. "Then why are your hands shaking?"

Raine stopped and held out a bony hand. He brought the other up and stared at it as if seeing the phenomenon for the first time. After a while, he rubbed his hands together.

"We are safe," he said again and motioned for her to follow him.

They walked past her shelter, along the ledge where it narrowed. Here she spotted the other shelters, places where the men slept. All were pretty similar to hers with the leather covering, the furs, and the grass beds. Raine's shelter had little bowls and different plants lined up to dry or ready for use. Aresen's shelter was neat and had different types of footwear tucked underneath the bushes. He loved his footwear. Zarac's bed was twice the size of all the others. She didn't find Jezero's area. A path turned off, behind a boulder. She wondered if he slept, hidden from view. Raine kept moving down the traveled path, so she had to follow with her crutch clicking as it hit the ground.

The rocks jutted high up from the ground as the ledge narrowed. The medicine man helped her around a huge tree, and then they squeezed between two rocks. On the other side, a path led into the forest.

"How far are we going?" Jezamina felt her leg weaken. Her crutch helped, but she wasn't ready for a hike.

"Only a short distance," Raine said. He slowed his pace and made sure she trailed close behind him.

His definition of a short distance wasn't the same as hers. The soft layer of black dirt cushioned the walk, but the obstacles—tree roots, rocks, and bumps—slowed her pace. She had to be careful where she stepped or placed her crutch, not wanting to fall on her face.

Jezamina opened her mouth to tell him to stop when Raine stepped off the path. He pointed to a log and motioned for her to rest. She accepted the invitation. The medicine man pulled out his flask and gave it to her. She drank while he scanned the forest, using his trained eyes. She knew who he was looking for.

"The Morlorns treated you in a horrible way, didn't they?" Veita had explained what happened to him, but she wanted him to tell her. She handed him back the flask.

"Aye," he said and took a drink.

"What did they do to you?"

He tapped his hand on his hip as if releasing nervous energy. His gaze moved about.

If he didn't want to answer, she'd respect his wishes.

Raine kept silent. He handed the flask to her again, and she shook her head. He latched it to his belt and signaled for them to continue. It wasn't until they turned down a second path that he responded to her question. "They left me to rot in the dungeon. I was too weak to work for the master, of no use to them."

"Did they capture you?"

"They attacked the village I called my home. They strung me up like an animal, tied me to a pole, and carted me off to the stone dwelling. They tortured me for days, a mere game to them. After a time, I became sick and too ill to be of use." His voice cracked as he explained but his tone showed no emotion.

"How terrible." Jezamina couldn't fathom the pain and suffering he endured. She shivered, thinking of the continual abuse, of Raine's spirit shredded like a rag. "I'm so sorry."

"Aye," Raine replied. His face gained a dozen more wrinkles and the lines near his lips fell to his chin. He sighed. "The dungeons are cold and damp, leaving yer skin raw and yer bones aching. Once there, it's only a matter of time before ye die."

"But you didn't."

"I am one of few who escaped."

He pulled a thick patch of ferns to the side for her to walk through. The other side was a clearing with three different gardens. Perfectly aligned plants greeted them as their leaves waved in the breeze. Raine said, "The gardens carry poisonous plants, plants for medicines, and plants for our meal and drink."

Jezamina loved the flowers growing in the third garden. The plants burst with deep, vibrant colors. The white ones seemed to reflect the blue from the sky. They reminded her of the flowers Jezero had showed her. *What were they?* Pentias and cyrolus.

Raine walked toward the middle section and showed her the plants they used for medicine. He pointed to each plant and told her its name, how he used it, and how he prepared it. Her lesson continued with him repeating everything he said twice, almost verbatim. The third time, he made her recite what she learned. If Jezamina had known what he planned to do, she would have listened more closely. He helped by mouthing the words. When she started fumbling her sentences—tired of talking—they sat to the side to rest. They ate bread and dried meat. He offered her a different flask. What she thought was water turned out to be ale.

"Holy shit." Jezamina coughed, the fizz going up her nose.

"Ye don't like it?" Raine seemed confused. "I don't know what ye mean by holyshit."

"I thought you were handing me water." She wiped her nose.

"I will get ye water. Holy shit," he said and grabbed an empty pouch.

Jezamina laughed. He had no idea what she meant by her words. She put her hand on his bony shoulder. "Stay. I will drink the ale."

"Why are ye laughing?" He gave her a blank stare.

The medicine man was so serious. She couldn't help but giggle. "Holy shit is an expression." He cocked his face to one side like a child trying to understand. Jezamina thought for a moment about how to explain. She mimicked surprise by putting her hands on her face and opening her eyes wide. She pointed to the tree with the highest top. "Holy shit, that tree is tall."

He nodded. "Holy shit, the ale is strong."

"Yes!" She clapped.

They spent the rest of the afternoon going over the edible plants and roots. Raine showed her which ones he used to make her hot drink. The frail man was like a walking instruction book, never faltering on his words. If she didn't pay attention, he would tsk-tsk. Jezamina began to hate the sound.

As the afternoon wore on, her eyes grew tired and her legs wobbled. Raine's sentences jumbled together. She believed the lesson was over, but he continued to talk.

"The blend is two to one."

"For what?" she asked.

"The herbs for yer drink." He rattled on, sounding like the birds chirping in the trees.

The emotions from Veita's leaving, the longer-than-expected walk in the forest, and then learning the different types of plants exhausted her. Her eyelids grew heavy. Sleep sounded so good right now. Raine expelled a long frustrated sigh.

He made her sit while he gathered the blue roots into a sack. She remembered them from earlier in his lesson. Veita liked putting them in her stew, and they had a nutty flavor. When her head nodded forward, Jezamina jerked upright and forced herself to stay awake. She asked, "How did you learn to grow all these different plants and roots?"

"My mother showed me," he said and lifted the sack over his shoulder, ready to leave.

"What happens if you come across one you're not sure about?" She arched her back to stretch out her muscles.

Raine stood next to her. "I'll test it myself."

Why is he staring at me?

"Oh!" Jezamina realized he waited for her, ready to leave. She rolled to her side and then used her arms to stand. She found her crutch. "Have you ever poisoned yourself?"

"Aye. On occasion."

"And you're not concerned by it?" She knew about food poisoning; the pain in the stomach and vomiting. She must have experienced it at some point in her life to know she never wanted to have it again.

"I'm still here, so no damage." He widened his arms to present himself. "Holy shit."

Jezamina chuckled. The medicine man had a sense of humor. He turned and headed up the slight hill to get to the main path.

She didn't want to walk. Her legs ached. "Can't we rest here for a bit? Close our eyes and take a nap?"

"Darkness falls soon. We need to return."

Jezamina groaned. The flowered plants wilted as the sun faded. She supposed Raine was right. She fell in line behind him, relying on her crutch to keep her steady. "Am I going to learn about the poisonous ones?"

"In due time. Ye learned enough for now."

Not quite. She had tons to learn. All of it was so new and different.

"How did you end up here, living in Dusken?"

Raine glanced back. She had fallen behind. She couldn't tell if he was annoyed at her or trying to think how to respond. He waited until she became his tail again before he turned down the main path.

"After escaping, I ran for my life. I hid in the woods. One day, I left my cave, the place where I stayed. Two of them saw me. When they were close on my heels, Jezero appeared."

Jezamina struggled to keep up. He walked fast, and she wanted to hear his story. His voice was already low with some of his words slurring. A long-term effect of being poisoned, she decided.

He continued without seeing how she panted for breath. "Jezero killed both. Others came. He stayed to protect me. When the woods became quiet again, he carried me to safer land. I had wounds and sores from being locked up. Most would have left me for dead. He did not. For that I am dedicated to him and the cause."

"The cause?"

"Teaching the villages how to protect themselves so they can fight back when attacked."

"Why don't you go after the Morlorns instead? Clear 'em out in one attack?" She had asked Veita the same question.

"They are evil and many. They are bred to kill."

Jezamina nodded. They were consistent with their responses. "How did Aresen and Zarac meet Jezero?"

Raine didn't answer at first. They came upon the ledge, and he motioned for her to stay hidden behind a tree. His right leg dragged and formed a line in the dirt when he walked to the ledge alone to make sure they were safe. The day had worn him out as well.

What a pair they were, she thought. Jezero protected his land alone. No wonder he seemed concerned.

A bird fluttered about in the trees. Another joined in. The yellow, fluffy balls hopped down the length of a branch with their stick legs. She didn't remember birds hopping like that before. When the low ceiling of leaves blew in the wind, the birds flew off. A storm must be moving in. The air turned colder too, not like the night air, but crisp.

Satisfied they were safe, Raine came back to help her up the stairs to the ledge. He left her at the fire and disappeared again. A few embers still glowed in the pit. Jezamina stirred the ash to bring up the heat. Some of the remaining pieces flamed up. She set a pile of kindling in the center of the pit and tended the fire, while Raine did his guard duties. Once the flames rose and emitted heat, she scooted back and used her favorite wooden seat as a rest.

A fur lay on the ground, used mainly for sitting on. She decided to wear it as a blanket. Jezamina clutched the ends tight near her chest and became mesmerized by the fire.

"All is well."

She jumped at the sound of Raine's voice. He crouched down and rubbed his hands near the fire to warm them. He then removed his sack and took his knife out and set both beside him.

A long, deep yawn overtook him. He scratched his face and said, "Zarac came to Dusken a few months after me."

Jezamina forced her eyes open when he spoke again. He remembered her question.

"His village was attacked and burned to the ground while he went on a hunt. Only the smoldering ash remained when he returned. Gone were his mate and children."

"Zarac had a family?" Jezamina's mouth gaped. She assumed all four men were forever single. How terrible for the burly man. She couldn't imagine losing her family so brutally, never being able to see them again. For her, life was a blank. She believed family waited for her return, but Zarac didn't have hope of ever seeing them again.

"He found Jezero, hearing of his cause."

No wonder he kept his distance. It explained his behavior. He suffered, like Raine, because of the Morlorns. If he didn't care about anyone else, he wouldn't need to worry about the same thing happening again. A chill ran along her back and spread to her shoulders. Poor Zarac.

He always grunted at her and used few words. She realized his effort to help her back to her shelter wasn't one to forget or be taken lightly.

"And what of Aresen?"

"A village was under attack as we traveled close by. We saw the smoke curl up to the sky, and we ran to help, knowing trouble brewed. We soon heard the wails and found blood smeared on the trees. As we ran, Aresen appeared and joined us. Jezero threw him a knife, and he stayed to fight. He's been with us since the attack."

"He has no family?"

"He doesn't talk of any." Raine frowned as if trying to recollect past remarks. "Before Dusken, he lived alone, traveling from one village to the next. He would help out, earn his keep, and often move on. He tried finding his own peace, like Jezero, and found it here."

Jezamina turned quiet. It made sense why Zarac and Raine joined forces with Jezero. With the tragedy they had faced, she understood their hatred for the Morlorns. She was still curious about Jezero, whom they referred to as their doyen. She wanted to ask more questions, but Raine stood up.

"What's the matter?" Jezamina straightened and the hairs on her neck prickled. "Morlorns?"

"The storm approaches. We must eat so ye can stay dry in yer shelter."

"Oh," she said. All the talk about attacks made her anxious.

They ate in silence, lost in their own thoughts. The tree limbs moved in circles as if trying to decide which way to go. Jezero was somewhere out in the forest. What if the Morlorns attacked him? Who would help him with two of his men gone? As she finished her last bite of the fleshy patara root, she sensed something wasn't right. Raine kept sniffing the air and looking out toward the forest. Even through hazed eyes, he focused hard on certain areas.

She didn't like how Raine seemed on edge. Was it the storm? Did he think Jezero was in danger? Were they in danger? She asked again, hating how scared she'd become. "Everything all right?"

"I'd say we're in for a holy shit storm." Raine smirked, proud of himself for using the words he learned.

Jezamina shook her head, relieved. She picked up from their meal and then cleaned their bowls and knives. Raine placed a portion of the roots and meat into a large leaf and rolled it up. He placed the meal near the coals. The leaves turned black but didn't catch on fire.

A black cloud soon covered the sky, making the forest ominous.

"Ye find yer shelter and stay there."

"What about Jezero?" She stood up and, with the help of her crutch, made her way to her shelter.

"He'll be fine." Raine's voice barely reached her through the rising wind.

She crawled into her leather cave and stayed to the back of the shelter to keep dry. The rain fell hard. The air turned cold. Jezamina couldn't remember a night being so dark. Not even the rock near her bed was visible. For all she knew, Raine could have left her. She could be alone on the ledge, alone within the vast forest. Or worse yet, a Morlorn could be watching her.

She pulled her fur blanket tighter across her shoulders. She listened as the rain fell in sheets and was thankful she couldn't hear anything else to make her paranoid. If someone were nearby, she wouldn't know.

Rows of lightning began to flash in a wicked display above her, while the ground vibrated from the thunder joining the storm. She tried closing her eyes to sleep, but her nerves were too shot. She was a tiny speck within the dark towering trees. Only a bed, furs, and a leather shelter kept her safe.

When the wind shifted, Jezamina curled into a ball near the corner of her area to keep dry. The top of her shelter snapped with each gust, and it was only a matter of time before the ties broke loose.

At any time, the storm could stop, she thought.

Another gust of wind blew into her area. She gasped for air as the rain sprayed her face. She sat up, held her knees close to her chest, and started rocking. She had no intention of sleeping now.

A new flapping noise distracted her. The corner strap had come loose, and the leather above her shelter flipped upward. More rain came in. Jezamina rocked up to her knees and tried finding the ties, but they kept getting away. The rain made it hard for her to look up as it came straight at her. Little icicles stabbed into her skin. She kept grabbing air.

"Stay down!"

Jezamina sighed with relief when she saw Jezero. He wore his cape so she couldn't see his face, but his voice was clear. She moved back to her corner as he secured the leather in place. He added another leather pelt to the front of the shelter, tying it to the trees on each side. Her little place turned calmer, snugger.

"Better?" he asked, ducking into the cocoon. He took his cape off and left it near the opening.

"Yes," she replied after realizing he couldn't see her nod in the dark.

A flash of lightning allowed her a quick glimpse of him taking off his tunic. He wiped his face and hair with it. She gave him one of her furs to stay warm, knowing his hard, bare chest was right next to her. His close proximity made her nervous, while he seemed unfazed, almost too comfortable.

Another shot of thunder ripped the air, and she jumped.

"'Tis all right," he said.

"I'm beginning to hate storms." She started to shake as the rain and coldness got to her.

"They should end soon. The weather will turn nicer."

An eerie noise began to rise above the wind, like a low, drawn-out howl. The trees creaked as if stretched beyond their limit. Jezamina let out a shaky breath of air. She had to stay calm.

Jezero didn't seem to be concerned. As it grew louder, he peeked out from the shelter. "We're in the eye of the storm."

"What's making that noise?" She wished it would go away.

"The wind is coming up through the valley and hitting the bark on the trees." He sat back again and brushed his hand against her leg. His fingers were like ice.

Without thinking, Jezamina took his hands and rubbed them with her own until the warmth returned to his skin. She gave him another pelt, the larger one that was soft and covered in thick, white fur.

He pressed his lower face against the fur. Her thoughts turned to their bath in the pool. How he didn't think she saw his arousal, even when he hid it under the water. How he helped wash her hair. How his fingers lingered a little longer than needed, catching a caress here and there.

Was it so wrong?

Jezero moved closer, as if knowing her thoughts. One hand slid behind her back. He pulled her tighter to him.

Jezamina sat straighter. Her breath quickened. His face was so close.

Oh my god! Her body wanted to melt into him. She didn't intend to lean closer to him but soon they were touching. She wanted him to kiss her. Her head tilted upward and her lips parted to invite him.

Jezero granted her wish. He kissed her lips ever so softly in welcome. She should've turned away, knowing it was wrong. Her willpower ignored her guilt. His sexuality permeated her senses.

The second kiss started soft, like the first. He then parted her lips, allowing his tongue to explore hers. Jezamina knew she should fight it. This wasn't right. Her head jerked back.

The move caught him off guard. "Do I disappoint you?"

She shook her head. "No, I'm just...I don't..."

Chapter 17

::: Jessie :::

Chicago, IL

Walt let the air out of his lungs, like a tire going flat. What the hell was she thinking, describing a kiss?

He couldn't believe it. He scratched his head and got up from his chair, having to pace.

"What's the matter?" she asked, her eyes widened. "Are you upset?"

Walt couldn't breathe. The room suffocated him. He didn't want to believe she acted so innocent. If she had said Jezero kissed her and she slapped him, then he could justify the situation.

"Why—what do you think?" Walt spluttered. "You cheated on me. You kissed him."

"But I knew it wasn't right."

"Really?" The sarcasm blew out of him.

She was about to say something as if to defend herself but then clamped her lips shut.

The atmosphere turned thick and tense. The silence hurt his ears.

Sam had advised him to hear her out. Let her speak her dream. Little did his friend realize how those words came with emotion. Jessie wanted Jezrezo, or whatever she called him. How was this going to help her recover? He had better things to do than listen to this made-up person. *They* had better things to do.

Jessie's attention turned to the door. He expected one of the staff to enter.

She said, "Your mother's here."

Walt waited, expecting her to enter. He rolled his shoulders to loosen his muscles. Still no mother. Was she imagining things? He walked across the room and stuck his head out. Walt waved in greeting to one of the specialists when the man made eye contact. Down the hall and near the elevator, his mother, chatting with Carol, carried a pink box. Treats from the local baker.

He retreated into the room. The last thing Walt wanted was for his mother to notice the tension between him and Jessie. Helen Arbol was good at reading her son.

"Good morning!" Her voice rang out when she neared. "Cupcakes are served."

The staff responded with upbeat chatter. His mother surprised him at times, but she usually had a motive behind it. He wasn't sure what she had cooking today. Walt took a deep breath to prepare for her visit. He turned to Jessie. "How did you know my mother was here?"

"I smelled her perfume when the elevator door opened. Your father is here as well."

"She's like...down the hall." Now the cupcakes made sense—his father's doing.

Jessie lowered her voice. "I don't want visitors."

"They're not visitors. They're family," he whispered back.

"Your family."

Another blow. Walt clamped his lips together. His jaw clenched.

Jessie rolled her eyes at his anger. "Your mother will never be satisfied with her boy marrying a commoner."

"My mother likes you. She doesn't feel that way." Walt defended her—she worried, that's all, typical of any mother wanting the best for her son.

Walt moved back to the side of Jessie's bed, his normal spot, before his mother walked in the room. His father came in a minute later and carried a coffee in one hand and a garment bag in the other.

"Mother. Dad." Walt let go of his anger, put up a front—just a day at the office. He walked over to kiss his mother's cheek and give her a light hug.

"Jessica." His mother forced a smile from ear to ear after she turned away from him. She put on a show and did it very well. Jessie was at least partially right saying his mother didn't like her. He hoped her feelings changed once they married.

Helen set her purse on the couch and then walked over to give Jessie a peck on the cheek. She only did this when Walt Senior was around.

"What's in the bag?" Walt asked when Walt Senior handed it to him.

"I bought clothes for Jessica to wear at the press conference," Helen said.

"*What?*" Jessie's voice cracked.

Walt winced and avoided eye contact with his fiancée. He felt her glare.

"The press conference," Helen stated again. "The reporters have been patiently waiting to cover what happened on the day of the fire. They want to see how well you are doing."

"Nobody said anything to me about a press conference." Jessie slapped her hands on the bed in frustration. Her cheeks turned rosy.

Walt meant to tell her yesterday, but he kept putting it off. The best way to handle it was to explain why. In his business voice he said, "You are international news, rescuing those kids from the burning house. Your story is heartwarming and people care about you."

"You're a hero," Walt Senior beamed and leaned down to give his future daughter-in-law a hug and a kiss. He held up his hand with the cup of coffee so he wouldn't spill it on her.

At least those two got along, Walt thought. He added to his father's comment. "You're known as the woman with a heart of gold."

Jessie turned her head after Walt Senior stepped back. She took a sip of water from her cup and the lines deepened around her mouth. She was pissed. Really pissed. Walt brushed his sweaty palms against his pants, anticipating another difficult conversation with her.

"Dr. Maguire will lead the press conference," Helen explained. "He's prepared to handle the media and their questions. We scheduled the event the day before your release."

Jessie's eyes popped open. "Release? They're letting me out of here?"

"A day or two after the press conference," Walt piped in.

Walt Senior took a sip of his coffee. He then said, "We've added a few more comforts to Walt's room for you—a chaise lounge, pillows, flowers."

Helen waved her hand in the air. "I don't know why our Walt insists on your staying in his room. We prepared another room for you, if needed, where you'd have privacy. You'll need rest."

"Wait..." Jessie raised her open hand as if registering what they said.

Walt saw the bull ready to charge. He intercepted with a red cape. "We know you're anxious to return to California, but my parents would like us to stay with them, closer to the doctors, if by chance some complications occur."

"But I'm recovering just fine."

"Heavens!" Helen acted like she wouldn't hear any more of the nonsense. "You can't travel to California, it's too early. We negotiated with Dr. Maguire."

She stood by Walt Senior as if two of them were an army. Walt wished his mother would let it go, but she wasn't finished. Her mouth opened. *Damn.*

"We hired a nurse to monitor your condition and give our son relief. Walt will be able to work while you're in our care."

Jessie closed her eyes as if counting to ten to keep her cool. She took a moment to gain composure. Thank God she didn't cause a scene. Arbols didn't throw or like fits of rage.

Between strained lips, Jessie asked, "Why do I need to be at the press conference?"

"The parents and those precious children you saved are waiting to see you," Walt Senior said. "Since the public has followed your story, we decided the press conference is the best option."

"Can't they come to my room, only allow a few of them in here?"

"Sweet child." Helen showed signs of impatience. She glanced over to Walt with pursed lips as if to say he was marrying a complete idiot. "The public wants to be there as well."

"Pops thought it'd be best," Walt said. He had a chance of reasoning with her by bringing his father into the mix. She respected him. "You requested no visitors. We can eliminate a lot of stress and continual noise this way."

"Noise?" she asked him.

"Constant phone calls, knocks at the door. Press out on the street."

Jessie didn't respond. A good sign, he hoped.

The rotating squeak from the food cart stopped at her door. Lunch was served.

"Helen, dear," Senior said. "Time for us to leave and let Jessie enjoy her meal in peace."

Helen turned to Jessie. "Please try on the pantsuit. I can request another outfit if needed."

Yes, they were leaving. Walt silently thanked God. He grabbed his mother's purse and handed it to her. "I'll walk you to the lobby."

***

Jessie breathed a sigh of relief when they left, needing the silence and the time alone. She wasn't angry about the press conference. She didn't want to do it but understood the reason for it. What Walt said made sense. The parents wanted to meet her. The nurses held them off due to her wishes. Jessie stared at her food—ham, scalloped potatoes, peas, and a brownie. She longed for a decent meal and a mug of Veita's herbs.

She set her fork on the rolling table, not hungry. Dealing with the outside world turned her stomach. No matter, the press conference would go on. The public and Walt's parents would get what they wanted even though the Arbols' motive wasn't for "the people." They craved the publicity—good PR.

A press conference.

What would she say? She didn't mind seeing the children. Jessie wanted to see how they were doing. But publicity wasn't her thing. The thought of all those reporters asking questions and taking pictures of her...she shuddered.

"I'm sorry." Walt raced to the door. "I got back as soon as I could. I think the elevator stopped at every floor. What...you haven't touched your tray."

"Why didn't you tell me about this press conference?" She was hurt more than anything because he hid it from her. He always talked to her. He kept her updated, even if it meant an argument.

"Pops mentioned the idea some time ago. I didn't know he was seriously looking into scheduling one."

"You defended them."

"I agree with them. The press conference makes sense."

"For whom?"

"All of us. I didn't like the idea at first. I wanted to keep you to myself." He paused as if thinking how he still wanted her alone. He took her hand and held it. "But the idea started to make sense. You won't have to say much as long as..." he looked at the door, the ceiling, at her hands, "you stick to the fire and kids. Keep your responses to a minimum." His voice trailed off.

Jessie pulled her hand away. "Ahh, I see. Make sure I only tell them the sane parts."

"They'll eat you alive if you mention anything about Dusken."

"I get it," Jessie snapped. The room turned ten degrees colder. She sighed heavily as if frustrated. "I'm sorry. I have no plans for telling the press where I've been. I'm upset because I'm not having a say in anything."

Walt's shoulders fell. He backed away and sat in his chair.

"You're not eating." He pointed to her food.

"Would you?" She shoved the tray away.

He snorted. "I guess not. Listen, if you don't want to do this press conference, I'll take care of it."

"I'll do the press conference." She never said she wouldn't do it. "Like I said, I'm not happy getting told by your parents."

"My apologies. I'm at fault." He raised his hand in full agreement.

She leaned closer to him, wanting to make her point. "And, just so you know, I will not stay at your parents' estate."

He nodded and rubbed his face as if tired of arguing. Walt changed the subject. "Did you learn more about the plants? The poisonous ones?"

Just like that, she thought. He had his act together, like the businessman he was. On to the next thing as if it were an everyday occurrence at the office.

"What's the matter?"

Jessie shook her head. Why bother telling him about Dusken? What if it was only a dream as he kept repeating? What if she was making a fool of herself? She remembered the nightmares haunting her as a child. The many nights she'd wake up in a sweat after dreaming about the accident that killed her parents. Had her childhood ordeal caused her reaction now?

"I would like you to continue. Please." A sad smile played on his lips. "I admit hearing some pieces upsets me. I'll get over it."

Jessie stared at him. He seemed sincere. For now.

Chapter 18

::: Jezamina :::

Dusken

"Off to the gardens?" Jezamina asked as she followed Raine down the ledge and to his spot in the woods.

"Aye, to the plants."

She had spent the last five days learning about plants, including roots. They even walked the forest so she could find them in their natural state. The garden was too easy.

Raine stopped and turned toward her, waiting for her to catch up. Jezamina's strength continued to build each day. She no longer used the crutch, but her leg was still weak. The scar on her thigh was shiny and tender as new skin grew over the wound. The medicine man showed her the plant to use and how to prepare the leaves to help her skin heal faster. Twice a day, she extracted the juice from the meaty leaves and then boiled the liquid down until it thickened. She spread the clear potion on her thigh and let the sun dry it out. So far she liked the results.

Instead of stopping at the midsection of his garden, Raine continued on. He smiled, showing his small, yellow teeth. "Are ye ready to learn about the poisons?"

"Really?" Jezamina's day brightened. Whenever they came near the section of his garden, he would turn away as if purposely ignoring them.

"Only if ye believe ye can use them with wisdom. Few know my secrets."

"And you're going to show me, tell me your secrets?"

"Aye."

Jezamina placed her hand on her heart. She'd gained his trust. "I'm honored. Of course I'll use them with respect." Her eyes widened. "Do the others—Jezero, Aresen, and Zarac—know your secrets?"

He shook his head. "They only know the common ones."

"I'm going to learn about the others? The uncommon ones?"

"Ye have a keen view for plants." He tapped his head near the temple.

"And because you like me." She smiled teasingly.

Raine fumbled for words. He gave up. The medicine man was so cute, the way his eyes went upward and his head twitched. Today, his hair was tied in a ponytail so she could see his face better. At one point in his life, she knew he had to have been handsome. Cruelty had left him older than his true age.

"I know ye like me," she said and used his accent.

"Come along." He started walking again.

"Jezero will have to sleep with one eye open now."

He giggled. Jezamina smiled at her success. She stopped at the flowery patch, but Raine continued on. She followed him but glanced back at the section they missed. She wanted to know about the purple tear-dropped flowers and the pink bell-shaped ones. "What about..."

"They're for show."

"They're not poisonous?"

"Not that I know of." He pointed to a garden at the side of a hill. "Here are the deadly ones."

"You devil." She was surprised yet not surprised. He was clever and she got it. If she went to use the ones she thought were poisonous, she couldn't be trusted.

The soft dirt under her feet turned hard. Rocks jutted out from place to place on the path. She watched where she stepped and took longer to get to the garden. A few times she tripped, not raising her foot high enough when the path narrowed and the ferns covered the hidden rocks.

"These here are the common poisons." He pointed to a small garden off the trail and between the trees, but he didn't stop. The path turned into a smaller valley. Like his other gardens, the plants were lined in neat rows with the taller ones in the middle. Most had some type of flower growing from their stems, but not as showy as those in the first garden.

Raine stopped before they entered his sacred place.

"This is amazing," she said in awe.

"Holy shit," Raine said with a smile.

Jezamina laughed. "Yes, holy shit."

"Follow me. Do not touch any of the plants."

He led her into the middle row where a group of dark blue flowers with dainty petals and tall furry stems bloomed high above the others. She noted the sweet, powdery scent but wasn't sure whether it came from the flower or the plant.

"These are the most dangerous poisons. One touch can put enough poison in yer system to make ye sick for many nights."

Jezamina froze. One touch?

She turned her head to the right and to the left. The leaves were less than a foot away from her shoulder. She swallowed hard. The muscles in her back tightened like the string on Jezero's bow.

"Here, in this area," he said while waving his arm, "not one mistake can be made."

He never touched one, even with his hand flying around. How could he be so relaxed?

Jezamina was afraid to move. Her heart pounded. Her legs shook. What if she fell? Lost her balance? She wore leggings, ones that Zarac made. Would the poison soak through the leather?

Raine said something to her. He got mad when she didn't pay attention.

Jezamina forced herself to focus on her teacher. Yes. Concentrate on Raine. Not the plants.

"When ye touch the flowers like I do, prepare them, or administer them, ye take a chance it may kill ye," he continued talking, unaware of her panic. "Never touch them with bare hands."

"Which ones? All of them?" Her voice squeaked.

"No, the drayens, the most dangerous. Reason for them being in the center of the patch. Less chance of touching them in error."

"So why am I standing here?"

Raine ignored her question. He walked to the other side, out of the danger zone, and stopped at a patch of yellow, speckled flowers. He wet his fingertips and then snipped one of the sprays from the plant. "This is a graelion. Use this for sleep. I make this for Zarac. I will show ye this one first."

Jezamina nodded, still afraid to move.

Raine headed through the trees to a clearing where a makeshift table held mortars and pestles. A few knives were stuck into a nearby tree, and he pulled one out.

"I can't show ye if ye intend to stay there," he scolded her.

Her feet wouldn't move.

"Hurry now."

Beads of sweat ran down her forehead. Her foot slid forward. She kept her shoulders squeezed in, closer to her body, while glancing right to left, making sure she stayed at a safe distance from the plants as she shuffled her way out.

Raine's eyebrows wrinkled together in a frown. He tapped his foot as he waited near the table.

Jezamina didn't care. She sank to the ground when she cleared the row. One move could have killed her. In one lesson she learned to respect all plants within the forest. Her hand shook when she opened her flask and took a long drink of water. Raine waited. His eyes burned into her. Damn him. No recovery time. Her legs still shook, but she got up, brushed off her hands, and met him at the table.

"Use a flat, dull blade to shred the stem. Like this. See how the center pulls out?" He started his lesson without batting an eye at her meltdown.

She nodded. The medicine man squeezed the center and a milky substance oozed out in globs. He put the serum into a small stone mortar.

"We'll pull off the smaller buds as well."

"I can use my bare hands?"

Raine nodded. "This one isn't as poisonous. But ye can only take the smaller buds."

"What happens if the larger ones are pulled?"

"Ye get the runs and yer stomach feels like it's been burned."

Now she understood why he waited to show her the poisonous ones last. Jezamina took her turn and repeated Raine's instructions.

"The medicine used on my leg, is it poisonous?" In his lessons, Raine never mentioned the plant.

"Queeno? The plant is deadly if eaten. Veita warned me."

"Can I see it?" She remembered the terrible odor permeating from her leg until the salve dried.

"I used the last."

"Shouldn't we replenish your supply?" Her leg hurt at night, and she noticed the wound had turned puffy and red again. She didn't want the infection to return. Veita's previous words haunted her. Jezamina did not want to lose her leg.

"Aye, but the plant is near the edge of Dusken."

Jezamina turned to the medicine man. "I'd be willing to go. I'd like to learn more about the plant."

Raine tapped his finger against his lips.

"What's the matter?"

"The river is a dangerous place."

Oh, yes, the Morlorns. They lurked near the edge of Jezero's land. But what if she needed the medicine tonight? The thought of being bedridden with a fever again made her stomach flutter. "We can get the plant and leave. You know where to find the plant, right?"

"Yer strength may not be fit enough."

"We can rest," she said and then quickly added, "away from the edge. If I can't make it, I'll stop and wait for you."

Raine pondered the idea. He looked to the woods. Was it Jezero whom he worried about?

"I feel good. Honest," she said. At least she would if they had the medicine on hand.

Raine muttered to himself, making an unrecognizable noise.

She pushed again. "If the Morlorns attacked, wouldn't you want the medicine handy?"

He toyed with the thought. "It's not too far from here."

"Even better wouldn't you agree?" She almost had him convinced. Jezamina gave him time to justify the reason for going. Oh, she was bad. "You need the plant. I want to go. We'll be careful."

His brain ticked away. "Very well."

"Yes!" They were going to find the plant.

Raine bent and lowered his head closer to hers. "Ye must tell me if yer tired." He raised a finger. "Even a hint."

"I promise I will." She crossed her heart.

He did the same, a pact made.

The walk was farther than she expected, but Jezamina would not complain. They climbed down the side of a steep hill, and she grabbed hold of tree branches and bushes to keep her balance. The river ran below them and sparkled as the sun reflected off the water. The cool water would be heaven now. She longed to soak her legs to relieve the ache.

Raine motioned for her to crouch down when they came to an open area. He put his finger to his lips and she nodded. The remaining hike down the hill was in silence and proved to be difficult for her strength. Every muscle running down her backside cramped from crouching so low.

Don't think about the pain. Keep going.

When the land turned flat, he led her into the woods, away from the path. They returned to walking normally, much to her relief. Jezamina shook out her legs one at a time.

"We're near the place," Raine whispered and held out his hand for her to stop.

Jezamina sat on a large rock, relieved to get the weight off her feet. She took a drink from her flask.

"See the stumps over there?" He pointed to a grove of fallen trees near the bank of the river. Dark green moss covered the bark. "Ye can see the queeno growing in that one over there."

She squinted. A few leaves stuck out from one of the stumps...or was it beyond the stump? No matter. She had a clear view of the land on the other side of the river. The edge of Dusken. Jezamina lost interest in the queeno. There was something different about the other land. The woods were still the same with all the trees and plants but something...

She scanned Dusken and followed through to the other side, comparing the two. The colors. Beyond the river, the land didn't have the rich browns or the deep greens. "Why is there such a difference between the two sides?"

"What?" Raine asked as if she had seen a Morlorn.

"The forest seems brighter over here."

"Oh, the land." He seemed relieved. "The soil here, in Dusken, is richer in minerals than the other side. One of the reasons why Jezero claimed it."

If she'd crossed the river and found the land, she too would have fallen in love. The forest seemed like Eden compared to the other side. Dusken held warmth and peace while the other seemed cold and lifeless with the gray bark and the faded greens.

Raine tapped her shoulder and motioned for her to follow. Again, they crouched low as they sprinted to the stumps. The open area left them vulnerable. Mostly plants and ferns covered the ground, unlike the tall trees residing in the forest. The noise from the river, the water rushing around and crashing against the rocks, deafened all other sounds. Not even the birds had a voice against the roar as they perched high in the trees.

"Here we are," the medicine man sang and rose to a kneeling position to examine the plant. He ran a finger along one side of a leaf. "The curl is what distinguishes queeno from the buire, which is similar but has no purpose."

Jezamina nodded, seeing the difference. She remembered the buire plant from her first lesson. "The veins are different too. The queenos are spidery and white."

Raine leaned forward to see for himself. He smiled and seemed pleased with her observance. "Good eye."

"Thank you." She relished the proud moment. His lessons paid off. Detail was key.

He removed the sack from his shoulder and found his digging tool. He let Jezamina pull up the plant while he used the tool to loosen the dirt. She lifted the full plant from the stump, careful to keep the roots intact.

Raine soaked a piece of cloth with water from his flask and then wrapped it around the roots. "We'll plant most of this in the patch. See if it will live with the others. The rest I'll use for medicine."

He tucked the digging tool and plant into his sack. He was about to put the strap over his head again when he froze. The wrinkles on his forehead deepened. His expression hardened. The medicine man's gray eyes pierced the woods across the river.

Jezamina's skin prickled. She ducked her head down, careful to stay hidden.

"We must leave," he whispered.

She nodded. His seriousness made her edgy.

"This way." He pointed toward a path leading north. "Ye must follow me close. No stopping until I say."

The blood drained from her face. In other words, he needed her to push her limits. They were in danger. Jezamina nodded in understanding. Even if she were in pain, she had to keep moving.

Raine ran across the riverbank, and she followed to the safety of the woods. His bow was ready with an arrow. Jezamina ran, keeping her focus on the medicine man. She prayed not to trip. The pace quickened as they darted between the bushes, the trees. They hurdled over a large, fallen branch. And then they started up the hill. A big, fucking hill.

Jezamina's heart pounded. Her lungs burned in protest. She pushed her limit. They were halfway up when he finally slowed down. Raine crouched and hid behind a thick bush covered with berries. She fell to the ground beside him and huddled like a turtle in its shell.

Breathe. She let out small shallow breaths. In. Out. In. Out. She forgot about Raine and the danger. Sweat poured from her face. She no longer felt her legs. Jezamina wanted to pass out but forced herself up. Raine disappeared. A moment of panic rushed her until she found him behind a different plant. She crawled over to join him.

"Don't you dare leave me!" she scolded him in a terse whisper.

"I'm right here." Raine frowned.

No matter. Jezamina had to reprimand him for scaring her—in a big way. Feeling better, she parted the branches, like he had, for a better view.

The medicine man pointed to a huge tree on the other side of the river. The large branches expanded over the water and the leaves almost touched the surface where the rapids began.

A slight movement to the side of the trunk caught her attention. A Morlorn!

Jezamina gasped. The Morlorn untied the waist of his leggings and relieved himself. She stifled a laugh. She spotted three more men in their odd, furred helmets. Flat metal plates shielded their backs but not their chests.

Raine pointed again. Two more were down the river. They seemed relaxed; their arrows were tucked into their belts. Even relaxed, the men looked mean. She studied their faces and how their jaws seemed wider than normal. They had prominent noses, almost pointed.

"The helmets and metal shields warn us," Raine whispered. "They are warriors, ready for battle, not the watchers."

"Will they attack us?"

Raine grunted. She assumed yes. He flicked his hand, signaling their time to move on.

They moved through the bushes until they came across a wider path. She recognized the odd-shaped tree with vines growing around it from when they journeyed to the river. She started up the pass, but Raine hissed between his teeth. He took a different route, one she hadn't noticed before.

Jezamina struggled to match his pace. He scurried through the forest like a wild critter. The medicine man wasn't strong or fit, but his thin legs moved. And he could hide. Many times she thought he had left her, only to find him nearby, blending in with the forest.

Raine climbed the hill, getting ahead of her. She fumbled, and her foot hit a rock. She couldn't yell at him to wait, but he stopped with a horrified stare when the rock bounced down the hillside. He peered down, in fear of the Morlorns hearing them.

Jezamina's leg gave out and she fell to the ground. She rolled off to the side to hide behind a tree. Raine scurried down to help.

"Leave me here." Jezamina said as she held her thigh. The pain seared through her leg.

"We're almost to the top." Raine's eyes showed his panic.

"You go. I'll hide."

He shook his head and pulled on her arm. "We can rest once we get to safer ground."

"Go!" she ordered.

"I cannot leave without ye." The way he said it, slow and forceful, caught her off guard.

Jezamina wiped the sweat from her face. Of course. Jezero trusted him just as he trusted her to follow through with their pact. Her head fell. This was her fault. Their lives were at risk because she pushed to find the queeno.

With a nod, she waited until Raine could survey their situation. She took advantage of the time and breathed in deep, slow breaths. She could do this.

"One more run up the hill," he instructed. "Rest at the top."

Jezamina got into position.

"Anytime," Raine coaxed her.

One. Two. Three. She kept her focus on the top of the hill. Jezamina used her hands to help climb when the terrain became steep, where the ferns grew thicker, and the trees denser. He stayed behind her, catching the rocks she unearthed. At the top, the path split in two different directions. Raine took the lead again, and she liked having him in front so she didn't need to think, only follow.

When she tripped for the third time, Jezamina completed a somersault and rolled back up to her feet. She was too tired to be impressed or remember what she did. When they covered enough distance to be safe, Raine helped her stop, keeping her steady so she didn't hurt herself when she collapsed.

Jezamina stayed in a curled position until her breathing became regular. She smelled the dirt underneath her, the bitter-smelling plant near her face, one of the fern leaves towering above her. Raine leaned against a rock with flask in hand. As promised, he allowed her to rest. He offered her water when she moved her head. She rose to her elbow. Her hand shook when she took the flask from him. She savored each swallow, careful not to drink too much.

"They know." Raine tsk-tsked his displeasure.

"The Morlorns?" She wiped her mouth with the back of her hand, then handed his flask back to him, realizing she could use her own.

"Aye." His face turned dark as if shadowed by a storm. "Are ye good?"

Jezamina rubbed her legs. No, she hurt like hell. She said to him, "I'm good."

She ignored the burn in her muscles, the ache in her back when she stood. She concentrated on moving forward, one step at a time, as she followed Raine. Dusken was no longer an adventure. She longed to be back on the ledge. Raine checked on her but never asked if she needed another rest.

A bird sang out. Raine stopped. "Aresen is back."

He cupped his hands and made a similar call.

"Huh?" Jezamina swayed, feeling lightheaded now that they'd stopped. She blinked. They stood near his gardens. She was about to ask Raine if she could stay there and rest, but he started walking again.

"Oh, this is not good, not good," he mumbled.

Chapter 19

::: Jezamina :::

Dusken

Jezero paced as night began to fall across the forest. Aresen sat near the fire with a large blade in one hand and a thick slab of meat in the other.

"They're using their heads this time," Aresen said. He chewed on a tough piece of meat while trying to talk. He gave up and spit out the remains to burn in the fire.

Jezero knew the Morlorns would soon contrive a way to penetrate his land. They wandered near the river on many occasions to test their grounds. A few ventured up the banks but the traps stopped them.

For the hundredth time he searched the forest for Raine and Jezamina. He tracked them to Raine's place with the plants, but then lost their trail. He saw no signs of struggle so they must have gone hunting for different medicines or food. Still, no plants seemed unsettled and no footprints strayed from the path.

"Where's the beauty?" Aresen took a swig of ale then ate the last chunk of meat in his hand.

"With Raine." Jezero grabbed a branch that had fallen from a tree. He snapped it in half with his knee and then tossed both pieces into the fire.

Aresen finished eating and wiped his hands on his leggings. He raised his head and made the chirping sound, a request for a response.

Jezero went to kneel near the edge of the ledge. He lowered his head and listened. Nothing. No call back.

"Should we go search?" Aresen frowned as he stood.

"We'll wait until you've finished eating." Jezero's gut reaction told him the two had lost track of time. Yet, something still nagged at him. He tightened his grip on his bow.

Aresen half-chewed, half-swallowed his bread. He drank his ale to wash it down. "One more time?"

He didn't wait for his doyen's response and repeated his call.

Raine called back, a cry for help.

"The gardens." Jezero pinpointed their location and jumped from the ledge. Aresen followed close behind.

The medicine man struggled to help Jezamina walk the path, a feat not easy to do with his frailness. She swayed, her eyes half closed.

"I can make it," she said to Raine as they approached. "I can do this."

Jezero caught Jezamina in his arms before she collapsed. With little effort, he picked her up and carried her to the ledge. Aresen offered the medicine man a ride on his back, but he refused.

"What happened?" Jezero asked as he maneuvered his way around the steps.

"We went on a hunt for queeno near the river." The medicine man hobbled after him.

"Did the Morlorns see you?"

"Aye."

"Did they see Jezamina?"

Raine's head lowered. His mouth quivered. "Aye."

Jezero set her down next to the fire so her back leaned against a log. Aresen handed her his mug of ale. She coughed out her first swallow.

"Were you attacked?" He spoke to Raine but looked at Jezamina for any signs of a fight.

"No. They were beyond the river."

"Did they leave?"

"Not sure." He shrugged. "Two hung around. Three others disappeared."

Jezero rubbed his beard. More than likely they'd be reporting back to Vyrone.

"Where's Zarac?" Raine asked after taking a drink from his flask. He held his shoulder; the one Jezamina had been leaning on.

"He stayed." Aresen moved in place to guard the ledge. "Veita's village was attacked the night before we arrived. Only a few remain. They have no doyen."

Jezamina sat up. Her eyes grew with concern. "Is Veita okay?"

"She is in safe hands." Jezero assured her. He set down his bow and found a cup. He dipped it into the pail of drinking water and then handed it to her. The ale would do her good, but she needed water.

"Was there a message?" Raine asked.

Aresen was about to tell him when Jezero interrupted with a hard cough. Jezamina didn't need to hear.

Raine cursed under his breath. He seemed upset with himself, once again. He should be. Jezero knew it was only a matter of time before the Morlorns saw her. He never expected Raine would present her for view. He understood the need to collect more queeno, but the price may have been too steep.

He handed Jezamina a bowl filled with meat and roots. She picked at her food but finished the ale. Jezero ate as well. He went to sit next to her. "Not hungry?"

"Not really."

"You need to eat. Keep your strength."

"You do too."

Jezero stabbed a root with his knife, showed it to her, and then popped it in his mouth. She did the same.

"What happens now?" she asked.

He wasn't sure what she meant or how much to give away. She seemed to have recovered from her adventure in the woods. He liked that. He said, "We continue on."

"And how about Veita? Now that her village is...gone."

"Veita is safe. Zarac will make sure of it."

"First watch," Raine said with bow and arrows in hand.

Jezero nodded. Normally, he liked to take the longer watch, but the change would help relieve Raine's guilt. Aresen disappeared as well. He left to sleep in his shelter.

Jezamina reached over and grabbed his mug. She took a drink after eating half the food in her bowl. Her blue eyes questioned him for more detail, but he offered her none.

"When you say continue on," she said and handed him back his mug, "do you mean you're traveling to the village?"

He couldn't lie. "It's my duty to help them. I must go."

Her head went down as if disappointed. Jezero braced himself. This was his life—what he had to do. She could not change his mind.

Jezamina struggled to get up from her spot. He held out his hand to help her up. She stared at it for a moment, as if struggling to contain her emotions. He wasn't sure if she was upset at him or just in general. Finally her head came up, showing a brave front, when she allowed him to help her stand.

Jezero let her be when she excused herself and headed for her shelter. He moved to the other side of the ledge, opposite Aresen. The forest was near black. Out there, the Morlorns waited. As Aresen noted earlier, they were getting smarter. They must have known Veita came to Dusken to help him with the woman. Clever of them to attack her village. Now he would be obligated to help in return.

***

Jezamina sat and tended the fire the next morning. The men stayed busy, preparing the ledge for attack. Arrows were stacked near the rocks along the edge. Small vials of poisonous liquid, filled and handled with care by Raine, were placed in different areas around their home. She wanted to ask questions, learn why everything seemed to be strategically placed in certain areas. Was this something routine?

She stayed to herself. They didn't need her distracting them from their duties. She already caused trouble for Raine. Jezero took him aside as daylight began. He carried a scowl on his face as they talked, while the medicine man's drooped in guilt. Should she tell Jezero she insisted on going after the queeno? Show him her leg?

Jezamina wondered if her lessons would stop. She'd adapted to Raine's mumbling and his quirks, tolerating him like a brother. When Veita left, he took her place. God knows she needed someone. Jezero was scarce, always on guard or practicing his skills.

"Why the solemn face?"

She snapped out of her reverie. Jezero stood between her and the fire. "No reason."

He squatted down on one knee and rested his arm on his thigh. "I bet your mind is racing in that pretty head of yours."

"Not all thoughts need to be shared."

He chuckled. Jezero was about to turn away when she stopped him.

"Please don't blame Raine. I wanted to hunt for the queeno. He was hesitant." She pulled her skirt up to expose her thigh. "We ran out, and I didn't want my leg to get infected again. See? It's not quite healed."

"I see," Jezero said as he stared at her leg. "However, Raine could have easily fetched the plant himself."

"I didn't want to be left alone." She shifted her legs and leaned forward. "Please."

She willed him to forgive Raine. Her blue eyes stared with such intensity at him.

After a time, Jezero let out a sigh. Slowly, his lips turned into a defeated smile. He nodded. "What's done is done."

His expression filled her with relief. Even though she had no place among them, Jezero's feelings affected her. She loved when he returned to the ledge after his rounds, and she'd catch him searching for her. His deep brown eyes would latch onto her, making sure she was good before moving on to other things.

Jezamina didn't want him to leave to go to Veita's village. She'd miss watching him practice his skill with the bow, and knowing he was there to protect her. Not that it mattered. She had no say.

She had no place among them. And this made her mad.

Aresen called for Jezero.

Before he left, a smirk crossed his face. "Holy shit."

It was her turn to chuckle. Raine must have tried his new words on Jezero.

***

Jezero covered his mouth and called out to his men before returning to the ledge. With the threat of an attack, he didn't need one of his men thinking he was a Morlorn.

He had relieved Raine and decided to stay out beyond the morning. He checked the traps in place and then set more near the river. Earlier, the medicine man had spotted a dozen Morlorns along the banks. Today, Jezero counted twenty.

Aresen responded to his call. All was safe.

Jezero reached the ledge and entered from the narrow side. Jezamina sat near the fire, talking to Raine. She handed the medicine man a bowl of steaming hot food.

He paused to watch her. She was the prize, worth any danger. The way she sat with her back straight, how her hair flowed across her breasts, her lips perfect to kiss, and her eyes...so blue...she had him mesmerized. This wasn't how it was supposed to be. Why did the calling tempt him so?

"Yer staring," Aresen came up from behind and joined him.

"Aye," Jezero said. "And realizing how high the stakes are if she's captured."

"The woman with fire in her ears." Aresen stated. He rubbed a melica stick between his teeth to clean them. "The Morlorns will fight for her."

"More of them are appearing near the river. Last night, the fires burned as they drank their ale and celebrated their victory." Jezero had listened to their laughter and the clank of their mugs as they boasted about the attack on the village. He toyed with the idea of surprising them, taking them on before they found the courage to step on his land but then changed his mind. The less noise made the better. Let them think their plan would work. They were high on one victory and would savor the taste for a few days if they didn't feel threatened.

"Anything I should do?"

"Check the traps on the valley side," Jezero said. Any Morlorn who set foot in Dusken would find it their final resting place. Their sanctuary would not be soiled by such a filthy presence. "The river side is ready."

"Easy to do." With orders received, Aresen headed off into the forest.

Jezero went to check on Raine. "Are we ready?"

"All set." Raine showed him the gear next to the rock. He still played with his food. The meat was burnt and the roots shriveled.

"Should I find something else to eat?" Jezero noted the blackened stew.

The medicine man glanced toward Jezamina. "She is not a cook."

He threw the rest into the brush. Jezero chuckled and took his advice to pass on the meal. He picked up his bow and said, "Extinguish the fire before darkness."

Jezamina showed no emotion when he walked toward her. She seemed to be mad at him, and he chose to ignore it. He tipped his head. "I shall return."

"I will be here," she said with an edge to her voice.

Jezero jumped from the ledge and ran into the woods, to the top of the cliff. He needed some time for himself—his last night in Dusken. He climbed up the spindled tree that seemed like an older, hunched man compared to the taller surrounding ones.

From his perch, he settled in to survey the valley. Two pillars of smoke rose above the trees. One was in the distance while the other was near the river. Both were too close to Dusken, making his sanctuary no longer safe with a woman to protect. His other choice, taking her with him, held the same danger. He needed time to think, to plan his next move.

Jezero listened to the forest while he said his farewell to Dusken. The faint lull of the water breaking over the falls, the birds nestling in for the night, and the slight rustle of leaves gave him peace. He never liked leaving his sanctuary, but duty called.

When the moon, a shimmering gold, rose against the black sky, he climbed down from the tree and headed back to the ledge. He went to Jezamina's shelter and was surprised to find her still awake. She sat with the fur wrapped around her head, only her blue eyes peeking out.

"You are awake."

"I am."

She backed into the shelter again so he couldn't see her face. "Permission to enter?"

She remained silent.

Jezero found a spot near her shelter to spend the night. He sat between the gnarled roots weaving above the ground.

"What are you doing?" she asked.

"Getting ready to sleep." He leaned back to rest against the tree.

"Why can't you sleep in your shelter?"

"One, you are in my shelter. Two, I am here for your safety."

"One, your shelter? Two, why? Am I in danger?"

"One, I gave up my bed the night you arrived. Two, the Morlorns are near the river."

When the silence spilled over, Jezero folded his arms across his chest and closed his eyes. He succumbed to listening to the lumazo's soft lullaby throughout the forest. The flapping of their wings was pleasant to the ears. Their silence would warn if someone approached.

"Permission granted," she called out.

Jezero sat up like an alarm had gone off. He didn't give her a chance to change her mind. He was in the shelter without missing a breath.

She sat near the middle of the bed but scooted over to give him room. She seemed hesitant, not knowing what to do. Jezero helped. He pulled her toward him so her head rested against the crook of his arm.

"Get some sleep," he told her. "Tomorrow will be a long day."

She sighed. "You're leaving tomorrow. Aren't you?"

"We leave in the morn."

Her head rose from his arm.

"I'm going with you?"

Chapter 20

::: Jessie :::

Chicago, IL

"Walt!" Helen Arbol popped her head through the door.

Jessie stopped telling her story.

"What?" Walt snapped upright. He wanted to find out if Jessie went to the village or stayed behind. Did the Morlorns attack? *Why in the hell is my mother here?*

"Walter." She gave him the look, the one saying to mind his manners.

He sighed, realizing the dream would have to wait. Jessie lay back in her bed. She wouldn't continue with his mother in the room. They had stopped the night before because the staff wouldn't leave them alone. She had started the story again this morning.

Walt wanted to decipher her dream or, as she put it, "Life in Dusken." How did learning about the plants correlate with the present? The Morlorns could be his side of the family, or the Arbol business. The man named Jezero could represent her freedom. If he thought of the man as a symbol instead of a love interest, he could handle what she said. Changing his perception made the kiss easier to accept. The kiss meant freedom.

"Did I come at a bad time?" his mother asked.

She always came at a bad time. His mood darkened. For once, he wanted to hear more about Jessie's dream. Her imagination was so vivid, he found himself thinking he was there with her. The details and emotions of being near the poisonous plants, fearing she would fall behind or get captured by the Morlorns kept him in suspense.

"Why am I finding it hard to get your attention?" Mrs. Arbol tapped her foot with irritation. She glanced toward Jessie as if blaming her.

Walt didn't want his mother throwing blame on his fiancée. He frowned, realizing she stayed near the door. The argument to find out why she didn't come in wasn't worth the effort.

Once outside the room, she took his arm and led him down the hall. "Did she try on her outfit?"

Walt had to think. The outfit hung on the closet hook. "I'm not sure. Why don't you ask her."

"We don't have time for procrastination. The press conference is tomorrow afternoon."

"Tomorrow?" This was the first he heard the news. He thought Carol was going to warn him.

"Will she be ready?"

They walked into the waiting room. His mother found the coffee machine. She took a Styrofoam cup from the stack and then poured coffee into it while balancing her Coach purse on her forearm.

His mother actually poured herself a cup of hospital coffee. A first. Normally she asked for tea, the safer route. He decided to grab a cup for himself. He wasn't finicky, not after the time spent waiting for Jessie to wake. He grew accustomed to the bitter taste.

"Well, do you think she'll be ready?" his mother asked again. She took a small sip of the black liquid, twisting her mouth in distaste.

"You didn't give me time to warn her."

"We had to schedule before she left the hospital. Dr. Maguire is saying she may be discharged in two days. She hasn't had any more seizures—his main concern."

Walt frowned. Why wasn't he told about her release? How in the hell did she know about all this? "Did you talk to Dr. Maguire?"

"This morning. Your father played golf with him."

Walt rolled his eyes. Of course.

"How do you think she'll handle the press?" She took another sip of her coffee to avoid eye contact.

"Isn't it a little too late for you to question her stability?" He knew Jessie was going to fume when she received the news—her life directed by his mother.

"Now, about this trip or odd behavior..."

"What do you mean?" His back tightened.

"Her outburst"—she made a noise as if to find the right words—"about living elsewhere. She cannot rattle nonsense at the conference."

Mrs. Arbol pointed a manicured finger toward her head and made a circular motion—only once, to be subtle.

"You can't judge her. Remember how you babbled after your surgery? She came out of a dream." Even if he had his doubts about his fiancée's sanity, he didn't need his mother branding her.

"You don't dream when you're in a coma."

"How do you know?" he challenged her.

Helen Arbol ignored his question. "We don't want the press or the public to get the wrong impression." She moved closer to her son, wanting to make her point. "She is representing us as a family."

How well he knew. Walt understood Jessie's anxiety. The pressure of being an Arbol was tremendous, almost like being royalty. He grew up with the press, the people, the associates, the clubs, and the money. She lived a quiet life.

His mother, with her chin pointed and eyes raised, showed disdain. Walt would think twice about marrying into his family as well if he were Jessie. Creating a fake smile, he said, "I'm sure she'll be on her best behavior."

The conversation turned toward Jessie's stay at the Arbols' residence and how the bedroom would be finished before her arrival. They added yellows to his room, along with some feminine touches, to assure she felt comfortable. Walt didn't have the heart to tell her;

Jessie wouldn't be comfortable no matter the changes. He buried the argument, knowing that continuing would only make matters worse between the two women in his life.

When Mrs. Arbol finished her coffee, she stepped back to scrutinize his appearance.

If he let her start the conversation, he'd be delayed another twenty minutes. "Don't worry, I'll shave and change. Are we set now?"

"Remember to let me know if she needs a different outfit or accessories."

"Will do."

Walt escorted his mother to the elevator. He waited, like a gentleman, and waved goodbye before the doors closed. With her off to her next event, he hurried back to the room.

He stopped short.

Jessie's bed was empty. The bathroom was empty as well.

He went out to the nurse's station, which was also devoid of staff.

What happened?

A hard knot formed in his stomach. What if she had a seizure, went into cardiac arrest while he was gone? Walt hiccupped after swallowing a rush of air. He spun around and went down the hall, holding his stomach, to find a nurse.

"Relax," Carol said as she came out of the room next to Jessie's. "She's out on the deck, getting some fresh air."

Walt spun back around. "She's okay?"

Carol nodded. She pointed to his stomach. "Are you?"

"I'm fine." He brushed off her question as his mind scrambled to figure out why Jessie was outside. He half scolded, "The temperature's too cold outside."

"I gave her a blanket," Carol said in an I-know-what-I'm-doing tone as they entered Jessie's room. "The sun's out. And the last time I checked, the temp was fifty-eight degrees."

Walt grabbed his sport coat from the chair. "Jessie's never left the room before."

"We do let our patients get away from the germs every once in a while. The fresh air will do her good."

"Ha. Ha." He got her stale joke.

"Wheel her back in for me, will ya?"

Without looking back, Walt raised his hand to acknowledge her request as he went to find his fiancée.

The glass door going out to the deck was down the hall and to the right. The door was hard to open, even using his shoulder to push on it. He wondered if it was to keep the weaker patients in.

The sun hurt Walt's eyes when he opened the door to the deck. He raised his hand to shield the brightness and find Jessie. The open space was square with a few steel chairs, a patio set, and empty planters meant to give the area some color. He found her standing near the corner of the four-foot-tall wall with a wheelchair nearby. She leaned over the edge of the wide cement rail to survey the street below.

"What are you doing?" Walt dashed across the deck, afraid she'd topple over.

She turned and smiled. "I'm watching the squirrels." She returned to a standing position.

"You could've fallen."

"No, not really." She made a face like he was nuts.

A steel object shined in her hand. *Oh shit!* She was going to kill herself—commit suicide. Slit her wrists. Slit her wrists and then hurl herself over the rail. His voice came out an octave higher than normal. "What do you have in your hand? Show me!"

"Walt." Jessie scowled. "What the hell is wrong with you?"

He shook his head to get a grip on his senses. He had to stop being so paranoid. This was just an innocent move for Jessie to get out for fresh air. Nothing more. She was safe. Nothing else would happen to her.

Jessie held up her hand and revealed a makeshift slingshot. She used a rubber tourniquet; the type nurses tied around a patient's arm before drawing blood. He wasn't sure what the steel pieces making the "Y" were, but they definitely came from the hospital.

Walt raised his hands in disbelief. "Why do you have a slingshot?"

"Because I can use it," she said and straightened up like a peacock showing its feathers.

"Really." Walt cocked an eyebrow.

Jessie's eyes gleamed with mischief and showed a spark of excitement he hadn't seen in a long time. "I learned how to use a slingshot to kill small game."

Walt laughed. He stepped back. Now she was taking her dream to a completely new level. "This I have to see."

Jessie dug a small rock out of her robe pocket.

He wanted to ask where she found the rock but waited, more curious as to what she planned to do with it.

"See the squirrel?" She pointed.

Walt followed her finger but only saw a bird pecking at the ground.

"Next to the bench."

"Got it," he said. The squirrel sat next to the tree, his coloring the same as the bark. Easy to miss, he thought.

Jessie rolled the rock between her fingers and then placed it on the rubber strap. She straightened her stance and raised the weapon.

No way, Walt thought. The squirrel was too far away, the rock too small.

With eyes focused on the squirrel, she pulled back on the strap and then let go. The rock flew, hitting the rodent in the leg.

Walt's mouth dropped open when the squirrel fell. "You killed it!"

"No, I stunned him. He's fine."

Sure enough, the rodent popped up and raced across the park.

"She's good isn't she?" Sam said from behind.

Walt turned his head around. His friend must have come for a visit while he was at the coffee machine with his mother. Sam held a dozen small rocks in his palm.

"I only found a handful," he said and passed them to Jessie.

How in the hell did he get the door open without making a noise? Walt wondered. And how did he know she needed rocks?

"Where'd you come from?"

"My mother," Sam said.

Walt shook his head in frustration. He left the room for less than half an hour. "When did you get here?"

Sam shrugged. "I don't know. Thirty minutes ago? Where'd you disappear to?"

"I was in the waiting room talking with my mother."

"I mentioned to Jessie how warm the weather was for February. Carol happened to be in the room and suggested we come out here."

"And he got me rocks." Jessie smiled at Sam while showing Walt one of the smaller stones. He wished she'd smile at him the same way.

"What do you want me to hit?" she asked Sam.

He shoved his hands in his dark blue Eddie Bauer jacket as he searched for a target three floors down. Walt noticed his friend had cut his hair. It made Sam look older, showing the baldness on top of his head.

Walt patted his own head. *Am I looking that old?* No baldness there.

"How about the stop sign at the end of the street," Sam suggested.

Within a split second, the ping of a rock hit the stop sign and echoed back to them.

"Whoooaa!" Sam laughed. "You did it! Can you kill a man with it?"

"I can." Jessie beamed.

Walt wondered if he needed to be concerned. Where did she learn to shoot? Dusken was a dream. She didn't mention anything about learning how to use a weapon.

"You want to try?"

"Not me." Sam held up his hands. "I'd hit someone and get sued."

Jessie offered the sling to Walt. He grabbed the handle, wanting to prove to her that it was simple to use. A slingshot. He played with one as a child.

"What's my target?"

"Try the paper cup next to the garbage can," Sam said.

"Or the garbage can." Jessie pointed to the larger target.

Walt eyed the two targets. They were across the street near the entrance to the park. Should be easy enough. "I'll go for the can first."

Jessie spread out the rocks Sam gave her. She found a midsized rock and handed it to him. "Be careful."

"Piece of cake," Walt said while loading up the sling.

A middle-aged man walked across the sidewalk. Jessie put her hand on his arm, telling Walt to stop. They waited until the man got in his Malibu and then sped off down the street. She removed her hand.

The rock was heavy enough to fly straight. The slight breeze shouldn't affect the direction. Walt placed the rock on the rubber band. He pulled back on the strap and lost his grip on the rock. It fell to the deck.

Sam snickered. "Way to go there, buddy."

Walt ignored him. He picked the rock up and took aim again, closing one eye. He wanted to hit the rim so it would make a loud clang.

One, two, three...

Walt released his fingers and the rock flew.

An explosion of glass. He hit the light in the lamppost.

"Shit!"

Jessie scurried to pick up the rocks and dumped them into her robe pocket. Sam grabbed the wheelchair and swung it around. Jessie plopped down in the seat while Walt grabbed her IV. They rushed for the door.

"Not even close," Sam said and harrumphed when they pushed the steel door open and entered the hospital.

"I was close."

"Close doesn't count if you're being attacked," Jessie stated.

"I'm only being attacked by you two harassing me," Walt said with a sniff. He should've hit the can. It was an easy target. The lamppost was five feet away from the garbage can and higher up. He had aimed downward. The wind must have taken it.

"All right, I'm out of here," Sam said once they got Jessie back in her bed.

"Find me more rocks," Jessie mouthed.

"Will do." He gave her a wink.

"I'll be back," Walt said and put his hand out to Jessie, palm out, for her to stay. He didn't want a heart attack if she wasn't in the room when he returned. He left with his friend.

"Any word yet on what you're going to do about Jessie staying at your folks'?" Sam asked as they walked to the elevator.

"You know, huh?"

"Jessie told me." Sam pressed the Down button.

"Was she pissed?"

"Extremely."

"I'm working on it."

"Stay at my cabin up in Wisconsin. Take off for a while."

Walt half-listened while fishing through the pockets of his jacket. He needed a favor from his friend. And paper. He found a pen. "Hey, can you research a couple of things for me?"

"What'cha need?" Sam zipped up his jacket.

Walt steered Sam off to the waiting room and grabbed a napkin off the counter. He wrote down a few of the names Jessie mentioned in her dream.

"Pentias, cyrolus, and queeno," Sam read aloud after he took the napkin. "What are they?"

"First two are flowers and the last is some type of medicine or a plant actually. Jessie's been telling me about her dream and she mentioned them. I'm curious whether they're real or not."

Sam's face lit with a mixture of curiosity and awe. He waited for Walt to say something.

Reluctant, yet knowing he owed an explanation to his friend, he said, "Yes, I've been listening like you asked."

"Is it interesting?"

Walt bobbed his head about, again not wanting to admit much. This was still a dream, and he had to keep reminding himself of it. He needed to remind Jessie as well. He said, "Different."

"Real?"

"She's got a vivid imagination. She does a great job describing where she's been." They headed back to the elevator.

"You should write her story down. It may make for a good book."

Walt laughed. "Fiction or non-fiction?"

Sam raised his finger in warning. The elevator door opened. "Later, Sharpshooter."

"Ha. Ha." Walt turned to head back to the room when he remembered. "Press conference is tomorrow afternoon at three."

Sam saluted.

Walt went back to the room. Lunch had arrived and Carol included a plate for him as well. Lasagna, roll, mixed vegetables, and lemon chiffon cake. One of the hospital dishes he could tolerate.

He took his plate and silverware and set them on the nightstand near her bed. Jessie lifted the Styrofoam cups. Milk or iced tea. He picked the iced tea.

"I have good news and bad news."

Jessie raised her eyes to him.

Walt took a deep breath. He had to tell her. "The press conference is tomorrow."

He saw her swallow hard. She broke off a piece of her roll and then popped it in her mouth. "What time?"

"Three."

She nodded.

He couldn't read her, but she didn't seem too upset. "Are you okay?"

"I don't have a choice."

Walt wished he could say she did. "Well, the good news...you're out of here soon."

"Amen to that."

She started eating her lasagna.

No anger? No words? She seemed too calm.

Jessie stopped, fork halfway to her mouth when she realized he was staring at her. She put the fork down. "I'm okay with it." She pointed to his food. "Eat while it's warm."

They talked about the conference, light conversation on what to expect. After he finished eating, Walt pushed his plate aside. "So were you attacked? Did you take off the next morning for the village?"

Jessie nodded while she finished eating the last of her cake. She drank some milk, then answered. "The Morlorns didn't attack us. We left early the next morning before daylight. We traveled in silence.

They taught me hand signals to use if I heard or saw anything unusual. The worst part is I knew I was holding them back."

Chapter 21

::: Jezamina :::

Savel's Village

Jezamina fought the pain as they traveled to the village. Her hip felt like it was going to dislocate. Her entire back ached. When they stopped for the night, Aresen doled out a small loaf of bread and chunk of cheese for her evening meal. He'd brought the cheese back from the village, a rarity for Dusken. He wanted to reward her for walking the distance. She only wanted to sleep.

Jezero made his bed next to hers. He closed his eyes soon after the meal. His breathing was soft and rhythmic, an orchestrated sleep with only so much time to perform. Jezamina lay still, not wanting to disrupt him even though finding a comfortable spot was nearly impossible.

Aresen stayed on guard for them all. She could've joined him as well. The continual swishing and scurrying of a plant or an animal disturbed her, not to mention the pain ready to burst out of her body. She didn't know which one was worse.

The next morning when they continued on, her leg went numb. She no longer felt her hips sway or her feet hit the ground. Jezamina kept moving without thought or emotion. The men expected her to keep up. Her first glimmer of hope came when she spotted the plant used to ease pain. She thought back to Raine's lessons. What did he teach her about the plant with the purple stripe?

She remembered him rubbing a plant leaf against his skin. He used it when they returned from the river, after finding the queeno. "A quick fix," he explained.

Lecture...lepure...leturp. Leture! Dark green leaves, purple stripe, and thick stem. Find the ones with dark green edges. Underneath was the milky medicine.

Jezamina grabbed two stalks of leaves. As they walked, she searched for more. They liked to grow near the taller, spindly bushes that shaded them from sun. Each time she found one, she snipped a couple of the leaves with her fingers and put them in her sack.

When they stopped to rest, she borrowed Raine's scraper to extract the milky substance. When the leaf was covered in white, she rubbed it against her leg, then up to her hip. The medicine took time to work, but when it did the relief was great. That night she made more and used it on her back as well.

Raine beamed. Aresen and Jezero approved as well. She was using her newfound skills.

She remembered Jezero's words: *learn to survive.*

On the third day of travel, when daylight faded, remnants of the village appeared. A pot with water rested on a stump. A basket lay on its side with berries scattered across the path. An arrow was half-hidden underneath a tree. She leaned down to pick it up when Aresen's hand gripped her forearm. "Poisonous."

Jezamina retracted her hand. He pointed. Rust-colored liquid coated the tip and the shaft. She placed her hand on his shoulder and smiled, thanking him.

Jezero slowed his pace to walk next to her. He slipped his hand in hers, giving a gentle squeeze. Aresen and Raine moved in closer. Her instincts told her they meant to protect her, but she wasn't sure from what. Morlorns? Villagers? Or worse, what she'd see?

The path widened. More traces of the attack began to appear. She fixated on the blood splattered against the tree bark, and the red dots on the plants. Now she understood why. Her stomach turned.

Jezamina tugged at Jezero's hand. Her eyes widened. She hesitated to move forward.

"Wait here." He let go of her and motioned for Raine to stand next to her. Aresen stood behind her with eyes to the forest.

The wind changed direction. Charred wood permeated the air. Jezero called out in their secret communication to each other. Raine gave her the nod.

Cautiously she moved forward. Dark gray patches marked the trees where the fire had burned. Everything was black: the ground, the ferns and bushes, the trees within the area, and even the stone well. All marked by the attack.

Jezamina gasped as the wind shifted and a foul odor mixed with the smell of ash. She covered her nose, guessing it was rotting flesh or old blood, and tried breathing in shallow pants to keep from absorbing the air into her lungs. She kept her head down as if it would help.

Aresen took her arm to guide her as she stepped through the remains and burnt ground.

Don't look.

When they reached the center of the village, she raised her head again, wanting to brave it like the others. Only one stray building remained. The roof was gone but the walls had survived the blaze. A few of the logs near the fire still smoldered. Pieces of metal remained; items that once helped them serve their dinner. Arrows were pitched in every direction, and random rocks dotted what was once a place many called home.

"Why are these rocks scattered about?" she asked Aresen.

"They were used by the women and children as weapons."

Her lip trembled. A lump swelled in her throat when she thought about elders or children trying to protect themselves from the Morlorns.

Jezamina then spotted a crude, straw doll with her arms ripped, buried halfway in the debris. Had the girl hung on to the doll, clinging to life?

The first tear rolled down her cheek. This was Veita's village.

Completely gone.

An eerie silence absorbed the village. Only the noise of their shoes crunched against the dead grass and ash as they reached the other side.

Aresen left her to talk to Jezero, who held a crude piece of paper in his hand. She wondered what it said. Raine veered off to find a healthy fern. He cut a few leaves and gathered them together, making a broom to sweep away their footprints. When the medicine man met up with her, she asked, "Where'd they go?"

"The villagers?"

"The ones..." She couldn't say killed or murdered. The words wouldn't come out. She picked softer words. "The ones who didn't make it."

"Proper burial," Raine explained. "Even the Morlorns who died."

"Why do they receive a proper burial?" Anyone who killed with such hatred wasn't worthy of decency.

"To clean the air."

Jezamina frowned, stumped by his words. "You mean for forgiveness or because of the rot?"

"The rot."

Jezero and Aresen joined them. Neither said a word but their set jaws and hard eyes told her whatever was on the note wasn't good.

"Zarac has taken the remaining villagers to Parnell's village," he said. "We'll continue on."

For a split second, Jezamina saw the pain in Jezero's eyes. He indeed had feelings for the villagers. The urge to kiss him hit her like a rock. To hold him and share in his pain. To become one with him.

Jezero caught her staring.

Jezamina lowered her eyes to the ground. Her cheeks burned and she wondered how red they were, if her embarrassment was noticeable.

When they made their beds, Jezamina forgot about her hip, forgot about her leg. Jezero slept beside her, as he had since they left Dusken. She listened to his breathing, more ragged than the nights before.

In the dark, she found his hand. She slipped her fingers into his and draped his arm around her. She moved toward him until their bodies nearly touched. He let out a deep breath and the warmth tickled her neck. His breathing stopped for an instant and then turned smoother, less ragged.

She fell asleep, hoping he knew her heart was with him. At the same time, she knew she was treading on dangerous ground.

Chapter 22

::: Jezamina :::

Parnell's Village

Jezamina's pain was in control as they continued their travel through the different forests. The smells, the hues, the ground—all changed every time they reached water or the other side of a valley. She studied the lands as they passed. She also studied Jezero. His walk was casual, but his eyes stayed alert. His shoulders were broad, his back straight. He took the lead with her close behind. At times, he slowed his pace to walk next to her. She learned to keep her stance like he did, to show confidence, not fear.

At those times, the sexual tension between them pulled on her, making her insides stir. She knew the attraction was wrong. Her heart fluttered every time he accidently brushed against her. Jezamina couldn't ignore it as her feelings grew for him.

Jezero was dangerous. He lived to fight, not to settle down with a family. He could shatter her heart if she let him in. And her struggle to remember the past, wasn't as strong as it used to be. This was her life now. She couldn't stop living and wait for the day when her memory returned to know if someone waited for her. She had to live for now.

The doyen tapped his hand against her back, signaling for her to walk behind him. He listened as he moved forward. All three men had their bows and arrows ready. Her skin prickled at their telltale sign of danger.

What if they were attacked? How could she help them fight or defend herself without a weapon? The knife in Aresen's hand shined, and she wanted one.

"Let me have one of your knives," she whispered after catching up with Jezero on the path.

"What for?" He motioned for her to stay back.

"To protect myself."

"We're protecting you." He frowned and became agitated when she tried walking with him again.

"But I can help."

He glanced at her for a brief second. "You don't know how to use one."

"I do too," she said, angered that he rejected her simple request.

Jezero shot her a look, and she immediately knew she spoke too loud. His nostrils flared.

"What he means," Aresen said into her ear and took her arm to pull her back, "is if ye use a knife to defend yerself, a Morlorn could take the knife and use it against ye."

The vision made her swallow hard. She didn't want to die by her own stupidity. "I feel so helpless. I can't just stand and watch. What if they grab me?"

Aresen placed his finger to his lips. His words came on a soft breath. "Trust us. We will tell ye what to do if needed."

They stopped for the night. A haze cloaked the forest. Jezamina settled against a tree and covered herself with a fur to keep warm. She dozed on and off while the men stood watch.

They left again before the sun rose. Jezero had said less than three words to her since she asked for a weapon. With signs of the Morlorns still apparent, he watched for potential danger. They quickened their pace to reach the village by nightfall.

Her entire body ached. Her head throbbed. She wanted to curl up in a ball and go to sleep.

Right. Left. Right. Left. She kept up with Jezero. They ate as they walked. No more breaks. How could the men manage the strenuous pace? They were driven, she decided. And crazy.

Her nose twitched. The haze thickened like fog through the trees. Smoke.

Voices. A child cried for her mother. A continuous clang of metal hitting wood.

"Is this the village?" Jezamina raised her head.

"We have arrived," Raine said.

A man's voice shouted out. Someone else laughed. People.

Her heart skipped a beat. How long since she'd set foot in a village? What if it were her village?

The closer they got, the more her heart raced. Her palms became sweaty. How were they going to react to her? What if someone recognized her? Would she recognize them? Would it trigger her memory? Jezero assured her that she wasn't from their lands, but from across the sea. How did he know for sure?

Jezero motioned for her to stop.

Aresen made the call. This time, a slight repeated chirp to announce their arrival.

Her insides turned.

The village must have responded for they continued on. The first villagers appeared. Two men almost hidden within the trees eyed them as they approached. A woman stood back to let them through. She had singed hair and eyebrows.

Jezero stopped in front of a younger, shorter man as they neared the edge of the clearing. He said, "My deepest regrets to you, Johan, and your village. Savel was well-respected and a brave doyen."

Aresen whispered to her, "Savel was Johan's father."

The men hugged. Jezamina saw the burn marks on the young man's arms. Johan said something to Jezero, his expression solemn.

Another woman with cuts on her arms and legs circled near the group. When her eyes made contact with Jezamina, the woman's face turned hard, her eyes cold. Jezamina shivered from the chill. Her anxiety increased.

"Jezero." Another man's deep voice echoed against the trees. "The days have been long since yer last visit." The man was tall and solid. He gave Jezero a hearty hug before turning to Aresen. "And ye." He puffed his chest out. "I will beat ye at Straightpoint before ye leave."

"Ye only hope," Aresen replied, and the two men laughed.

Jezamina assumed they were talking about a competitive game by the way they held their chins high as if daring each other. She was about to ask what Straightpoint was, but Jezero stepped back and held out his hand to present her. "Parnell and Johan, I'd like you to meet Jezamina."

She jerked to attention.

The shorter one set his chiseled jaw. He looked into her eyes but not in greeting. He masked all emotion.

Jezamina moved closer to Jezero. Aresen, behind her, said, "Johan's father was the doyen of the village, the one attacked."

Her heart went out to the grieving young man. "I'm deeply sorry for what happened."

Johan looked down as if almost ready to spit on the ground. This wasn't grief, but someone unhappy to see her. Jezamina stepped back.

Parnell's greeting was warmer. He bowed before her. "Ye are a breath of beautiful." He glared at Johan for a moment and then turned back to her. "Welcome to my village. Come join us near the fire. Yer journey was long. Be warmed and eat our food."

He led them to the main area of the village where a community fire roared with life. Jezamina searched for Zarac and Veita. Two older women walked around the fire and monitored the different pots of food cooking over the flames. A few men sat on logs as if chatting about the day's events. She hoped Zarac and Veita were okay.

People milled about. They walked down paths and disappeared into the woods. They sat near the fire to eat. Others carried water in woven baskets. Shacks made of sticks, mud, and hay surrounded the area. The little square homes stretched toward the other side of the clearing. Jezamina could tell which ones were new with the brighter, yellow straw. A few, in the process of being built, had no walls. New homes for the new people. Was Veita in one of them?

Jezamina searched for the medicine woman near the newer shacks and then by the main fire as more people gathered. She caught Parnell staring at her as if a hunger burned in his eyes. She pondered which one made her more uncomfortable, Johan's contempt for her or Parnell's lust. This wasn't the welcome she expected. She wanted Veita to come rescue her.

Parnell motioned for them to sit. "My father may be ailing, but his eyes are still like the birds in the sky. He will know ye are here. For tonight he will only meet with Jezero."

Aresen tapped Jezamina on the shoulder and motioned for her to sit next to him. She did as directed and then watched as Parnell and Jezero walked up to a tall, hollow tree stump.

The tree moved. Jezamina squinted. The shadows deceived her. An old man sat inside the stump, cradled inside the bark. His broad shoulders and thick neck provided signs he had once been a solid man. His leathered face and arms were hidden within the curved walls of the tree. His hand shook as it held a gnarled walking stick.

"Drago is well respected in all the lands," Aresen explained, indicating the old man sheltered in the stump. He removed the sack from his back and settled in. "He recently passed his duties as doyen to Parnell."

She watched as Jezero greeted Drago. He dropped to one knee and offered his hand. Parnell's smile widened as if appreciating how much his father meant to Jezero. He leaned down to be part of the conversation.

"Parnell is Drago's only son. If anything should happen to him, Johan would be doyen of the village." Aresen adjusted his quiver and let his bow rest against his leg.

"Is that good or bad?" Jezamina guessed Aresen didn't approve. When he grunted in response, she assumed bad. She changed the subject. "I haven't seen Zarac or Veita. Have you?"

"Huh?" Aresen had found a smudge of dirt on his bow and cleaned it off.

"I haven't seen either one."

"Veita is more than likely in one of these shays helping a poor soul wounded from the attack. Zarac is over there."

Jezamina followed to where he pointed. Zarac stood near a tree with his bow and arrow ready, on guard as his doyen talked to Drago in private. Parnell left his father and headed toward them. He chose to sit near Jezamina.

Musk and sweat. Not unpleasant, but a little more than she wanted to breathe in. She readjusted, twisting so their arms didn't touch. Aresen became her close friend.

"How's Savel's village adjusting to their new home?" Aresen asked the doyen.

Jezamina tried placing Savel again. Oh yes, the doyen of Veita's village. Johan's father.

Parnell scanned the village before him. He nodded as if pleased with the progress. "We embraced many villages over time. This one did not have many survivors."

The village grew peaceful as dusk fell around them. No chaos or anger. Only people trying to cope and others wanting to help. Everyone seemed to get along. Yet, she still sensed tension in the air. Was it in fear of the Morlorns attacking again?

"Are ye cold?" Parnell asked when she shivered at the thought of the burned ruins she witnessed two days earlier. He moved closer so his arm brushed against her shoulder.

"No, I was thinking about the unfortunate circumstance." She had nowhere to go. If she got up and moved to Aresen's other side it would be an insult.

"When my father was young, he formed this village and helped others who had lost their land to the Morlorns. By taking in a village, he built a stronger village. The same goes for Savel's village. They will make us stronger." He smiled again, but this time his eyes lowered to her cleavage. "That is how my father met my mother. When she walked into his village for the first time, he knew instantly she was for him." He raised his eyes to stare into hers, as if insinuating the same just happened to him.

Jezamina's back tightened. She searched for Jezero. He was still with Drago. She looked to Aresen, who contained an amused grin. He picked his teeth with a twig. He was of no help to her. Jezamina gave him the most icy, cold stare she could muster, but he ignored it. She turned back to Parnell. "Are you hoping for the same?"

"Fate will answer my wish."

His words struck Jezamina. Not in the way he wanted, for love. She rubbed her face, the day wearing on her. Fate. What did she do to deserve this turn of events? No memory. No history. Should she be thankful to be alive?

"Ye be tired after yer journey." Parnell became the host again. "I invite ye to stay in my shay."

"Yer offer is kind." Aresen stood. "But we'll stay where Zarac has made us a place to rest."

"Jezamina will be more comfortable and protected in a shay."

"She will stay with us," Jezero said as he returned to hear the last part of their conversation.

"As ye wish," Parnell said. Disappointment showed on his face. He rose and helped Jezamina up as well. She had no choice but to accept his hand.

"The journey was long," Jezero said to Parnell. "We'll meet again in the morning."

"The morning," The doyen bowed. He squeezed Jezamina's hand before letting go, as if telling her he wasn't giving up.

***

Jezero poured another mug of ale and drank half of it down. They finished eating a meal of fresh bread and seared meat near their own fire. Zarac had picked a spot away from the village yet within view of all the activities.

"Why are we so far from the village?" He overheard Jezamina ask Raine as they unrolled their furs.

"We're not so far," Raine responded.

Not far enough. Jezero wasn't happy with Parnell's eyes on Jezamina. The new doyen was respectful, but lust could overshadow honor. Not only would he worry about the Morlorns but possibly Parnell's desires as well.

A loud shout came from across the clearing. Two men argued and their voices carried across the night air. Jezero wasn't in the mood for breaking up fights. He stood, ready if needed. Issues always occurred when two villages united. Parnell's voice called out. Soon the men turned quiet, settling their dispute. Jezero was pleased. He stretched his back, hoping to relieve the ache in his shoulders.

"Get yer sleep." Zarac passed him on the path. "I'll cover the area."

Jezero patted him on the back. "You're a good man. We'll talk in the morn." He hoped to spend time with Jezamina, to see how she was doing, but found her asleep in her makeshift bed. He slipped off his boots and set them aside. He pulled a top fur over him when he lay next to her. They shared a ground fur to keep them dry from the earth.

Jezamina slept on her side with her back toward him. He memorized the curve of her body and how her hair fell in soft waves. After a time, she turned toward him, and Jezero didn't bother moving away. He kept his distance when they traveled, not wanting to get too comfortable or be distracted by her beauty. An occasional touch satisfied his need.

When did he start feeling for her?

Jezero had to put up his shield. She would find her memory. She would leave. His heart didn't need to be broken.

The sun rose toward the treetops when Jezero woke. He slept longer than expected. Zarac was gone. Aresen was still asleep, and Raine sat under the tree with Jezamina near his side. The two were deep in conversation when he rose from bed and left to relieve himself. He then walked to the lake to wash away the grime from traveling.

He returned to find Raine had moved to the fire. "Where's Jezamina?"

"She spotted Veita."

"Who's with her?" He tightened up, ready for action.

"Veita."

"I meant one of us." Jezero gave him an eye, not liking his response. "Where's Aresen?"

"In the village. Within sight of her."

Jezero nodded. His day had begun, and there was no room for error. He sliced off a chunk of meat roasting above the fire. His stomach growled and he aimed to satisfy his hunger. He grabbed a small loaf of bread.

"She asked why we surrounded her." Raine pointed to their beds and how they were placed. "I told her we needed to be kept safe without Dusken to protect us."

"Did she ask why?"

The medicine man grinned. "She thinks we're keeping her safe from Parnell."

Jezero chuckled. There was some truth to her words. He ate in silence, losing his thoughts to Jezamina. She did well with the plants, learning to use them. She helped Raine and kept track of him. She wanted to explore and learn their ways. The safety of Dusken gave her the chance, only the time had been cut short. Now in the village, life would be different. Acceptance had issues.

He sensed the anger within Johan and others. Zarac had filled him in as well. Tension would grow with Jezamina in the village, but he had made a promise to Drago to come. They needed his help to protect their land, to show them how to fight and bring back their faith. The men must be prepared, work together, before the next attack. The warning was out. Another attack would occur. At the same time, if they wanted him, the village needed to accept her.

"Jezero." Raine called his name as if impatient.

"Aye?" He snapped out of his thoughts. The medicine man waited for him at the path to the main circle, the center of the village. "Are ye coming with me?"

"Let's begin." Jezero stood. He grabbed his bow and the quiver stacked with arrows.

Veita's new shay was off from the main path but accessible. She sat near the fire, smashing leaves in a bowl. Jezamina sat next to her and stripped strings from a green stem. They seemed to be catching up with events.

A few villagers walked by; some with curious stares and others with their heads down as if ignoring the new woman. Jezero frowned but continued on. The path widened as it curved to the main center where Parnell sat with a few of the men. Again he frowned. Parnell should be leading by example, preparing for battle and not chatting like the village women. As he approached, the villagers turned silent. They stared in his direction. When he stared back, their eyes turned away. Something was amiss. He moved forward with caution. Near the fire, two women stepped aside. Behind them, a woman with straight, brown hair parted down the middle stood off to the side.

Jezero's mouth clamped shut. The long, pale face with full lips and haunting brown eyes told tales of collecting hearts and then tossing them away. Jezero knew this for a fact.

Leota.

When his eyes met hers, Jezero gave her one long stare before turning away. He shook his head. *Son of a bitch*. He had no time for her.

Raine stood next to him and clicked his tongue. He seemed equally surprised. "Why is she here?"

"That is what I'd like to know."

Jezero went over to Parnell. His anger continued to rise. The woman created trouble. She had a black tongue, one that didn't care if she created havoc or pain. He snapped at the doyen. "Are you ready to plant the traps?"

"I am." Parnell stood. He stretched before picking up his bow. He seemed oblivious to Jezero's anger.

Leota smiled and moved out to the open, a deliberate move as if to say, "Yes, I'm here."

He scowled. "What brings Leota to the village?"

Parnell hesitated for a moment as if questioning the anger in his words. "She was my friend's mate. He died while hunting."

"When did she arrive?"

"Two days earlier," Parnell said. He turned to face him. "What is yer concern with her?"

"Did she know I was coming here to the village?"

"No..." He thought for a moment. Parnell's eyes flittered as if something triggered his memory.

He didn't respond, but his reaction made Jezero believe differently. She knew. He said, "Gather the men."

"Hello, Jezero," the woman's silky voice purred when he walked over to her.

He stopped, his back twitched. She seemed so delicate, so innocent. He shook his head to rid his mind of the image.

"What? You're not happy to see me?" She pouted.

"What brings you here, Leota?" He posed with his hands on his hips.

"You haven't heard?"

Jezero raised his eyebrow, ready to listen.

"Tovet died while hunting."

Leota slid closer to him. She brushed her hand against his shoulder and smiled. "I heard of your precious find." She walked around him. Her moves were catlike as she eyed him like prey. Jezero kept still. "So you found her on Morlorn territory? What a shame. You stole Vyrone's property."

"Humans can't be property."

"Oh, really." She stopped in front of him. Being the same height, her eyes aligned with his. "When did you change your mind?"

Jezero stayed devoid of emotion. He wouldn't commit or play into her game, but his ego had to address her accusation. "I've never considered you property."

"I remember when you promised to protect me." The bitterness rose in her voice. She leaned forward, putting her hand on his chest. "Did you promise her as well?"

Jezero stretched his neck, annoyed. He stepped back. "And do you recall what happened the last time I tried to protect you? How many unwarranted deaths had you caused? Twenty?"

"As many as you," she said with her face now in front of his. Her voice turned hard when she added, "We are the same."

His stance widened when she moved in, a few inches from his face as if ready to kiss him. Leota licked her lips. "We are meant to be together."

Jezero took a long, slow breath.

Her hand went to his chest.

He grabbed her wrist. "Not anymore."

"I will prove to you differently." She vowed and then walked away, swaying her hips seductively.

Aresen met her on the path. He increased the distance between them and held out his hands to keep her away as they crossed. "Ah, the evil one now lurks within the forest."

"You are only a pawn, Aresen. Only a pawn," Leota said with a sneer.

He laughed her off and then met up with Jezero. "Well, she's a delight."

Jezero wasn't ready to make light of his encounter. "I need you to watch Jezamina. Do not let that woman near her."

"As ye wish."

"Not as I wish," Jezero said.

***

Shredding stems, Jezamina raised her head when Veita stopped telling her about the attack on her village. She focused her attention to the center area, and her mouth dropped open.

"What's wrong?" Jezamina searched and found her answer. A woman stood with Jezero. She had unique features—a full mouth and deep-set eyes. She was extremely thin yet fluid. By the look on Jezero's face, he wasn't happy to see her. The tension between them was noticeable. Jezamina's heart lurched. They knew each other.

"Who is she?"

"Leota." Veita didn't seem pleased to see her either.

"Is she from your village?"

"No. She has drifted from one place to the next."

"Then why is she here?"

The woman kept her neck straight as if carrying a heavy, gold crown on her head. The woman placed her hand on Jezero's chest, more intimate than a kind gesture. A rock landed in Jezamina's stomach. The woman's eyes fluttered, calling out to him. Jezero grabbed her wrist, bringing Leota's hand down.

Realization hit like an arrow to her heart. "They were lovers."

Veita coughed and began to pound the grain in front of her with a new vigor. Her actions said it all.

Jezamina sat, immobilized. She was too shocked to say anything. Never had it crossed her mind that beyond Dusken, Jezero may have a different life. Aresen talked on occasion about his love interests, a few here and there to keep him company. Zarac had no interest in women. But Jezero? Of course it was possible. He was handsome, rugged, and sexy. She remembered him standing before her, at the beach, with his chest exposed; the flat, muscular stomach.

"How long?" A pang of jealousy shot through her.

"Long enough for him to learn her ways." The medicine woman had regained her composure.

Leota turned from Jezero and sauntered away, making sure he noted her hips. Aresen met up with her. She exchanged words with him and then looked up, directly at Jezamina. The expression was cold and calculating. Jezamina refused to break the stare.

"You best keep away from her," Veita warned.

Leota seemed to smirk before continuing down the path. Jezamina wondered how complicated her life would get.

Veita tossed another pile of stems in front of Jezamina to keep her busy. She picked one of them up and began shredding the stringy skin into a pile on the ground.

Leota's stare stayed with her throughout the day. Another one who didn't like her presence in the village. How many others? No one came to greet her. If she smiled at them, they ignored her or walked in the opposite direction.

"Why don't the villagers want me here?" she asked when the medicine woman brought her a new basket for the shredded stems.

Veita, for the second time, stumbled over her words. "What makes you think they don't want you?"

"No one has welcomed me here, besides Parnell. People walk away, avoid me."

"'Tis your imagination," Veita said as if dismissing the thought for her. "Anyone with Jezero is welcome here."

The words didn't hold any meaning for her. "So you're saying they will tolerate me since I'm with Jezero."

"Oh, goodness! That isn't what I meant. You are welcome here, child."

"I don't think anyone got the message."

Veita made a face. "The message. What are you talking about?"

Jezamina frowned. Why was the medicine woman acting so strangely? She loved Veita, but the woman seemed so tense compared with how she was during her stay in Dusken.

The last of the plants were shredded. Jezamina excused herself and went back to her area. Aresen followed.

"Why the long face?" he asked and grabbed another piece of wood to throw on the fire.

She shook her head, not wanting to talk. She didn't need him to say it was all in her head. Jezamina wished it were true, but the actions of the villagers spoke louder than words. She missed Dusken. Now she felt useless, not part of anything.

"What do you do when you're down?" She found a small stick and made lines in the dirt.

Aresen thought for a second. "I guess I'd think of a sweet memory to make me smile."

"I don't have any memories. Can you share?"

He scratched his head, shook each foot, pushed up the sleeves on his tunic. He nodded. "I was fishing in the river with my father. He helped me make the spear I used to catch my first big fish. For the life of me, I couldn't spear one for our dinner, while my father had five on shore. Frustrated, I tossed my spear into the woods. We heard a loud bellow, and we raced through the trees to see what happened." Aresen laughed. "I killed a juntabe."

Jezamina made a face. "What's that?"

"A juntabe is one of the hardest animals to hunt in all the lands. They're low to the ground and fast. That night we celebrated, and my father let me drink ale for the first time. I became a man in his eyes." He drifted as the memory took him back to a place long ago. "He died not long after."

"It's a good memory to treasure in your heart," she said and nudged him with her shoulder.

Aresen's eyes lit up. "How would ye like to learn how to use a slingshot?"

"I'd be willing to try."

"Then follow me."

Aresen grabbed his sack near the base of the tree. He placed the smooth weapon in her hand.

Jezamina ran her thumb against the handle and prongs. She wasn't sure whether it was made from an antler or bone. The sides were smooth and white with a slight indent near the base where her hand fit perfectly.

"I made it for ye."

She wrinkled her nose. "For me?"

"Ye need to learn to protect yerself. Feed yerself."

She liked the idea. Aresen showed her the best rocks to collect based on the size of her target. He showed her how to hold the slingshot and place the rock near the center of the band that stretched between the two points. She had a knack for knowing where to point and release. Soon they played a game, seeing how many targets they could hit. She missed half. Aresen was always dead on.

The night made them call it quits; it was too dark to continue. Jezamina gave him a hug. "Now you have given me a memory I'll always cherish."

Chapter 23

::: Jezamina :::

Parnell's Village

Jezamina woke with the slingshot still in her hand. She wanted to show it to Jezero, but he had left their area. Or maybe he never returned. The thought of Leota made her stomach turn again.

Stop it.

She had no right to feel betrayed. Jezero made it clear from the beginning he was only there to protect her. He was called to her and not by choice.

She tucked the slingshot away and then went about her normal tasks. She helped Raine with the fire, pulling up the beds, and cleaning their area. Jezamina appreciated how her men were tidy and clean, unlike the people of the village. A few shays smelled of old urine and rotted food mixed together. Finished with her chores, she took the path to the lake and then changed her mind. She'd find Veita first, see if she needed help.

Heading toward the main area, Jezamina took the cutoff for Veita's shay. She wasn't sure what made her look, but she stopped. Jezero and Leota sat near the village fire, deep in conversation.

Her legs wouldn't move. It was rude to stare, but she couldn't turn her eyes away or walk down the path. Seeing the two together stung. She had no right to be mad.

I'm here to protect you.

Jezero caught her eyes on him. He slid back to create distance from the woman as if guilty at being caught. Leota turned to see why he reacted. She smiled in triumph. Jezamina forced her legs to work. She followed the path and kept her head down.

Veita wasn't near her shay. Jezamina took the longer route on the edge of the clearing to avoid seeing Jezero with the woman. She walked to the river. Aresen promised he would spend time with her again, once the men returned from the hunt. She wanted to be prepared. The shoreline carried different-sized rocks, so she decided to collect a pile of them.

"Jezamina," Jezero called out for her when she began. He skidded down the side of the hill instead of taking the path. Rocks kicked up from the ground and tumbled toward her. A gold mine of ammunition for her slingshot rested near her feet. She resisted the urge to collect the mix of smooth and jagged stones.

"You shouldn't be alone." He landed, standing in front of her.

"I'm not." She didn't want to sound cold, but the words came out sharp and hard. In the back of her mind she wondered how much he cared for Leota. Did the woman still have a soft spot in his heart?

Jezero assessed Jezamina for a moment with his hands on his hips.

"I get it," she said, having no right to feel angered.

"Get what?"

"I'm here because of the calling."

"In truth, aye." His slow speech and stare deemed him clueless to what she meant.

She didn't want to have this conversation. He had a chore to do and that was taking care of her. No more. Why couldn't he soften and show affection when they were together?

Her head spun as he mesmerized her with his dark brown eyes. She breathed in his presence, wanting him. Yes, she could easily fall in love with Jezero. She ignored the tug of someone waiting for her. This one was alive and standing in front of her.

Jezamina turned to walk away and distance herself from him. Jezero grabbed her arm. He frowned. "What's wrong?"

They stood face to face. She raised her chin. "I don't want to be pitied. I don't want you to think you have to take care of me like I'm some charity case."

His mouth flickered with slight amusement. "Charity case?"

Jezamina turned again to leave and tried pulling away. Jezero's grip was solid. He pulled her in, closer. She put her hand to his chest to keep distance between them.

"The calling was for me to find you, to protect you on your journey."

"It's not what you wanted. And now I am a burden." Jezamina hated herself—hated the jealousy and hurt squeezing the air out of her. Leota wanted him, desired him. "I'm just another. You were called to Leota as well."

Jezero's nostrils flared. His body stiffened. She pushed the wrong button. She tried pulling away again, but he wouldn't let her.

In slow, controlled words he said, "She means nothing to me."

"She did at one time."

"At one time."

"Exactly." Jezamina proved her point.

Jezero turned his eyes downward.

Chapter 24

::: Jezamina :::

Parnell's Village

Jezero let go of Jezamina, and she ran up the path. Again he remembered why he didn't get involved with women. Instead of feeling anger, her actions hit his heart. He didn't like seeing her run from him.

Zarac called his signal, announcing the men were gearing up to leave. Jezero made his way up the path and saw Veita near the well. He went to speak to her.

"We are leaving to hunt. Will you inform Jezamina?"

"Can't you tell her yourself?"

"She's not exactly speaking to me at the moment."

"And whose fault may I ask?"

Jezero kept silent. She already knew.

"You can't live in fear, Jezero. You can't let the past determine your ever after."

"I have no fear nor am I concerned."

"I am still here. You are here. She can be too."

"She can also leave. She will leave."

"If the desire is strong to come back, she will find a way."

"As did Leota."

She had come back with a vengeance. Power became her motive. Jezero cut his ties from her when she didn't use her knowledge wisely. She was similar to Vyrone, an enemy to the lands, yet the villagers were blind to the fact and let her stay on.

The flutter of wings, a light shrill called from above. Zarac motioned they were heading out. Jezero asked again, "Will you tell her?"

"I will."

Jezero turned to leave. With the addition of new members, the village food supply was low. As much as he preferred to stay in the village, they needed this hunt. Raine would guard Jezamina and hide her if necessary.

"Jezero," Veita called after him. He turned to face her again. She placed her hand over her eyes to shield them from the sun. "When you return, give Jezamina reason to want to be here."

***

Jezamina scowled and swore under her breath when Veita gave her the news Jezero had left. *Let him go*. She didn't need him here.

The day turned long. Veita had to make visits to some of the villagers still healing from wounds suffered in the attack. Jezamina offered to help, but the medicine woman declined, not wanting her around those with fever.

She stayed near the main fire for a while to watch the women go about their daily chores. The children played a game with animal ears and sticks. Jezamina hoped someone, woman or child, would befriend her. She was wrong.

Even the man named Drago, hiding in the tree, gazed at her with old, shadowed eyes. No smile. No welcome. Not wanting to deal with the stares or total avoidance any longer, she headed back to her area.

Raine was busy sanding a long, narrow shaft that would soon turn into an arrow. He had a pile of the sticks at his side with only one shaft done. Jezamina decided to help. She grabbed a pile of the sand near his foot and picked up one of the fresh cut, debarked sticks.

"Raine, am I a prisoner here, with Jezero?" She rubbed the sand against the wood.

"Why would ye say that?" He stopped sanding. The question seemed to take him by surprise.

"I guess I don't see myself as being free."

"Odd way to look at it."

"Well, think for a minute. You're here to protect me. I can't roam about. I'm frightened the Morlorns will find me, even though I never met one. No one from the village is talking to me." She let the sand fall through her fingers.

"I talk to ye."

"You and few others," she said, disheartened. "I guess I don't feel like I belong."

"Ye will. Ye need patience. Yer purpose here will come."

"What is yours?"

"My wisdom of medicines. I can cook. I can find my way through the stone dwelling, the place where Vyrone lives. I knew about the cave we kept ye in, after finding ye in the sea. I found it when escaping the Morlorns. My knowledge has helped others."

"What is Jezero's purpose?"

"He is a protector. He will fight to help those who are in need."

His voice was solid and committed to his doyen, the one who saved him from the Morlorns. Was her purpose the same? To follow and help Jezero?

She asked, "What do you think mine is? Why am I here without a memory?"

Raine made a noise under his breath. He lowered his head and started sanding the stick again. Avoidance, similar to Veita the other day. This made her even more curious. "What does it come down to, Raine? A few simple words? Is my purpose to help you? Jezero?"

"I can't answer yer question."

"Because you don't know the answer or because you can't tell me?

A high-pitched laugh echoed across the late afternoon. It came from the area near the main fire as people gathered to eat. Jezamina straightened, holding her head higher to see above the tall grass. Of course it was Leota. She stood with an injured, younger man, her hand on his shoulder. Whatever he had said made her laugh, even snort. She seemed to be flirting with him.

"Who is this Leota?" She returned to sanding the shaft. "Tell me about her."

"We don't talk about her."

"Was she found in the sea as well?"

"No, not in the sea." Raine got up to stretch. He placed his finished stick to the side.

"How did Jezero meet her?"

Raine leaned over so his head ballooned in front of her. Steam left his nose like an animal snorting. "Like I said, we don't talk about her."

Jezamina raised her hands to hold him back. "Okay. Okay. I get it."

The next morning, she woke with puffy eyes after a restless night. She was sure a Morlorn lurked in the woods. The villagers' noise near the center fire made her jump at times when they became too loud. She also listened to Raine snore. Jezero wouldn't be too happy if he knew her protector was out cold. She didn't care. Raine needed the sleep. Later when he woke, he seemed refreshed, with less darkness under his eyes, as he prepared their morning meal.

The medicine man tapped on the large gourd used for water. The stew in the pot over the fire was ready to boil. He couldn't leave.

"Do you need water?" she asked after putting their beds away. "I need to freshen up. I can get water at the well."

"Ye stay by the villagers. Ye don't be alone."

"I will," she said and then sighed. She couldn't help but mumble, "Here's to freedom."

Raine snorted. He wasn't too pleased with her remark. *Oh, well.*

Jezamina took the gourd and made her way to the lake. Three middle-aged women were wading in knee-deep water while washing their clothes. A young mother bathed her two children. All turned their backs to her. They moved further away—subtle but noticeable.

Another woman appeared from behind the tall grass growing near the shore. She had beautiful long, black hair that shined in the sun, and she seemed to be around the same age as Jezamina.

"Good morning," Jezamina said and waded into the cool water.

The woman's brownish-gray eyes turned large. She brought her hands up to her chest as if protecting herself and then glanced over to the women washing their clothes. No one noticed the exchange.

Jezamina's heart dropped when the woman walked away. What made her think this one would be any different? No one wanted to be near her.

She washed her face and fixed her hair, pulling it into a loose braid. Again, after collecting water for Raine, she would seek out Veita, spend time with her, and then help Raine. Maybe today she'd also practice using her slingshot. So much excitement, she thought, rolling her eyes. Her spirits fell.

"Jezamina." The voice was silky and unlike the dialect spoken in the village.

Leota had sneaked up on her.

She stood and turned. They eyed each other. Jezamina admired the woman's porcelain skin, and her full, soft lips. Her eyes were dark and soulful, like someone who had survived a rough life. She was beautiful yet venomous.

"Leota."

The woman raised her eyes, seeming impressed. "You know who I am. Jezero must have told you."

"No, I learned from Veita."

Leota laughed. "Of course. The medicine woman."

Jezamina wasn't sure how to respond. She remembered the warning to stay away from her, given by both Raine and the medicine woman.

"I'm sure she has you fooled." Leota nodded as if validating her statement.

"How do you mean?" The question came out before she could stop it. Jezamina should have excused herself, but she was drawn in by Leota's demeanor. What secrets did the woman keep under her sleeve?

Leota smiled like an animal pacing around its prey. "Nobody warns you or tells you the reason why you are here or why they want you to leave. In time, you will learn to live with it."

"As you learned to do?"

"Yes." She stepped closer and her chin went up. "I survived. I *know* what I want."

A chill ran up Jezamina's arms, knowing she meant Jezero. Leota's eyes hardened as if she wouldn't think twice about taking her down if she got in the way.

"Jezamina," Veita called from the path. She picked up her skirt and watched her steps as she came down the bank. The medicine woman seemed frazzled for early morning.

"Ahh...Veita to the rescue," Leota said. "How convenient."

"There was a time when you needed my help as well," Veita said, as if reminding her.

"Which I am grateful for."

There was something deeper between the two women. Neither shared any kind of love for the other.

Veita turned to Jezamina. "I need your assistance today. I'm running out of pain medicine for those burned in the attack."

"Of course. What would you like me to do?" She picked up the gourd for the water.

"We need to make the salve," she said and motioned for her to follow as if trying to get the two of them away from Leota. "We can then coat the bandages with it and redress those with infection."

"They will let her help?" Leota seemed surprised.

Veita scowled. "Why wouldn't they?"

As fast as the words came out, the medicine woman seemed to regret saying them.

Leota's expression changed as if those words had opened the door she was waiting for. "Why, Veita, you should know the reason better than I. It was your village that was attacked. Your village received the message."

The medicine woman cried out in protest. She covered her mouth. Leota had struck a victory.

"What message?" Jezamina asked.

The medicine woman glared at Leota.

"They didn't tell you?" Leota asked. She waited for the medicine woman to respond.

"Enough." Veita's tone was sharp. "The Morlorns attack at random. This was no different."

Jezamina's world became still. She recalled the words she heard in passing. The little hints, the secret looks. She remembered the time before they left Dusken when Aresen began to say something about the message. Jezero cut him short.

Realization hit. The attack on the village was her fault.

She swayed when her body began to shake. She couldn't breathe.

"Child..." Veita grabbed her by the arm to keep her steady.

Jezamina wanted to hear it from the medicine woman. She demanded to know. "What was the message?"

Chapter 25

::: Jezamina :::

Parnell's Village

Jezero sensed the prevailing mood in the air long before entering the village. The men still hunted with Parnell in charge, but Jezero and his men were close enough to return and check on the safety of the village. He found Veita, Leota, and Jezamina at the water—instant trouble in his mind. Only one seemed to be enjoying herself. The other two were visibly upset. He took in a deep breath. Let the battle begin.

Jezamina's anger flared when she spotted him. She climbed up the bank with the water gourd tight in her fist. He noted the weapon as she stomped toward him. The diamond in her right ear sparkled, causing a few gasps from the women standing nearby. Jezamina normally kept them hidden, annoyed with Raine for always staring at them.

Like the villagers, who now listened in, Aresen and Zarac stayed back to let Jezero face Jezamina on his own. He started to ask what was wrong, but she cut him off.

"Don't you fucking talk to me, you bastard, unless you're ready to tell me the truth."

Jezero glared at Leota, wondering what she'd said. The woman raised her eyebrows, shrugged her shoulders, and then walked off into the woods. Veita rubbed her hands together. Tears welled from her eyes. She shook her head toward him, but he wasn't sure what she meant by it.

"You fucking prick. You lied to me." Jezamina's cheeks burned red. Her nostrils flared as she pointed the gourd at his chest.

"What do you mean I lied to you?" He grabbed her wrist to keep her from hitting him with the gourd. He took it away from her and then tossed it to Zarac for safekeeping.

"What was the message?"

Jezero stayed calm in hopes of inspiring the same in her. "How did I lie to you?"

"You didn't tell me that I'm the reason for the attack." She choked on the words. Tears welled in her eyes. She twisted her hand out of his grip.

"I didn't lie. I protected you by not telling you." He didn't like seeing her so angry, but he couldn't let it affect him. He made the right decision.

"You think you were protecting me?" Jezamina's voice rose. Her hand shook when it came up to wipe away the tears from her cheeks. "Do you know what it's like to be rejected before you're even given a chance and not understand why?"

He tried placing his hands on her shoulders to calm her down. He needed to reason with her and quickly before causing more of a distraction with the villagers. The Morlorns could be hiding and waiting for the perfect moment. Jezamina jerked away.

Her voice turned cold—done with the nonsense. "What was the message?"

Jezero contemplated what to tell her. The truth? Partial truth? His hesitancy made matters worse. Jezero gave in. If it didn't come from him, she would learn from others. No doubt, Leota would be glad to tell her all she could. And then some. "Vyrone is claiming you as his possession. We found you on his land. According to him, you are his property."

"Is this true?" Jezamina turned to Aresen, who was still within listening distance of their conversation.

She caught him off guard. He stepped closer, holding his bow to his chest as if it would protect him. He glanced to his doyen for a sign on what to do or say. Jezero nodded. Aresen turned to Jezamina. "He speaks the truth."

She swayed, trying to compose herself. Again, she continued in her hard voice. "Did Vyrone come to claim me?"

"He sent his men."

Jezamina turned pale. She looked away. Jezero cringed. Her chest heaved with burden. He decided to explain before her imagination took over. "The Morlorns knew I would leave Dusken to help the villagers once attacked."

She swallowed hard. Her stance weakened. Jezamina rubbed her forehead, clearly upset. "They were attacked because of me."

"Ye're not at fault." Aresen tried to help.

She shook her head. To Jezero, she said, "The Morlorns know I'm here."

"Aye."

She stepped to the right and then to the left, unsure where to go—shock overtook her.

He wanted to rush in and hold her but he refrained.

Jezamina stuttered. "What will happen to the village, with me being here?"

"I can't say," he answered, not knowing.

"Will the Morlorns attack this one too?" She seemed calmer.

"There's a possibility."

"That's the reason you're preparing the village," Jezamina said more to herself. She turned to walk away.

"They will not take you."

She stopped. Her eyes glazed with new tears. "Do you think I care about myself?"

***

Jezamina sat in the tall grass, away from the village and away from their area. She knew Raine stood nearby, but at least he respected her need to be alone. The thought of her being the cause of the attack to Veita's village made her sick to her stomach. She would welcome a knife to her back, an arrow to her heart—anything to rid herself of this guilt.

She thought of Johan and his cold stare when they first met. He had every reason to hate her. Every reason. A long sob rolled from deep inside her. Jezamina covered her face with her hands as she sat with her legs folded beneath her and leaned forward. She cried for Johan, for Veita. For those who lost their lives and their homes. Every part of her shook. How could she face the villagers again? Everyone glared at her with hatred, and for good reason.

Jezamina couldn't catch her breath. She gasped for air and an arm reached out for her. She jerked away.

"Child." Veita tried soothing her. She sat next to her and held her, not letting Jezamina push her away. "This isn't your fault."

"Yes, it is." Jezamina stared at the grass. The blades rose higher than her head. "Your village died because of me."

"Vyrone ordered his men to attack our village, wanting Jezero out of Dusken."

"Because I lived there."

Veita stayed quiet.

Jezamina took her silence as acknowledgement. She wiped her eyes. "I don't get why he wants me. What good would I do for him?"

"You come from a different place. The fire in your ears brings mystery."

Why would her earrings be of importance? The women in the village wore skirts and tunics with different designs sewn into their clothing. She couldn't recall anything around their necks or in their ears. She still didn't understand. "They are only diamonds."

"Remember Raine's reaction?"

"Of course." He was the reason she covered her ears; his continual fascination with them annoyed her.

"He sees the fire, the life in them."

"Some life." Jezamina let out a puff of air. She'd tried taking the earrings off at one point, but learned they were locked. "If it's the diamonds he wants, Vyrone can have them."

"You are who he wants."

There was only one logical answer. "I must find him and end this now."

Veita gasped. Her eyebrows knitted together. She scolded her. "Don't you ever think that way, child."

"I am not worth the attacks, all the lives lost." Jezamina rubbed her temples. Her head throbbed from her forehead to the back of her neck. She couldn't see straight.

"You cannot let Vyrone win," the medicine woman said between clenched teeth. "He cannot be allowed to think that he has more power by taking you. Our lives would be worse. He will continue attacking the villages." She grabbed Jezamina's chin and turned her until they made eye contact. "Promise me, child. Promise me you won't go to him."

"You have lost so much," Jezamina said and began to cry again.

Veita pulled her forward until her head rested on Veita's lap. She stroked Jezamina's hair. "So have you, my child. So have you."

***

Jezero had wanted to follow Jezamina. Veita stopped him. Let her handle the mess. He tried putting up a front. Damn Jezamina for getting under his skin.

He took his meal near the fire. They would head out again to take advantage of the day. This time, he let his mood direct the hunt.

Jezero and his men stayed out in the woods for two additional days. They found a place on high ground where a herd of walatos wandered in the open; plenty of meat to last the village for a season. Jezero kept the men moving. He orchestrated their hunt, circling the animals and then having those with bows and arrows strike at once. The chaos of animals and men mixed together as the non-hunters moved in to haul away the dead animals ready for slaughter. The work was hard. Jezero had little time to think of Jezamina until nightfall when he made his bed and watched the stars sparkle like her diamonds.

Jezamina had every right to be upset at him. He hoped she didn't get any ideas about becoming a hero. She would not survive Vyrone. If she thought her life was miserable now, she would take her own life if she were ever in Vyrone's control. During his time in the dungeons, Jezero had contemplated the same notion many times over.

Veita's words popped into his head. *Give her a reason to stay.*

What the hell did she want him to do?

Chapter 26

::: Jezamina :::

Parnell's Village

With their hunt a success, Jezero left the men early, knowing they could skin the hides and prepare the meat. The women in the village would soon join them. With sweat and the smell of the hunt on his skin, Jezero shed his clothes and cleansed himself in the lake. He vigorously scrubbed, wanting to be refreshed and clean before finding Jezamina.

"Jezero!" Veita scurried down the path from the village. She wrung her hands.

A pit opened in his stomach. He wiped the water from his face. He took a quick dip to rinse off the remaining soap and then headed to shore. Jezero assumed Leota was up to her antics again. Veita held up the new pair of leggings he left hanging on a plant.

"Jezamina's gone."

"What?" Jezero came out of the water and grabbed his leggings. "When?"

She grabbed his tunic, ready to hand it to him. "She was sleeping the last time we saw her. Raine is out looking for her now."

He tied his leggings. His stomach balled into a hard knot. He pulled his tunic over his head. The first step was to figure out when she left. The Morlorns might be involved in her disappearance. So could someone else. "Where's Leota?"

"She is in her shay." The medicine woman couldn't keep up. Jezero stopped and helped her up the bank.

"Any signs Jezamina was taken?" Jezero grabbed his gear and headed down the path toward their area. He covered his mouth with his hands and made the call to his men. All his senses were on fire. "What happened while I was gone?"

Veita relayed the conversation she had with Jezamina in the field. "But she promised she wouldn't leave." The medicine woman wiped the sweat from her forehead with her arm. "I should've made her stay with me."

"This isn't your fault."

They headed to their area.

"Last night, I checked on her. She was asleep in her bed," Veita said.

The furs were still on the ground, smoothed out. Raine may have grown suspicious if she had rolled up her bed and put it away. The grass around their area, toward the woods, showed no signs of foul play. The Morlorns weren't swift or careful and would have left evidence. Nothing seemed to be out of place.

Aresen and Zarac arrived. Zarac positioned himself, ready with bow and arrow. Aresen hung on to his fighting knife with a tight fist. Judging by their hard, angered faces, they'd heard she was missing.

"No sign of the Morlorns near the village," Zarac reported.

"Her footprints start here." Jezero found the spot where she headed into the woods.

"She left on her own." Raine appeared. The men eased their weapons and turned their attention to the ground, searching for additional clues.

"Jezamina has her slingshot." Aresen dug around near her belongings. "I guess it's a good sign."

"She doesn't know how to survive on her own," Zarac snapped, which startled them. "She's had almost a full day to travel."

"I'm guessing she's headed back to Dusken," Aresen said, "the only safe place she knows."

Jezero agreed. He turned to Raine. "Did you check the path we took to get here?"

"Aye." He nodded. "No sign, but then it's been traveled well."

"From what I can tell," Aresen called out from the tree line, "she cut through the woods from here." He continued to move the ferns aside. "She took this path out." He pointed to the one going around the outskirts of the village.

Distant thunder rolled through the sky. The hint of rain blew in with the breeze. Jezero cursed. Her trail would be lost once the storm hit.

"What were her last words to you?" he asked Raine, trying for any type of clue.

"Ye be a fucking prick."

Jezero smirked. Aye, she was mad. Parnell and Johan walked toward their area.

"I've asked around the village," Parnell said. "No one saw her leave. Veita was the last to speak to her. They did remember the two together."

"Beforehand, one of the women witnessed Leota sharing words with her," Johan added.

Jezero paid attention. His blood boiled, ready to find her.

Raine stepped in to calm him. "That was before she'd been with ye by the water. Not after."

Jezero didn't care. The rage still burned in him.

"We'll divide the men," Parnell said. "We can cover each path."

"No," Jezero said flatly. "My men will search. Your men need to stay here. The Morlorns will take advantage of both situations. We can't leave the village unprotected."

"Very well." Parnell grunted. He seemed disappointed at having to stay behind. No doubt he wanted to be the one saving her.

"Johan," Jezero called out when the two men started back to the center area.

The men stopped.

"You found Jezamina guilty of a crime she did not commit. She was called to me. And for that, we need to protect her. Do I make myself clear?"

Johan took a step forward. The muscles in his neck tightened. "My village is mourning. They suffer because of her."

Jezero's hand clenched. His nostrils flared as he controlled his emotions. One blow with his fist would knock the man out. But this was Savel's son. He would refrain.

Johan moved another step forward as if ready for a challenge. Parnell slapped his hand across the young man's chest. "This is my village." He turned to Jezero. "I will make sure she is welcome."

Jezero nodded to Parnell. His people were guilty as well. The doyen would fulfill his promise. He pointed to Johan and said distinctly, "You have no village."

"One day," he said, "one day I will."

Precious time was lost. Jezero turned back to his men. They headed into the woods with their quivers full of arrows and their bows in hand.

"We won't have long before the rain falls," Raine said and sniffed the air as they left the village.

"Think she'll stop for the night?" Aresen asked. He eyed the two paths now forcing them to choose a route. "She learned to hide herself while we were travelling here."

"The rain will stop her," Jezero said and thought about her incident at the ledge when she tried walking to the fire pit. "She has experienced what it's like to be in wet clothes, to be soaked and cold."

Raine checked their surplus. "She didn't take any supplies with her, only a small amount of food."

One path led them deeper into the woods toward Savel's burned village, and the shorter distance to Dusken. The other followed the river. She had good reason to choose either route. He tried thinking in her head. Jezamina would consider following their steps to get here. If she found the remains of the village, she'd be on the right path. She also knew the river would take her back as well. If she recognized the spot where Raine found the queeno, she could then find her way to the ledge.

"Aresen and Zarac, take the path to Savel's village. Try to find signs of her trail before the rain starts. Raine, stay in this vicinity. She may be near or circle back. I will take the river."

"Aye," the men said in unison.

Jezero zigzagged through the trees and ferns, checking the hidden spots between the rocks jutting out from the earth. He searched under bushes, and for divots under fallen trees.

The forest turned quiet, the air heavy. The animals sensed the rain and had already found their shelters, a sign the storm would come before nightfall.

He made it to the river as the rain started. He doubted if she would cross, knowing the Morlorns lived on the other side. Jezero kept to the path. Even for him, it was too dangerous to continue when the forest turned dark and the territory unfamiliar. He found a tree with a thick trunk and low limbs—perfect for a nighttime perch.

The bark was smooth and slick. Twice he slid down, unable to get a firm grip on the first limb. Jezero tried a different approach, jumping up to grab another limb and then swinging over to the one he wanted to straddle. Making it to the alcove between limb and trunk, he kept his legs up and rested his back against the trunk. The spot would work, giving him a vantage point over the path. He would see if she returned or if a Morlorn passed by.

The storm moved through rather quickly, but the night grew cold. Jezero's patience wore thin as he sat, chilled from the rain. He couldn't sleep for fear of falling out of the tree.

Both Jezero and his men more than likely lost her trail. He hoped she found a place to hide. Raine taught her how to find food and medicine. If she didn't panic, she'd be fine until he had her safe in his hands again.

Jezero rubbed his face to stay awake. How long had it been since the rain stopped? The moon, buried within the clouds, offered no clue as to when the day would start.

He had been wrong to keep the message from her. Jezero growled under his breath in frustration, kicking himself for his stupidity. She had a right to know the danger.

A rustle of ferns brought him back. A brown-furred anole grazed on the flowers near the river. The morning light fanned across the horizon. Jezero shifted, letting his legs dangle from the branch as he stretched his back. The animal took a drink, dunking his head into the river, before wandering away.

Jezero's descent from the tree was less than graceful as he missed a foothold and fell to the ground. He scanned the area, hoping no one noticed. After brushing the dirt from his hands, he bent down to pick up the satchel that had fallen from his shoulder.

As he came up, he spotted the green shell of one of the common nuts near the base of the tree. He found another. Jezamina liked to eat the fleshy inside of the plant but not the bitter outside. Few people discarded the shell. She had been there! Right under his perch.

The forest otherwise seemed in order. The rain left on the ferns and trees sparkled as the sun came up. The smaller animals scuttled about as they started their search for food. The birds began to chirp.

He rubbed the ends of the shell to determine how long ago she'd been there. The outer rim was tougher than the inside. They weren't fresh but neither were they dry.

Jezero resumed his search, following the narrow path near the river. He wanted to call out to her in case she was hiding, but the likelihood of her responding changed his mind, and he didn't need the Morlorns catching on.

The day moved on with no other trace of her. He guessed she followed the river. The rain would've erased any trail from the day before. He searched for fresh tracks.

Jezero walked the long stretch before the river turned again. When he stopped to drink from his flask, his stomach growled, and he realized he hadn't eaten since the night before. He was about to pull a slice of dried meat from his bag when a snapped branch caught his eye. Looking closer, he found a fresh-made footprint stamped into the wet ground. Next to it was another footprint with three distinct holes punched into the ground. Footwear the Morlorns wore when walking long distances.

The Morlorn moved fast, his heel mark lighter than the rest of the print. Jezero found the next step, heading down the bank to the edge of the water. Where the river turned shallow, two more sets of footprints met with the other pair. A small distance down, the footprints made their way up the bank again to the path.

Jezero's jaw hardened. He grabbed an arrow from the quiver and placed it on the rest of his bow. The tracks seemed rushed as if chasing something or someone. He followed their path, staying low yet keeping a steady, quick pace. The tracks stopped. Some of the footsteps slid to the side as if hiding. Still, no sign.

If they were on her trail, they would wait for the right moment to take her. They would use her as a shield if he tried saving her. Jezero raised his head to the sky and listened for the birds. One, in the distance, seemed distressed. A sign he could be close.

Jezero continued, staying on the path with the dense forest to the left and the flowing water to his right. If he remembered correctly, the river would soon turn shallow and narrow—a perfect time to capture Jezamina and drag her across to safer ground. He could only hope they hadn't yet.

The river turned and the rocks became jagged. A few rapids could make the crossing difficult. A reflection of light caught his attention. Jezero ducked down and surveyed the bank where the water turned again. The shine came from a Morlorn's shield and bounced as the man started running.

Jezamina's cry rang through the air. The birds squawked and flew to safety. Jezero's arms and legs prickled. The Morlorns found her.

Jezero raced down the path. His feet barely touched the ground. The Morlorns were a distance away, but still on the same side of the river. He got to the point where they found her. The dirt was scuffed with footprints, including hers. She must have run.

A Morlorn yelled out. Jezero stopped and ducked into the woods. He pinpointed their direction and inched forward.

"We got 'er, Dode." One of them laughed in victory. "We found our prize!"

Jezero darted between the trees to get closer.

The one named Dode removed a knife from the sheath attached to his leggings. He pointed the tip at Jezamina's face and sauntered toward her. She was pinned by another, stockier Morlorn who locked her arms behind her. She struggled to get away, but he jerked her back to keep her in line.

Dode stepped closer and pointed the knife under her chin. Jezamina raised her head in defiance. Her chest heaved as she waited for the blade to pierce her skin. Her nose flared, part in anger and part nerves. Jezero knew her signs. Hold still, he thought. The enemy wouldn't think twice about slitting her throat if she angered them, even if it were against Vyrone's wish.

Jezamina looked toward the river and then back at the Morlorn. The third Morlorn, off to the side, sneered. He said something to Jezamina, and her eyes grew larger. She eyed the river again as if searching for an escape route.

"Don't do it," Jezero said under his breath. The current was too strong for her to handle. The rocks would cause her to slip if she tried running in the water.

He kept one ear trained on the woods. The three Morlorns seemed to be alone. Jezero raised his bow and closed one eye. His fingers curled around the string, and he pulled back to aim.

The arrow sliced the air, straight toward Dode's back. Before the tip pierced his heart, the second arrow was loaded and released. The third Morlorn went down with a thud. Jezamina cried out as the arrow he held in his hand came up and grazed her chin. The Morlorn holding her turned to see what happened. It was enough for Jezero to aim at his head.

Jezamina pushed away from her captor. He held her tight, until she slammed her foot into his shin. Free, she ran for shelter behind a tree. She took the sleeve of her tunic and began rubbing her chin.

Good girl. She remembered Aresen telling her about poisoned arrows.

Jezero stepped away from his hiding place. Two of the Morlorns were dead. The third gurgled as he tried pulling the arrow from his neck. Jezero put him out of his misery. In one fluid motion, he took his knife out of its sheath and slit the man's throat.

A choked cry came from behind the trees. Jezamina paled with horror when she witnessed his action. She grabbed a stick from the ground and raised it up as if to hit him. She was in shock and trembled as if he would attack and do the same to her.

"Jezamina." He cleaned off his knife on the Morlorn's shirt and put it back. He raised his hands to show he wasn't going to hurt her as he slowly stepped closer. "It's all right. You're safe."

Jezero grabbed her. She fought, but he managed to walk her down the path, away from the Morlorns. When they reached a comfortable distance, he stopped and pushed her hair away from her face.

"Jezamina." He shook her chin to get her to refocus. Her entire body trembled as she gasped for breath. "Listen to me. You're safe."

He covered both sides of her face with his hands and gently slapped her cheeks.

***

Jezamina's head swirled as if she were drowning in a body of water. The last two days paralyzed her.

Within a short time, she had realized her mistake in leaving in such a rush. The forest was larger, scarier than she'd thought. She hid under a cluster of rocks as night fell. Raine passed her twice, and she bit her lip to keep from calling out. Guilt crushed her, knowing he trusted her. But what could she do? Going back to the village wasn't an option.

She wanted to return to Dusken. Start over. Live in seclusion. But her plan failed. Without the security of Jezero or his men, she lost her courage. Every sound made her jump. She imagined seeing faces behind trees, an arm, or a leg pass by a tree.

The Morlorns. They found her.

She jerked her head up. Someone called her name. Jezero? She became focused, back to the present.

"Jezamina!"

He held her close until she looked him in the eye. He placed a finger over his lips.

"I had no rocks," she whimpered. She couldn't protect herself when the Morlorns grabbed her.

"What are you talking about?"

"My slingshot. They were too close. I didn't have a chance..."

Jezero held her and kissed her forehead. "Your slingshot wouldn't have done any good. Come back to me. You're in shock."

Her blue eyes widened. His words triggered her to shake out of it. She remembered the Morlorns. "Is it over?"

"Aye. You're safe."

Jezamina shuddered. The surprise in the Morlorn's eyes when the arrow pierced him stayed with her. The sound of the knife coming out of the sheath and slitting the other Morlorn's throat rang in her ears. She wanted to believe Jezero hadn't killed the men, but he was a warrior. His job was to protect, no matter the cost. He saved her life.

Jezero picked her up and carried her down the path. Jezamina rested her head on his shoulder, feeling safe again. She replayed her capture. How one of the Morlorns stepped from behind a tree and blocked her path. The other two surrounded her. The beady eyes and nasty smiles would forever play in her head.

She wasn't a prize. There wasn't any reason for them to want her.

The message.

Jezamina wanted down. When Jezero didn't take the hint she pushed against his chest and said, "I can walk."

He wouldn't let go. She twisted her legs until he had no choice. The reason she was in this position stood in front of her. Her anger rose. He should've told her why Veita's village was attacked. And now she worried about the goddamn arrow piercing her chin.

Her hand shook when she reached out and tore a small leaf off one of the ferns. She checked her chin. The bleeding had stopped. No bubbling or discoloration wiped off on the leaf—all good signs. Her skin wasn't being eaten away. She let the leaf fall to the ground.

Jezamina glared at Jezero before walking away from him. If he'd only told the truth.

"Listen," he said. "You can't—"

"You!" She spun around and hammered her hands into his chest.

Jezero, caught off guard, tripped. He grabbed her forearms and wouldn't let go when she tried to hit him again.

"Let go of me," she cried out.

"Jezamina..." He squeezed tighter as if scolding her behavior.

What an asshole. She hit him full force with her weight, determined to take him down.

Jezero fell backward and hit the ground. She landed on top of him and felt the *whoomf* of air leave his lungs. She hit his chest, his arms, and his sides with all her strength. He wrestled with her, coughing to catch his breath, yet trying to pin her down. They tumbled off the path and rolled down a hill covered with ferns.

Jezamina didn't stop. All the frustration, anger, and hurt came out. She pounded him. He tried calming her down. When it didn't work, he flipped her on her back. She yelped when his weight came down on her.

"Enough," he said between gritted teeth.

"I am not done," she said and tried bucking him off her. "Let go of me."

"Shhh!" Jezero cupped his hand over her mouth.

She tried biting him, but he squeezed harder so her lips puckered.

"We'll both be dead if you don't stop." His words were precise and hard.

She understood. Jezamina stopped moving. For a moment, only their breathing joined the chirping of birds overhead.

"Are you going to be quiet?" He spoke the words as if soothing her with a lullaby. She nodded and he removed his hand from her mouth. "I know you have your reasons to be angry with me."

"Angry?" Jezamina said a little too loudly. He threatened to cover her mouth again. She created a whispered shout. "Most of the villagers are dead because of me. You hid it from me."

She squirmed to get away from him. Jezero applied more pressure against her, the length of his body weighted against hers. Her lungs fought for air. She wheezed in noisy gasps while pushing up on his chest for relief. He moved slightly to allow her to breathe.

"Would you have come with me if I'd told you in Dusken?" He didn't wait for her to answer. "The Morlorns are out to find you,

Jezamina. I couldn't risk an argument or having to force you to come with us. We would have all been in danger."

"They still found me," she snapped.

"Your own fault. You left."

Point taken.

Jezamina lost the energy to fight. She lacked sleep. She learned the forest carried evil along with good.

"You win." She wanted to go back to the village. If they hated her, she would put up with it.

"This isn't about winning," he said. "I don't want you hurt."

"It's too late for that."

"Then let me make it up to you." The tone of his voice changed. He stared into her eyes as if wanting her to know life had changed. His breathing was shorter, yet controlled. "Almost losing you got in my way. You are what I live for now."

Jezamina melted. The forest went away. It was only the two of them, lying in a bed of ferns. Jezero cradled her head in his hands as the intensity in his eyes progressed to desire. Her heart fluttered as his lips moved closer to hers. The depth in his eyes changed. She moved slightly to connect with the hardness in his leggings.

Jezero's lips found the soft curve of her neck. The thrill of his touch sent shivers of delight throughout her body and awakened her tired mind. He kissed her jaw and moved upward. If she let him continue, her life would turn into his life. She would have reason to stay, her unknown past left behind.

Jezamina waited for the pull, the one telling her to stop. The reminder she had someone waiting for her. Jezero's kisses made her forget. She didn't fight when he placed his hand on her chin and covered her in a long, tantalizing kiss. Her hips rose, wanting him.

Jezero slid his hand underneath her tunic. She moaned as his fingers played with her nipple, turning it hard. She moved her hand down to his tunic and then came up underneath. Hard, solid muscle greeted her. He untied his leggings with his other hand. She helped pull them down until her hand cupped the treasure between his legs. His breath turned ragged while his hands rushed to undress her.

Jezamina's head swam. She stroked his desire and allowed all her senses to focus on him. Gone were the Morlorns. Gone was her fear of being alone. Gone was the guilt of creating havoc. The moment carried her away.

Lust and longing took over as he caressed the soft patch between her legs. She helped guide him inside her. Jezamina's breathing turned to short pants as he kissed her open mouth, her nose, her forehead. Their bodies aligned together, their legs tangled in a dance. Jezero rocked her, allowing the rhythm of their bodies to build his desire until he exploded. He cried out as he came and buried his head into her shoulder to muffle the sound.

Recovering, Jezero rocked again. He cupped her ass, pulling upward and staying with the motion. She moved her hips in tune with his. He covered her mouth with his hand when she started to groan. This time she didn't care. The rush of desire spread between her legs and spilled over like the world had just turned upside down. The release left her intoxicated. She couldn't move. The sounds of nature took over as they enjoyed their closeness, confirming their chemistry.

After a time, Jezero caressed her face with the back of his hand, having recovered first. She purred to his touch. The tenderness in his face and the warmth wasn't something she saw very often. He smiled and kissed her.

Someone shouted.

Jezamina, still caught in the pleasure of their lovemaking, didn't recognize it as a voice. Jezero's body tensed and he rolled them under the bushes, keeping her close to his side. He raised his head, focused on the path above them. When the voice shouted again, she paid attention. The person seemed closer than before.

She mouthed, "Is it a Morlorn?"

Jezero nodded.

Jezamina's fear erased the remaining pleasurable moments she had with Jezero. She tried sitting up, but he held her down and placed his finger over her mouth.

She listened as he did. The birds turned quiet. The wind picked up. They waited. Jezamina closed her eyes but opened them again when Jezero slid off her.

The rustling of leaves and the shuffling of footsteps grew louder.

She grabbed Jezero's leggings and held them up to her chest, as if they'd protect her. Jezero reached over her to find his bow but only found air. He searched for his quiver—also missing. He cursed under his breath.

Jezamina traced where they had fallen down the hill. She spotted the quiver, now empty as the arrows had spilled out. She nudged his shoulder and pointed. If the sun hit right, the Morlorns would see the reflection of the shiny points. They searched for the bow. Jezero nodded toward the trampled ferns. The bow was wedged under the large green leaves.

He patted the ground between them and turned. He mouthed, "My leggings."

She scanned the area around them and found hers near their feet. His were missing. She shook her head, not able to find them. He glanced back.

Jezero scowled. He grabbed his leggings from her hand. Jezamina wrinkled her nose, embarrassed. She forgot she held them like a security blanket.

He searched and found the knife strapped to his leg. He removed it from the sheaf and held the blade behind him. She assumed he did it to keep the sun from reflecting against the metal. How easily the weapon could slice her skin. Her breast hung close to the sharp edge. She inched back, but Jezero grabbed her hip to hold her still.

The top of a Morlorn's helmet came into view. Jezamina held her breath. The man stepped closer to the edge of the hill with his back toward Jezero. In his hand, the Morlorn held a large club with sharp points lining the middle. He seemed young and inexperienced by the way he rested the weapon against his leg as he adjusted his helmet. No matter the age, he was still dangerous. If he turned his head slightly, he'd see the trampled ferns.

Sweat beaded on Jezero's forehead. He lay naked, like her, under the ferns. One little noise could be their downfall. They weren't in a position to fight.

Why was the Morlorn standing there?

Jezamina didn't dare move. Jezero kept still, like an animal watching its prey. His hand clenched the handle of his knife, the point touching his back.

The Morlorn grabbed his club when it fell off his leg. He looked up and down the path to make sure no one had witnessed his clumsiness. Another Morlorn shouted, louder and higher pitched. They had found the bodies. The younger one ran off toward the shouting.

Jezero went into action. He rolled out from under the brush, pulled up his leggings, and grabbed his bow. He motioned for her to stay hidden, while he crouched to retrieve his arrows and quiver. She watched as he effortlessly maneuvered his way up the hill without a sound.

Chapter 27

::: Jessie :::

Chicago, IL

"You're not listening," Jessie said in a sharp tone, causing Walt to jerk back.

"I am," he said matter-of-factly. He played the game. He listened as Sam told him to, and it took every piece of his willpower to stay in control. What did she want him to do? Rant and rave about her making love to a figment of her imagination? He had to think the guy was himself, only in a different body. To listen to her speak so passionately about Jezero, when Jessie forgot *he,* her damn fiancé, was in the room.

She crossed her arms in front of her. She shut down, and he didn't know what to do to change her reaction. The sad part was she ached for the guy in her dream. It stung.

Why did he promise Sam he'd get through her dream?

In truth, he said, "I'm just taking it all in. I find your story fascinating with all the details you're remembering. How the Morlorns had fur on their helmets, how the village looked and smelled when you found the burned remains. How the villagers made you feel. And you should be pissed at Jezero for not telling you." He paused to make it clear Jezero was the bad guy. "He lied to you."

She frowned. "He explained why. Vyrone has this venom about him." She waved her hands around as she tried explaining. "One of evil and danger combined. Very powerful but in the wrong way. I sensed the ugliness about him the first time we met."

"You met him?"

Jessie nodded. "I'll save that *story* for another day."

She took a long drink from her cup of water. She did seem tired.

Walt leaned in so his elbows rested on his thighs. He rubbed his hands together. "I will admit I hate when you talk about Jezero." He shook his head. He competed with a dream. "How could you give up? Forget that someone was waiting for you? That was me!"

Carol called out from the doorway. "You're still here?"

He glanced up at the clock—close to midnight. Dinner had come and gone. They had picked at the food, Jessie sharing with him as she told him how she learned about the message. Where did the time go?

"You need to leave, Mr. Arbol. Get some rest. Tomorrow's a big day. Jessie needs her sleep." She brushed her hands at him as if shooing him out.

Chapter 28

::: Jessie :::

Chicago, IL

Jessie's stomach churned as if a war battled inside her. She hated being the center of attention. Why couldn't her meeting with the kids be private?

Get used to it, she thought. The Arbols tended to get what they wanted. A press conference.

The pantsuit was hanging in the closet. Navy blue pants and jacket with a cream-colored blouse. Funny, no bra. Really? Not that she cared to wear one. It was ironic Helen would forget the basics, her sole focus on outward appearances. She asked Carol to call Walt to bring her a white bra. She wasn't ready to use electronics. Her cell phone stayed in her personal drawer near the bed. Besides, she was still irritated by Walt's reaction.

Walt seemed interested in Dusken until she mentioned her closeness to Jezero. When she did, he would sit back in his chair with his mouth twisted in a false smile. He nodded out of politeness. Where was the open-minded Walt she'd once known? She respected his feelings and didn't want to hurt him but not telling him would be worse.

Her grandpa always told her to tell the truth. Even if it meant suffering the consequences, the weight in her heart would become unbearable if she held it all in. What she did was wrong, falling for Jezero, and Walt needed to understand why she broke their promises to each other. Everything was so different in the other world. Jezero saved her.

Jessie waited until half an hour before the press conference to put her clothes on. The pants draped over her legs like a curtain. She could fit her hands between the fabric and her waist. Even the length was too long as she stepped back and almost tripped when the fabric caught under her foot. She wondered if Helen bought the oversized clothes on purpose. Would people be more sympathetic, seeing how much weight she'd dropped? How her clothes sagged? She waited for Carol and Walt before putting on her top. The nurse arrived first to unhook the IV line from the catheter attached to her arm.

"Why can't we get rid of this thing?" Jessie looked at the capped needle bandaged to her skin.

"Hospital policy," Carol said. "That thing makes sure you get enough fluids. You're a little low on potassium and iron."

Jessie rolled her eyes.

"Need help putting your top on?" she asked.

"I'll help her," Walt said as he walked in the room with a Victoria's Secret bag in hand.

"Holler if you need anything. I'll come back in a few minutes and hook you up again."

Jessie laid the blouse and jacket on the bed. Walt handed her the bra—white lace with underwire for support. She ran her hand across the satin fabric. She forgot how sexy it felt to wear one. She loved the leather tunic and halter top Zarac made. He had excellent tailoring skills, and the leather was soft, supple. But today she'd welcome something silky against her skin.

Walt excused himself to take a phone call. She put her arms through the straps and then reached around to latch the two hooks. Her shoulders were too stiff and sore to reach around. She still had issues from falling off the roof, which she vaguely remembered doing. Three tries and she managed to hook her bra together.

The heat got to her, and Jessie fanned herself. If she was hot now, she imagined the press conference room would be worse. She wanted to wait and cool off before she finished dressing, but time was running out.

She put the blouse on with the buttons in the front. She wiggled her shoulders. The shirt didn't feel right. Jessie unbuttoned the top button. The label stuck out. Nice. She had the blouse on backwards.

"Need some help?" Walt knocked on the doorframe before popping back into the room.

"Yes," she said with frustration. Jessie pulled her hair to the side. "Could you please?"

He chuckled.

"What?" She glanced over her shoulder.

"Let's fix your bra. You missed one hook and even the one that's hooked is wrong."

Jessie laughed at her attempt. "I guess I forgot how to dress myself. I put the blouse on backward as well."

Walt unlatched her bra, and she shivered from his touch. His hands stopped for a moment. She turned, thinking he was done.

"Hold on." He made her turn again and he hooked her bra.

"What's wrong? Am I okay?"

He scratched his head. "I don't remember the scars on your back. Your skin used to be smooth."

Jessie grew concerned by the expression on his face. She swept the back of her hand across the middle of her back. She had bumps or marks rippling her skin. Her face paled. She knew what they were but had to see for herself.

Walt followed her to the bathroom. She took the hand mirror off the cabinet. He pulled open the blouse and ran his fingers along the scars. "They look like...like lines going across. That's odd."

"No, it isn't." The jagged lines marked the pain she endured. She smiled inwardly and mimicked Raine's dialect. "Holy shit!"

"What is it?" Walt seemed as if he were almost afraid to ask.

She raised her chin. She never thought to check herself for evidence until now. Jessie found the tiny scar made by the arrow when the Morlorn captured her the first time. Small in size compared to Vyrone's wrath when he used the whip on her back. She flinched, remembering the pain she endured every time it struck. How her body jerked as the leather tore her skin. A cry escaped her lips.

"Jessie, talk to me," Walt pleaded.

"Please finish buttoning me." She leaned her stomach against the sink. Her blue eyes stared back at her in the mirror. Eyes full of experience, pain, hatred.

Walt quickly buttoned her blouse. He placed his hands on her shoulders. Through the mirror, he asked, "What are you remembering?"

"Vyrone." She swallowed hard. The palm of her hand pressed against her forehead as she closed her eyes. "I remember the grin, how his eyes glistened with pleasure when he raised the whip. He used his entire arm, striking me with all his strength."

"He whipped you?" The disbelief showed in his eyes. "Like a slave?"

"A prisoner."

Jessie left the bathroom. She massaged her shoulder as if the pain returned. How could she forget the searing burn. The warmth of her blood against her skin as it seeped from the wound.

"I've been there. The marks prove it."

"That can't be," Walt shook his head as he followed behind her. "Those scars could be from anything. You fell from the roof of the house. You could've been banged up or landed on something."

"On what?" she snapped. "You saw the lines crossing my back. *Really?*"

"I thought Jezeno...Jesero..." he gave up, "saved you from the Morlorns."

"He did. The first time."

Walt huffed in frustration. "I don't get what you mean."

Jessie's head went down. "There's more to my life, my story, with Jezero."

The marks on her back were from Vyrone. Veita's skill and medicines healed her. She was fitter and stronger than she had been before the fire. She knew how to use a slingshot. All signs telling her Jezero and his world existed.

Helen Arbol's timing was impeccable. Her heels clicked on the tile floor and stopped at the nurse's station. She greeted Carol with airy cheer.

"And so it begins," Jessie mumbled under her breath. She composed herself when Mrs. Arbol entered the room and gave her son a kiss on the cheek.

"Oh!" His mother clapped her hands once and pursed her lips. "We didn't make an appointment with the beautician." She wrinkled her nose as she moved in closer to Jessie. "You're sweating." She dug in her coat pocket. "Here, use this tissue." She handed it to her but continued to scrutinize her. "Can you put your hair in a bun or at least comb it?"

Jessie used the tissue to blot her upper lip. She handed it back to Helen and smiled. "Excuse me."

She went into the bathroom and styled her hair into a messy bun. She looked ridiculous. The pantsuit was too fancy for the press conference—not to mention too big.

"Makeup?" Mrs. Arbol raised her voice to ask. "Do you have any here? You're a little pale, which isn't good in the lights. Don't forget to put your jacket on."

"I'm fine." Jessie came out of the bathroom and put the jacket on. She buttoned it up.

"Where's Dad?" Walt asked, clearly needing a break from the two women.

"He's down in the meeting room where the conference will be held. He's talking to the doctor. Did you know they're old golfing buddies?"

"Yes, we've been told a few times," Walt said.

Carol walked in. "Everybody out. Give me five minutes alone with my patient."

"I have makeup in my purse." Helen Arbol rummaged through her Coach bag and came out empty-handed. "I must have forgotten it on the dresser. Your father—"

"She'll be fine." Walt cut her off and escorted his mother out of the room.

"One of the aides is getting a wheelchair," Carol said. "It should be here shortly."

"Can't I walk?" Jessie asked.

"Not while you're here as a patient." The nurse said and took her blood pressure. "Besides, we need a place to hold your IV."

Jessie closed her eyes as Carol put the cuff around her arm. She imagined Jezero's smile with his perfect white teeth. His deep brown eyes would sparkle when he returned to the ledge to see her waiting for him. He would walk over, lift her up, and embrace her in a full hug. The mix of his scent with the fresh air would make her swoon forward, ready when he leaned in for a long, passionate kiss. She would give anything to be with him again.

"A bit overwhelmed?" The nurse broke into her thoughts.

"That's an understatement." She wished she could confide in Carol, tell her about Jezero. The nurse would listen and get caught up in her story. She'd want to meet Jezero and his men—even Veita. She'd then call the psych ward.

Chapter 29

::: Jessie :::

Chicago, IL

"There you go, m'lady." Walt arrived with the wheelchair. "Your carriage waits."

Some carriage, Jessie thought. Jezero lived for danger. He was there to protect with no fear. And she? Having to ride in a wheelchair like a spineless hero.

So what went wrong? Why did she return? Why couldn't she stay in Dusken?

Carol unhooked the IV bag from the stand in her room. She reattached it to the steel rod protruding from the back of the wheelchair. She then attached the drip to Jessie again. "All set."

Walt wheeled Jessie to the elevator. They stayed silent as they rode down to the first floor—no discussion of Dusken, Jezero, Vyrone, or the scars. She could tell he was all about the press conference.

A crowd gathered in the room, waiting for her. Jessie's knuckles turned white as she squeezed her hands around the padded blue armrests. Walt leaned down and whispered in her ear. "Don't worry, you'll do fine."

"Do I have to do this?" Her mouth went dry.

"Yes."

The room turned quiet when he pushed her through the door. Eyes focused on her. Jessie took in a breath. Her heart raced. She was petrified of having to talk, of saying something she shouldn't. They looked at her—some with blank stares, some with sympathy, others with curiosity. She relived her parents' wake and being the little girl lost in a sea of people. Jessie drew in a deep breath.

The cameramen went to their posts in the back of the room and started filming. The photographers focused their cameras and waited for the right angle. Jessie held her head up as the flashes went off. She tried not to squint. Walt pushed her to the front and positioned her at the long table covered with a white tablecloth.

The first two rows of chairs were empty. The rest of the chairs held the curious. She thought she recognized the woman with long, chestnut hair from Arbol Publishing. Behind her sat a man with a slight pouch, drinking coffee. She wondered if she knew him.

A commotion outside the door had heads turning. Moments later, a group piled into the room, kids with their parents. They sat in the empty rows up front. Jessie recognized the redheaded boy. Aaron. He walked with a brace on his leg. She tilted her head and smiled at him. He blushed and smiled back. The cameras loved it. She recognized the other kids, the ones she saved from the fire. Now it made sense why the first rows were empty.

Dr. Maguire entered the room soon after the kids. He could've been the star of a television show with his golfer's tan, silver hair, and perfect smile. Out of all the doctors who flew in and out of her room, Jessie liked him the best. The doctor didn't probe her as much as the other doctors about when she woke and spoke others' names. If he mentioned Jezero or Dusken, she would change the subject. He knew she hid something but didn't push. He hugged her when he sat in the chair to her left.

Mr. and Mrs. Arbol sat in the chairs on the other side of Dr. Maguire. Walt took his place to her right. Jessie took a short, quick breath. The press conference was about to begin. She glanced over at Walt, thankful he sat next to her. He had his arm around her chair, not to be the loving fiancé everyone expected, but to support her, knowing she was scared shitless. *Don't screw up!*

Dr. Maguire leaned over and squeezed her hand, which still gripped the handle of her wheelchair. He smiled. "You'll do fine."

His reassurance offered little comfort against the people crowding into the room. More were coming in and they stood like sardines in the back and to the sides. Jessie let go of the wheelchair and put her hands on the table. Her palms sweated.

The room turned quiet.

Dr. Maguire introduced himself and then turned to Jessie. He didn't have to say anything, only smile. The crowd cheered and whistled.

Jessie blushed. Why would so many people want to see her? She thought of the village destroyed. How Jezero and his men helped the remaining survivors adjust to Parnell's village. They did not cheer him on. It wouldn't have been natural if they did.

She focused on the kids in the front seats. When the cheering quieted, she turned to Dr. Maguire. She wasn't ready to speak, nor did she have a clue what to say. A mere thank you wouldn't cut it, and she had no speech. Dr. Maguire had turned to Mr. Arbol, listening to whatever he was trying to say. *He was supposed to lead this damn thing*!

She turned to Walt and pleaded for him to start.

He cleared his throat. "Thank you for coming. Your presence today means a lot to my family and of course to Jessie." The people clapped. "This has been a long journey for us. For Jessie, for me, for the doctors and nurses..."

Walt explained their story from the beginning. How on the morning after their engagement party, she left the house to go for a run. How worried he became when she didn't return. The arrival of the police as he left the house to find her.

Jessie somewhat listened as he spoke. Her mind wandered to Jezero. Was she there in a coma with him taking care of her? Would she wake again to find him sitting next to her? Or was she still a prisoner? Vyrone's cry of rage filled her ears.

Pay attention.

Her eyes popped open to the glaring lights above them. She shifted in her chair.

When the questions turned to her, Jessie kept the answers short yet polite. She wouldn't embarrass Walt, not with all he'd been through. She still had feelings for him—maybe not the passionate kind, but the type made from respect.

The questions continued. How did she feel? Was she scared when she ran into the burning house? Some she answered. Some she couldn't. The details of the fire were too vague. Others she avoided.

Perspiration beaded on her forehead. The lights beaming down on her were ten times worse than the sun. The questions became more demanding.

"You lost your engagement ring in the fire. Was it found?"

The question tripped her. Jessie stammered, not knowing what to say. She didn't wear the ring in Dusken. She wasn't wearing it now, taking it off after she woke and placing it on the end table.

Walt cleared his throat before leaning forward to talk into the microphone. "I have it. My father and I searched the property the day after the fire. We found the ring in the grass where Jessie fell off the roof."

"You're not wearing it? Has the wedding been postponed?" Another reporter shouted from behind the cameras.

Jessie bit her lip. She didn't like the questions anymore. They were getting too personal. When she didn't respond, the reporter asked again. All ears tuned in as if waiting for some newsworthy dirt.

"Please." Walt came to her rescue. "Our first concern now is her health."

"Walt," the man with the slight pouch and coffee raised his hand. "You gave her rare diamond earrings the night of your engagement party. Were they from the same jeweler as her ring?"

Odd question, Jessie thought. She then saw the thick gold chain around his neck, the large diamond ring, and the bracelet. He must be a competitor.

"Yes, they came from the same jeweler."

"Where?" he asked.

The girl with pigtails, Aaron's sister, interrupted them. She pointed to Jessie's ear. "How come you're not wearing the other earring?"

"She lost it," Walt explained.

"No," Jessie responded. "I gave one..." Her mouth clamped shut. She almost slipped. She had given the earring to Jezero.

Walt jerked back. He regained his composure, but his eyes hardened. He knew her other life had something to do with it.

"I gave it to someone. To fix. The lock broke." She stumbled out her excuse.

Jessie wished the conference were over. The man asked another question about the ring. Finally someone else spoke up. "Where do you plan to stay? Are you heading back to California?"

"We'll decide later," Walt chimed in before Jessie could say anything.

He had probably cut her short to make sure she didn't set his mother off. Or say something else she shouldn't. Jessie let him take over. He liked being center stage with the media. She grabbed the glass of water in front of her and took a long drink before setting it down again.

One light hurt her eyes. She moved closer to Walt. He took the opportunity to put his arm around her shoulders, showing the world they were a happy couple. He beamed.

Jessie gave Walt, the cameramen, and photographers their moment. She focused her stare to the side of the room to avoid the flashes. In the corner, one woman stood out. She wore a yellow scarf draped over her head. She had dark brown skin and exotic eyes like a Jamaican queen.

Their eyes locked. The woman gave a slight nod.

Jessie caught her breath. She glanced over at Dr. Maguire, who now answered medical questions about comas and her condition. She squirmed in her chair.

The queen.

All of it came back to her—the little shop, the coffee, the conversation.

"A brew to help you with your troubles." Words from the queen.

Jessie shot a glance toward Walt, to the doctor, to those in the crowd. She had no choice but to stay locked behind the table, unable to disrupt the press conference.

The queen started it all. She *knew* what happened. Jessie held her hand to her chest to keep it from pounding out of her body.

"A special brew just for you."

Was the coffee laced with poison? Did she cast a spell on her? Some type of voodoo?

Walt noticed her fidget. He followed her eyes to the Jamaican woman.

"Who is she?" he whispered into her ear.

Jessie shook her head. Now wasn't the time or place. She pulled away from Walt and took another drink of water. She shot a glance over to the corner again. The queen was gone.

Walt grabbed Jessie's hand to keep her steady. He squeezed hard, not to hurt her but to keep her still. He was right. No need to cause a commotion.

The conversation in the room shifted. The media directed their cameras toward the first two rows. A woman motioned for the kids to come forward. The parents stayed in their seats, while those saved by Jessie came up to the table. One by one, they introduced themselves. Jessie vaguely remembered the two boys, the ones she first found. She remembered the little girl and then of course the redheaded boy.

Aaron waited by his sister, who came up to the table with him. She handed him a royal blue gift bag with a yellow chiffon ribbon tied to the handles.

"Hi, Aaron," Jessie said and smiled at him. From the way he bit the edge of his lip, the boy seemed nervous.

"Hi," he whispered. He glanced toward the cameras and at the other people now staring at him. He wiped his nose with the back of his hand. His eyes grew larger.

"There're a lot of people here, aren't there?" Jessie said and leaned forward. She tried keeping his attention on her and away from the cameras. "How old are you now?"

He turned around to find his mother. She sat in the front row.

"Aaron." Jessie grabbed his attention again and waited until he looked at her. "I hear you had a birthday."

He turned back to Jessie and vigorously shook his head while his eyes popped wide. "Not yet. I'll be eight in five days."

"That sounds like fun."

Another nudge from his sister reminded Aaron of the bag he held in his hand.

"This is for you." The bag came out and Jessie leaned back to keep from getting hit. A few chuckles came from the crowd.

Jessie smiled and took the bag. "But it's your birthday coming up, not mine."

He shook his head so his entire body swayed back and forth. "This is yours. I get my gifts at my party."

"Can I open it?" Jessie asked, holding the bag to her chest.

He nodded and moved closer, putting his upper body on the table so his legs kicked out. Walt moved the water glasses before they spilled. Aaron played with an air bubble in the tablecloth, poking at it with his finger. He then returned his attention to Jessie, unaware of the near accident with the water.

Jessie put the bag on the table, and the boy lifted his head to peek inside the bag when she did. Aaron gave her a big smile. The cameras loved it.

A stack of thank-you cards were inside the bag. Each one was handmade with detailed pictures of the fire, the house, the sun, the stars, and little stickers with fun designs. The detail amazed her. One was like a mini book with different pages telling her about their family. Aaron's sister beamed when she told Jessie how she made it. Other cards were short and sweet. All touched her the same way when she went through the stack to admire the artwork.

She got the sign from Walt to speed it up. Their time was up.

Of course, business as usual.

***

Walt glanced over at his mother. According to the smile on her face, the press conference was a success.

"You can be proud of her," Sam said as he came up from the back of the room. "All went well and only one stumble from Jessie about the earring. Any guess as to what it was about?"

"Can't say that I do, and I'm not sure if I want to." Walt shook his friend's hand. "I'm just glad she caught herself. And I'm glad you made it."

"Wouldn't miss it for the world," he said with a half smile.

Everyone moved to the room next door for coffee, punch, and cake. The children took care of Jessie, wheeling her to the cake. She would be busy for a while. If needed, Carol could take her up to the room. The thought of coffee or punch did nothing for Walt. Scotch sounded better. "You in for a drink?"

"Lead the way." Sam waved his open palm toward the door.

Walt raised his finger. He went over to Jessie and explained he was taking off with Sam for a while. "You'll be okay?"

"Of course," she said. She turned to see his friend and waved, and then her attention shifted to the girl as she tried climbing on Jessie's lap.

He had no worries. In fact, it was nice to see his fiancée laugh. The children seemed to lift her spirits, something he hadn't been able to accomplish since she woke. This was good for her. He hoped the kids would get her to realize she should be here, not in some godforsaken village.

"Carol," Walt called out to the nurse, who was making her way out the door. He motioned if she would wheel Jessie back to her room when it was time.

Carol gave the thumbs up.

With his main concern taken care of, Walt patted Sam on the back, a sign for them to get the hell out of there. He didn't want his parents seeing him leave. They wouldn't be happy knowing he hadn't stayed to talk to the reporters.

They walked the four blocks to a quaint French hotel. The front desk was bustling with activity, but the bar was quiet. They sat at a table near the corner window. The seats were comfortable, leather and curved. Walt sank in.

"I bet you can't wait until she's out," Sam said as he pulled off his coat.

Walt made a point to nod his head up and down. "I've seen enough of that hospital to last me a lifetime. But then her leaving is another issue."

"How do you mean? Your parents?"

He nodded again. Their conversation stalled when the bartender arrived to take their order. When he left, Walt continued. "They want us to stay with them. Jessie wants to fly back to California."

Sam shrugged. "Makes sense. She's been away from her home for quite a while."

"Yeah, I get it. I don't blame her." Walt glared at the bartender. He wanted his drink. "However, I wish she'd stay in Chicago for a few days. Stay close to the hospital to make sure she's ready to handle...," he searched for the right words, "handle the outside world."

"Ah," Sam said and raised his eyebrows. "You're afraid she'll flip."

Walt rolled his head to say yes but no. "Somewhat. The doctors can't regulate her heartbeat. She has this fluttering going on inside her that has me worried. We're not sure if it's her heart, her chest muscles, or who knows what. Carol, the nurse, is the one who updates me. Jessie won't say anything to me because she knows I'll order a specialist to find out what's wrong."

The bartender came with their drinks.

"What else?" Sam frowned. "I've hung with you for a long time, my friend. What else is eating you?" He raised his glass to Walt and then took a sip of his scotch.

"I saw her back." Walt raised his glass as well and took a drink. He let the gold liquid burn down his throat. Exactly what he needed.

His friend leaned in, curious.

"She had scars on her back. Deep lines I don't remember seeing before." Walt shook his head. "I know they weren't there. Her back used to be smooth as silk." He remembered their last night in Carmel and running his fingers in a line from her neck down to her cute little ass. He loved touching her skin, enough to make her shiver and then laugh. He loved her laugh.

"Were they from the accident?"

Walt stared into his drink. "Her face dropped, turned pale when I mentioned them. No, they weren't from the house fire."

Sam raised his glass. "Ah, Dusken. How'd she get the scars?"

"She said she was whipped." Walt downed the rest of his drink. He hailed the bartender and ordered another two.

"What?" Sam asked as if to make sure he heard him right.

"I can't remember the name she said. Byron...Viloin." He raised his hand and waved his fingers around. "The king of the Morlorns."

"Morlorns?" Sam wasn't following. He downed his drink as well.

"Jessie told me about the place in her dream. About the village and how this group named the Morlorns were after her. She was the cause of someone's village being attacked and left in ruins. All because of this Vyrone wanting her."

Sam sat back in his chair with his mouth open. He seemed to be digesting Walt's words, but gave up. "Sounds like a wild dream."

"A nightmare for me." The second round of drinks arrived and Walt needed it. He raised his glass to toast. Sam met him halfway and they clinked glasses. After taking a drink, he continued. "She believes, or remembers, how Vyrone whipped her." Walt shuddered. "What's creepy is that the scars do look like she's been whipped."

"What did she fall on? A fence maybe?"

Walt thought back to the scene of the fire. "There was splintered wood, the shingles, the gutters. I can't picture what could have made them." He let out a growl and rubbed his head with one hand. "I don't get it, Sam. One minute we're this happy couple, and the next I'm listening to her tell me about falling in love with a man who doesn't exist."

He couldn't bring up to his friend how she fucked the guy. She was brief, as if it were a casual event like a stroll through the woods. Walt finished his drink and set the glass on the table for the bartender to get him another.

Tears welled in his eyes. Walt had to control himself. He wasn't one to cry. "I'm telling you, Sam. She's slipping away from me, and I don't know how to stop it."

Chapter 30

::: Jessie :::

Chicago, IL

"What an afternoon!" Carol commented as she helped Jessie to bed. "You should be pretty dang proud of yourself, saving those kids."

"I am glad I was there." Jessie never thought about her actions. Running into a house on fire wasn't something she had set out to do.

"Those kids were cute. They wouldn't be here today if it weren't for you."

"They were pretty cute." Jessie smiled and shook her hair out of the bun. She ran her hands through the twisted strands and changed the subject. "Did Walt say if he was coming back?"

The kids had consumed her time after the press conference. Helen stayed by her side and talked to the reporters as if shielding her. For once the woman helped her out, even though she knew Helen's motive was to keep her from blabbing about the "dream."

"I didn't talk to him. He only motioned if I'd wheel you up to your room." She finished tucking Jessie into bed. Her expression changed, her lips turned down. "We're going to miss you around here."

"Me or Walt?" Jessie joked and raised her arm to let Carol take her blood pressure.

"Both," she said and smiled like a good nurse.

Walt treated Carol like his personal assistant. At times, Jessie saw the irritation in Carol's smile, ready to give him a piece of her mind.

"What time do I get out of here?"

"With a little luck, early tomorrow afternoon."

"That late?" Jessie needed to find the Jamaican woman. If Walt and his parents came to pick her up, she would lose her chance.

"First of all, you're getting released a day early. Second, the doctor plans to make one last check on you before he signs the release papers. I'm not sure where you are on his list."

"I should be first. I've been here the longest."

Carol laughed. "Seniority doesn't work for patients. The most critical get first dibs on our doctors."

Jessie rolled her eyes. The doctor didn't need to examine her again.

"Are you excited to stay with your future-in-laws?"

"We're making final arrangements," Walt said, overhearing their conversation. His smile drooped to the side. He leaned against the doorframe when his leg wobbled.

"Well, tomorrow's the big day." Carol folded a blanket and laid it across the end of Jessie's bed. "And this one here needs her rest."

"You're right. It's getting late." Walt checked his watch. He stepped closer to the doorframe to make room for Carol to pass.

"You can go inside the room to see her," she said and seemed to keep her distance from him, which puzzled Jessie. The nurse hugged the other side of the door to get out. Jessie saw her wrinkle her nose before disappearing into the hall.

Walt made his way to the side of the bed and grabbed the rails. He leaned down to give Jessie a kiss on her forehead. She smelled scotch on his breath and understood Carol's reaction.

"Did you have a fun time with Sam?"

"I did." Walt twisted his mouth into a smile. He slurred his words. "A much-needed relief."

The color drained from Jessie's face. Ouch. The truth comes out with a little liquor. Her shoulders drooped. "I've been a pain. Life hasn't been easy for you."

"No fucking shit." He almost fell onto her and then popped up. "I gotta go."

"You're not driving, right?"

"Sam's waiting. We're taking a cab." Walt's hair flipped in front of his forehead, and he tried smoothing it back in place.

Jessie preferred the less-than-perfect look to the controlled, businesslike, slicked-back style that never moved. He needed to lighten up, be more simplistic.

"I'll be here tomorrow." He hiccupped. "First thing in the morning."

Jessie nodded. She opened her eyes wider to keep the tears from falling when he swung around and headed for the door.

"Walt!"

He stopped and turned, using the door again to keep his balance.

"Thank you for listening. Being here for me, even though I was being a burden."

"You still need to tell me the rest of your dream." He winked.

Jessie nodded, unsure if it would ever happen. Her heart sank. He deserved better than her.

Chapter 31

::: Jessie :::

Chicago, IL

The light of dawn cracked the sky and spread a deep violet hue across the horizon as Jessie hailed a cab one block from the hospital. She plopped into the backseat, wanting never to see the hospital again.

"Where you heading?" the driver asked, tossing his clipboard to the passenger seat.

She gave him vague directions to the coffee shop, not knowing the street name. He typed in *Secret Endeavors* on his phone and verified the location. He asked no questions, but he seemed curious about her lack of wearing a coat in the middle of winter. His eyes narrowed as he peered at her through the rearview mirror. Finally, he clicked on the meter and sped off when she offered no explanation.

Jessie settled into the seat and dug through her purse to see how much money she had. Plenty. She had replenished her funds before the flight to Chicago, knowing she'd need money for the "engagement" weekend and for her next trip to New York as well.

Funny how one event could change her entire life. Walt had cancelled her scheduled photo shoots with her being in a coma. Her clients were waiting and had called to reschedule.

They would have to keep waiting.

"You can drop me off here," she told the driver when they were within one block of the coffee shop. She paid him before slipping out of the vehicle.

The coffee shop appeared to be the same as she peeked through the window. The two lights above the bar cast a warm glow. Another light filtered from the back room. The shop was closed, but Jessie sensed the Jamaican queen would be inside preparing for the day.

The handle on the door turned. The latch clicked, and it seemed to open on its own.

"Hello," she called out.

The warmth inside the shop was like bathing in rich, thick coffee. She welcomed the heat and shook the cold from her arms and hands. An oven door creaked open in the back. The heavenly scent of cinnamon and pumpkin swirled through the air, and she slowly breathed through her nose to take in the aroma. Her stomach growled. Jessie had forgotten such simple pleasures.

The scrape of a pan sliding across the oven rack and onto the counter brought her back to her purpose. Jessie followed the aroma and noise to the back of the shop and found the Jamaican queen busy in the kitchen. She wore an emerald green tunic with a matching skirt. A thick necklace of wood beads hung between her breasts, and a scarf covered her long, braided hair.

"You found my shop once again." The Jamaican queen turned toward her and smiled in welcome. She didn't seem surprised to see her.

"I had to come," Jessie replied. This woman was the key to her getting back to Dusken.

"I made a nice brew for you," she said. The words rolled from her tongue like waves cascading across the sea. From the table nearby, the Jamaican queen picked up a lone cup filled with steaming liquid and handed it to Jessie.

"You knew I was coming?" Jessie asked, but she already knew the response. Of course she did.

A small pool of white floated on top of the coffee like an island. The whipped cream began to melt, making Jessie believe the dollop was added when she entered the shop. She wrapped her hands around the cup to warm her fingers and raised it to her lips. The rich drink tasted like the best coffee ever with hints of chocolate, butter, and vanilla included in the blend.

"The coffee is good, eh?" the queen asked, proud of her concoction.

"Very," Jessie agreed, and was surprised people weren't lining up at the door, waiting for the shop to open.

"Go have a seat at the counter. I will bring out a treat for you," the Jamaican queen said as she turned away to check on a pan of muffins baking in the oven.

Jessie walked out to the front. The painting on the wall captured her attention. She set her cup of coffee on the counter, then went to examine it. She remembered studying the oil before and how it had intrigued her. The vibrant yet mystical forest scene drew her in again. She loved the trail winding through the woods, the ferns and orange flowers covering the ground, and the sun's rays beaming through the trees. Jessie gasped.

Dusken.

She swooned and grabbed the back of the chair next to her to keep her balance. She looked closer. Yes, the path curved near the tall, thick tree with the limb hanging down like an arm to show the way. The orange flowers, cyroluses, were only found in Dusken. The Jamaican queen had said the land was special to her heart—a sanctuary. *Jezero's sanctuary.*

Jessie's heart swelled and ached with pain. She wanted to cry with sadness and joy. This wasn't a dream.

The Jamaican woman walked toward the front of the shop.

"Have you been there?" Jessie asked while she continued to stare at the painting.

"I have not," the Jamaican queen said.

"How did you...get this?"

"It was a gift."

Someone else knew about Dusken—lived there and returned. Jessie stared at the forest scene, thinking back to the ledge and when she woke for the first time. Jezero had said she wasn't from around there. Did he know where she was from?

Jessie wanted to take the painting down from the wall and hug it close to her chest. She wanted Jezero to know how much she missed him. How she was determined to return.

"I have a treat for you. Eat while it's still warm."

Jessie forced herself to turn away and sit at the counter. The pumpkin muffin had a drizzle of frosting over the top and looked delicious. She stared at the treat but didn't have much of an appetite.

"You seem sad." The queen placed another cup of coffee in front of her.

Jessie's throat tightened. *Yes, I'm sad.*

"You have mixed feelings like when you entered here the first time."

She nodded. "I am not seeing my life here, in this world, anymore."

"Are you sure?"

Jessie stared into the exotic brown eyes. "I don't want to lose Jezero. I belong there, with him."

The queen, standing in front of her, had delivered her to Dusken. Whether it was voodoo, magic, or a dream, it didn't matter. The woman carried the knowledge and means for Jessie to return.

"What of your life here? You had regrets before. Do they still carry with you?" The queen kept her eyes locked on Jessie's.

"My regret is that I'm here, that I woke from the coma."

Jessie loved Walt, but he deserved someone other than her. He needed a woman who would fit with his Rolls Royce lifestyle, and someone whom his mother would approve of him marrying.

The Jamaican woman's expression turned to empathy. "Listen to your dreams and peace will settle within your heart."

"I don't know what you mean." Jessie was confused.

"You will."

She shook her head. Life with Jezero wasn't a play with a break between acts. She needed to be with him. Her biggest fear was that he thought she had run away—deserted him. His eyes had widened and expressed fear, sadness, and longing before she faded into the smoke.

Jessie bit her lip to keep from crying.

"Be patient, my child. To start again takes time. For now, you can only wait for a sign," the queen said and moved away from the counter. She turned and grabbed a box off the back shelf.

Jessie wanted direct answers. She was tired of the vague conversation about her future. "Will it come? This sign?"

"What you *need* will be placed before you." The queen pointed to the muffin waiting for her to eat.

Jessie took a bite of her muffin. The icing was a soft cream cheese that blended well with the pumpkin and cinnamon. *Oh, yes. Heaven.*

"You like?"

"This is extremely good."

The Jamaican queen placed four muffins in the box, closed the lid, taped the edges together, and then placed it in front of Jessie.

"You go, child. The answers you want will come in time. You'll see." She placed a to-go cup of coffee in front of her. "Drink all of it."

The conversation was over. Jessie savored the warmth from the cup in her hands and stood, preparing to leave. The Jamaican queen folded her hands together, gave a slight bow, and then stepped back. Jessie wanted to hug the woman but didn't dare put herself so close to the queen's powers. Instead, she expressed her appreciation in a smile. The queen nodded in return.

Jessie stood alone outside *Secret Endeavors*. With her steaming to-go cup in one hand and the box of muffins tucked under her arm, she had no place to go. If she went to the airport, Walt would follow. She could rent a car and drive to Carmel. She missed her little house near the beach. Maybe the ocean would provide a clue to what she should do. Jezero dragged her from the sea. There had to be a connection.

Jessie didn't feel the draw. Not to mention, her house would be the first place Walt searched. Where else?

She took a sip of the coffee and enjoyed the liquid as it heated her throat. The familiar taste brought her back to the morning before the fire. Would her life end here? Would something happen, causing her to fall into a coma again? Jessie shuddered, thinking about the pain she endured.

She would take the pain if it meant being with Jezero again.

Snowflakes floated down from the sky and joined the thin layer of snow blanketing the sidewalk. Her fingers were getting cold without gloves. She took another drink from her cup.

A Ford Escape turned down the street and passed her. The license plate was from Wisconsin.

A sign?

Wisconsin. Walt would never think to search for her there. He knew she preferred sunny, hot days to the cold winters of the Midwest. She'd have to do some research. Lake Geneva was a popular place for those living in Chicago. Maybe there?

Jessie moved her cup from one hand to the other. She dug into her back pocket for her phone to call a cab. She stared at the black screen with her thumb close to the ON button and laughed. Out of the hospital, she now used it again like an old friend. The modern conveniences of this world. Had they simplified or complicated lives with all the electronics and new inventions? For her, she was fine without. The phone landed in the garbage can to the side of the coffee shop door.

A taxi turned the corner, just as the Ford had, and moved toward her. She stepped out to the street and raised her hand. The driver pulled to the side of the road. As she was about to enter the car, Jessie glanced up at a billboard advertising Log Cabin syrup.

"You getting in?" the cab driver ducked his head to see her better when she hesitated.

"I am," she responded and slid into the back seat.

"Where to, ma'am?"

This guy was younger than the first taxi driver. He reminded her of Sam, Walt's friend, when they first met.

Sam. A smile played on Jessie's lips. Sam had a cabin. A log cabin in Wisconsin.

Jessie knew where she would stay until she returned to Jezero.

Author's Biography

Beth M James lives with her husband in Northwestern Wisconsin and loves being surrounded by nature. As an author and writer, she's been interviewed for *Time* magazine and published in *USA Today*. She's taught classes to other authors/writers and to the public. Her passion is writing stories full of adventure and with twists and turns. You can read Beth's blog, sign up for her newsletter, or find out more about Beth and her books at: **https://www.bethmjames.com**

Note: Reviews are important and appreciated for independent authors, especially when it comes to book ratings and visibility. Please consider reviewing this book at one or more of the major online bookstores or review sites.

Novels by Beth M James

(Contemporary Romance)

Gitana – Life Plan

(Dream or Reality Series: Adventure, Time Travel, Romance)

The Calling

The Promise of Return

The Calling's Return

(Romantic Suspense)

Peaceful Plots

(Action/Adventure, Magical Realism)

The Orb Lady – Cali's Story

The Promise of Return

Excerpt
A Dream or Reality Series Book 2
By Beth M James

:::::: Jessie ::::::

Chapter 1

Chicago, IL

Walt steered his Mercedes off the exit ramp from the freeway toward the hospital.

Fifteen minutes late.

His parents wouldn't arrive for another hour, giving him enough time to have Jessie released from the hospital—and out of Chicago. He wanted to avoid his mother and her continuous rant. She liked to butt heads with his fiancée, and the less they saw of each other, the better.

"Make it happen. Make it happen," he said under his breath. Walt popped another two aspirin into his mouth and then grabbed the paper coffee cup from the beverage holder in the middle console. He took a gulp of the lukewarm caffeine to help down the pills. Another right turn and the hospital came into view.

His head pounded from the effect of drinking scotch the night before. Walt kicked himself for many things he'd done in life, but he'd gotten over them. This time, his drunken words may have caused some damage. He cursed at himself for his stupidity and tried justifying his actions. The guilt played on.

Yesterday, after the press conference, he'd needed to get away from the hospital and the stress that went with it. Managing the reporters and TV crew, making sure Jessie behaved, and keeping his mother in line wore him out.

The public witnessed firsthand how his fiancée was doing after rescuing the kids from the fire. His mother liked that Jessie didn't say anything to ruin the Arbol name. He did his part in making sure the event was a success. With everything under control, Walt disappeared with his longtime friend to a quaint French bar at a nearby hotel. Going out for drinks had been a necessity. Checking on her afterward before heading home—dumb on his part.

Walt kicked himself for his stupidity. Now, he worried about whether he'd given her more reason to cut him out of her life. The shattering glass of his plans continued to spread—and not in his favor.

He cringed, replaying what he said when she asked him if he had fun going out with Sam. He confessed that he did and how it was a "much-needed relief."

She apologized for being a pain in the ass.

"No fucking shit." The words came out like a devil spewing fire. The color drained from her face. The shock in her eyes haunted him all night.

For chrissake, she'd been in a coma for weeks. For forty-eight days, he prayed for her to wake, staying by her bedside and ignoring his job. The doctors couldn't guarantee that Jessie would come out of it. Walt promised God if she woke, he'd keep her happy. And she did wake.

He failed his first promise.

His second mistake was letting his parents insist that she should stay at their estate upon release from the hospital. Their rationale made sense. She needed to be near the doctors and specialists who took care of her. And should an emergency arise, his parents' place was fairly close to the hospital. They even hired a nurse for her, knowing that he had a two-week business trip in New Orleans, which he had to leave for tonight.

Another sore subject. Arbol Publishing. The family business. Walt shook his head. Today he could make it right with Jessie. Her repeated requests to go home and recover at her cottage in Carmel had fallen on his deaf ears. Now he agreed California would be great. Sun and beaches. She'd enjoy her alone time and more rest, while he worked out a contract with a new advertising client, one his father wanted to obtain. Walt would close the deal, something he was good at, and then fly back to her place. Once there, they could decide where to go for a nice, long vacation.

He smiled, rewarding himself for his clever plan. A tropical island far away would give them peace and an added surprise—to elope without his meddling mother getting in the way.

Walt pulled the sedan around to the side entrance and glanced up at the building. The last time. He never wanted to set foot in the hospital again. Over three months, including recovery, were spent in the square, sterile room. The doctors drove him crazy as they kept changing the time frame for her release.

He parked in the slot marked "Patient Pick-Up" near the emergency entrance. The doors were locked, and the attendant buzzed him in. Walt waved his hand to the man behind the camera before he entered. The staff knew him well.

A whiff of bleach and lemon-scented cleaner hit his nose. He never liked the welcome in.

"Hey, Pete," he said to the volunteer behind the counter. No time for idle chatter today.

Walt glanced at his watch as he walked the hall toward the patient wing. His parents said they'd arrive at eight-thirty. Fifty minutes remained. The doctor should be in the room signing Jessie's release papers now. He'd called in a favor, wanting his fiancée to be seen first thing in the morning.

The elevator hummed, stopped, dinged, stopped. Why was it so slow? He turned away, ready to find the stairs, when the doors popped open. Walt spun back around. Sam, his friend, stepped out, shocked to see him.

"Hey, man, don't you answer your phone anymore?"

"What?" Walt had better things to do.

Wait, my phone. Sam's words triggered the thought that he hadn't used it in a while. When was the last time? He stepped into the elevator while fishing underneath his coat and into his pants pockets.

"Son of a bitch. I forgot my phone." He patted his suit coat to make sure he hadn't dropped it in one of the pockets in his rush to leave that morning.

Sam went into action when the steel doors began to shut. He used his foot to jam the door and then hopped in. "Where you heading?"

Walt noticed the button to the third floor was unlit. He quickly pressed it.

"Did you leave it at the bar? In Jessie's room?"

Walt grunted at his friend but was too preoccupied trying to remember where he left the damn thing. His hand felt something hard inside his breast pocket. Relief swept over him. Taking it out, he checked the screen.

"Damn it." His phone had been powered off. He hit the button and waited as it fired up.

"You're looking a little frantic, buddy." Sam watched him with some amusement. He leaned against the back-corner wall while holding his briefcase with both hands near his crotch.

The elevator jerked to a stop. Walt glanced at the top numbers. Second floor. The door opened to an empty hall.

Walt hit the button to the third floor again. He stepped back and checked his phone. Five missed calls—one from his mother, two from Sam, and two from the hospital. He scowled and turned his head toward his friend. "What the hell is going on?"

"I was hoping you'd tell me."

Walt inhaled a sharp breath through his nose to keep from blowing up. All he wanted to do was get Jessie out of there, get on a plane to California, and then get her home. He'd fly with her, making sure she was settled in before catching the red-eye flight for New Orleans. Simple plan.

Sam yawned. Walt frowned. His friend usually wasn't up this early in the morning, especially after a night of drinking. The guy liked to sleep until noon when possible. Even one Scotch would give him a.m. withdrawals. "Why are you here?"

"I came to find you. Can you give me five minutes of your time here?" Sam expressed a touch of impatience. "I don't know what the hell is going on with you right now, but I have some information that may make your trip to New Orleans even better."

"Oh yeah? What?"

The elevator door opened. They stepped into the hall. Walt glanced around. He sighed with relief. No sign of his mother or father.

"Pentias. Cyrolus. Queeno." Sam held up a finger for each one.

Walt shot his friend a look, paying attention.

"You know those plants you wanted me to find? All three names were in one article. Can you believe that?"

"And you're telling me now? Not last night?"

"I just got the copy last night, buried in my emails. Jeez, man. Give me a break."

The day before the press conference, Walt had given Sam a list of plants. His friend was good with research—one reason he was a successful lawyer. Jessie had mentioned the plants in her dream. The information could be what he needed to convince her that the coma played a trick on her, making her think she was in another world.

Dusken. He snickered. How could anyone believe a place like Oz existed? She tried convincing him that it was real. The trauma affected her more than anyone realized. Their secret. If the doctors found out, she would still be in the hospital—locked up.

Why was this happening to him?

"Fucking insane," he muttered to himself. His heart tightened. Hearing her tell him how she fell in love with a man from that world made his anger boil.

Staff were milling about. He and Sam needed privacy. Walt motioned for his friend to follow him into the waiting room. He checked his watch—forty-five minutes remained. The doctor should be done. "We have to make this quick."

Sam sat on one of the yellow chairs and set his overstuffed briefcase on the coffee table. "Last week, I found an interesting article at the library in New Orleans, but the librarian had trouble uploading the document to print it out. The copy was blurred. She said she'd clean it up and then email it to me." He unzipped the leather bag.

"Why New Orleans?"

Sam shrugged. "Since I was in the city on business, I thought it was worth a shot. And bingo. Hit the jackpot."

Sam cleared his throat after finding the manila folder with "Jessie" written in pencil. Walt sat next to him. He drummed his fingers on his leg while his friend turned to lawyer-mode, being meticulous in setting the file on the table before opening the cover. *I have time to do this. I have time. Jessie's not going anywhere.*

"Like I said, the copy isn't the best. I tried different settings on my computer, hoping it'd print better." He slid over the first paper. "The article is about a patient who disappeared about five years ago from one of the treatment centers near the city."

Walt studied the picture. Two male resident nurses escorted a man by the name of John Arlington through a set of doors. The guy had curly black hair and looked fit, like a trainer. He stared into the camera as if daring anyone to take him on. He didn't look insane, just angry. The photo was taken two weeks before his disappearance.

"How does this relate to the plants?" Walt didn't have time to read the full article, but he skimmed the print, looking for names or words Jessie may have used.

"This John guy became friends with the janitor at the center. When the janitor cut his arm on some type of equipment at his other job, John told him about a plant called queeno. He claimed the medicine inside the plant would heal the infection. The two began to talk about plants and that's when John told the janitor about where he lived." Sam leaned over to see the article. He hit the paper with his finger near the end of the first page. "There it is. Dusken."

Walt's stomach muscles squeezed in. He didn't like where this was going. "So where is this place? Dusken?"

His friend shook his head. "Not sure. I couldn't find a city with the name. The guy told the janitor how he lived on a ledge." Sam laughed. "The guy claimed his home was in a forest. He mentioned something about the flowers, the other plants you wrote down." He rolled the names off like a song. "Pentias and cyrolus."

Walt rubbed his chin. He wanted to know more, but ten minutes had passed.

"I can try to set up an interview for you...to talk to the janitor. He's retired now but still lives in New Orleans. You want me to call him?"

"Hold off," Walt said and stood. He folded the papers in half and then tucked them in his coat pocket. "I'll read the article once I'm on the plane. If it's worth the trouble, I'll contact you."

Now twelve minutes had passed since he entered the hospital. His left eye twitched.

"No problem," Sam said. He grabbed his briefcase and the empty manila folder. "The janitor's phone number and address are on the backside of one of the sheets. Give me a call if you need anything else."

"I will. Thanks, my man." He held out his hand.

Sam sidestepped away from the coffee table, then came back around to shake Walt's hand. "I'm surprised I caught you, going up. Is she in the car? Did you forget something?"

"Huh?" Walt made a face. "Jessie's in her room."

"At your parents' house?" Sam looked at his friend as if confused. "How'd that go with your mother?"

Walt made a face. "My mother?"

"Yeah. Jessie couldn't have been happy."

"What the hell are you talking about?" Walt's voice rose an octave higher than normal. His chest tightened in pain.

"Jessie's with your folks, right?" Sam pointed to her room and then to Walt. "She's not in there."

"Not in—" Walt said and spun around. He placed his hand on the wall for balance as he nearly hit it. He stepped away from the waiting room and stared down the hall toward the room. Everything was quiet, no rush of activities near her door. Heading toward the room, he said over his shoulder, "I came to get her out of here before my parents show up."

"Maybe they showed up early."

Sam wasn't helping. Walt glared at his friend as Sam caught up to him. Nothing made sense and he cursed his headache. "She better be in there."

His feet moved like lead weights down the hall. He passed the nurse's station—not one nurse or aide in the area. Walt swung into her room, hanging on to the doorframe for support. He stopped short.

The bed was empty. The sheets lay crumpled on the floor.

"Jessie?" He stuck his head into the bathroom and found no one.

"Walt." The nurse's voice called from the hall. It was Carol, her normal cheery voice cracked with distress.

"Where is she?" He spun around.

The nurse shook her head. She glanced at Sam as if needing his support.

"Where is she?" Walt growled. He stepped over to Jessie's bed to examine it more closely. The catheter to the IV and the tape, which had held it secure to her arm, now stuck to the sheets.

"She left early this morning. Between rounds."

"Why didn't you call me?" His head pounded. He leaned forward and rubbed his temples.

"We tried. We left a message."

His phone. He'd forgotten to turn on his cell. Two calls from the hospital.

"Fuck!" He kicked the bed, and the metal frame rattled like a snake. As the noise died down, the familiar click of heels on the tile floor snapped his head back.

His mother arrived.

To read more, "The Promise of Return" can be purchased on various online retail stores. Links can also be found on the author's website:

https://www.bethmjames.com

Don't miss out!

Visit the website below and you can sign up to receive emails whenever Beth M James publishes a new book. There's no charge and no obligation.

https://books2read.com/r/B-A-VCEBB-MKUZC

BOOKS 2 READ

Connecting independent readers to independent writers.

www.ingramcontent.com/pod-product-compliance
Lightning Source LLC
LaVergne TN
LVHW100516110826
845146LV00002B/669

9798989344932